BLUE
MOON
HAVEN

Don't miss any of Janet Dailey's bestsellers

JANET DAILEY

BLUE MOON HAVEN

ZEBRA BOOKS
Kensington Publishing Corp.
www.kensingtonbooks.com

CHAPTER 1

At age ten, Kelly Jenkins dreamed she would live in a quaint two-story country home with a red roof, operate a highly successful cotton candy business in her spacious backyard and fly fighter jets in air shows on the weekends (part-time, of course!) to the cheers of adoring crowds comprised of thousands.

At age thirty-four, Kelly, homeless, stood in a field of knee-high weeds in Blue Moon Haven, Alabama, with seventy-one dollars in the pocket of her ripped capris and two abandoned siblings—one of whom despised her—at her side.

Life had always had different plans than Kelly did, and the world hadn't always been kind, but deep down, she still clung to the secret hope that things might one day improve.

"It has wheels." Todd Campbell, ten years old, with the shrewd gaze of a middle-aged litigator, frowned up at her. "You said we'd never live in a place that had wheels again. You said when we moved here, there'd be a house." His eyes narrowed. "You said—"

"Yep." She nodded vigorously. "Yep, I know exactly what I said."

And two weeks ago, when she'd emailed her (sorely lacking) résumé to Mae Bell Larkin, owner of the Blue Moon Haven Drive-In, and accepted a management position, that's exactly what Kelly thought she would acquire—a home. That, along with a thriving drive-in–theater business exuding nostalgic appeal.

Instead, the massive sign, fourteen feet high and forty-eight feet wide, marking the drive-in's entrance, was covered in moldy grime, and the large letters comprising BLUE MOON HAVEN DRIVE-IN were faded or dangling precariously. And the lot itself was even worse. Weeds and briars were everywhere; patches of them rustling in succession as though small, unseen creatures scurried about. Two massive projection screens, one obscured by the sprawling branches of a pecan tree, had gaping holes and seemed to be covered in the same grime that slicked the entrance sign they'd passed earlier. Leaves, cigarette butts, beer bottles and other debris littered the concessions building and one of the two tall projection booths slumped to the right as though it had a bum leg.

But the worst—the absolute worst—was the ancient, poky trailer slumping at the back edge of the lot, its metal surface glinting beneath the early-spring Alabama sun, heat rolling off it in hazy waves despite the morning chill still lingering in the air.

"'Living quarters,'" Kelly said quietly. "'Homey living quarters.'" She twiddled her fingers by her sides. "*Homey* to me meant *home. House.* Not a mobile home." Cheeks heating, she winced. "I guess I should've ask—"

"Yeah, you should have." Todd crossed his arms over his chest. "You should've asked about the structure, how many rooms, where it was located. You should've asked how much you'd be paid, if you'd get health insurance, bonuses, retirement." He stamped his foot. "You didn't ask anything, did you?"

Gifted. Kelly grunted. That's what the school psychologist had told her six months ago when she'd been called to Todd's elementary school to discuss his unruly behavior. Behavior that had strangely involved Todd dressing down his new seventh-grade teacher (Todd had recently skipped two grades) for having made an absentminded mistake in a mathematical equation on a worksheet he'd given the class to complete. Todd had thrown his math worksheet and laptop out of the classroom window, then marched to the principal's office, reported the teacher as incompetent and demanded he be reassigned to another class.

All of this had happened because Todd was intellectually gifted far beyond his years, the school psychologist had said. He possessed an unusual combination of creativity, insight and innovation. Unfortunately, according to the psychologist, Todd's personality also included extreme sensitivity, a keen sense of justice and a volatile temper.

Kelly shook her head. Too bad empathy and politeness didn't seem to be in as plentiful supply at the moment.

But . . . considering all Todd had lost over the past year, most especially his mother and father, his anger was to be expected and easily forgiven.

"I did ask, Todd. I'm not completely inept." She breathed deep. Choked back her pride. Counted to ten. "I asked how many rooms and where it was located. I asked about all those things, except for the structure part. But the simple truth is, I had no choice but to move on from where we were. You're incredibly intelligent, and I know you'd understand if you knew all the details, but there are some grown-up things I can't discuss with you."

Like the fact that her former boss had been a micro-managing dictator with no heart, focused on dollars and cents instead of compassion and rewarding hard work. Of the twenty-five job applications she'd submitted, only one job—this one, in fact—had resulted in a callback. With no income and two extra mouths to feed, she'd had no choice but to . . .

"I need you to trust that I made the only decision I could for us at the time," she said softly.

A soft breeze rolled over the empty lot, ruffling Todd's thick hair. His brown eyes glistened, and his chin trembled.

Heart aching, she reached out, smoothing back his bangs with her fingertips. He flinched and jerked away.

"I'm sorry," Kelly said. "I know this isn't what you expected. What either of us expected, really. But it doesn't have to be bad. It can be whatever we make it." She studied his rigid back, then set her shoulders and smiled. "All we have to do is look to the birds."

He eyed her over his shoulder, examining her from head to toe as though she were a piece of crap stuck to the toe of his well-worn tennis shoe.

"From the Good Book," she prompted. "Birds are always provided for and never worry about tomorrow. Your mom used to say it all the time. We just gotta be optimistic."

Pain flashed in his eyes. He scowled, lifted his chin, then bit out, "This place is abandoned. There aren't any birds out here."

She laughed. "Of course, there are. There's"—she tipped her head back and scanned the blue sky—"well, there's . . ."

Nothing. Absolutely nothing. No wings, no beaks, no chirps. Not even a cloud.

A small hand tugged the hem of Kelly's T-shirt. Daisy, Todd's six-year-old sister, blinked her thick eyelashes and crooked her small finger. Over the past year, she rarely spoke, and when she did, it was only to Kelly or Todd. Daisy's words were as precious and valuable as she herself was to Kelly.

Kelly bent, placing her ear close to Daisy's mouth, and waited for Daisy's little lips to brush her cheek.

"Over there," she whispered softly. So softly, Kelly barely caught it. Then Daisy, clutching her well-loved doll named Cassie to her chest with one hand, pointed toward the tree line in the distance.

Lo and behold, a black-and-gray figure emerged, leaping from the towering tip of a pine tree, flapping its wings and ascending high above the weedy lot.

"Hot dog!" Kelly kissed Daisy's cheek, nudged Todd with her elbow and bounced up and down as if her exuberance alone would ignite a spark of interest in Todd. "Daisy spotted one right over there. Look at that beauty go. She knows how to live. Spreading her wings, soaring without a care. A strong red-tailed hawk who has tossed away her worries and is poised to conquer the world."

Todd glanced at the bird, then smirked. "That's a turkey vulture."

Kelly stopped bouncing. "Oh."

The vulture circled them twice on the swift breeze, then glided away over a thick clump of trees in the distance. The spring wind picked up, whistling over the abandoned lot, and the weeds started rustling again, the strange scratching sounds of creatures hidden among the overgrown grass growing closer and closer.

Biting her lip, Kelly hugged Daisy close to her side. "I think we need to pay our new boss, Mae Bell Larkin, a visit."

The drive into town didn't take very long. Blue Moon Haven Drive-In was located only five minutes from the

Blue Moon city limits and the drive through rural fields, colorful wildflowers and budding trees was just pretty enough to lift Kelly's spirits.

Along Center Street, the heart of Blue Moon's quaint downtown, small mom-and-pop shops with old-fashioned storefronts lined each side of the road; cherry trees, their blossoms still closed in anticipation of full-fledged spring, waved their graceful limbs in the light breeze; a three-tiered fountain stood confidently in the center of a roundabout, though it remained inactive. A few people milled about the sidewalks, and a golden retriever, barking playfully, shot across a grassy lawn in pursuit of a squirrel.

Kelly grinned. Sweet heaven, the town looked like the feature photograph in *Best Homes and Towns* magazine. This was why, from the moment it had snagged her attention, she'd clicked once-a-waking-hour, every day, on the ad for an assistant manager of Blue Moon Haven Drive-In. Even the owner's name, Mae Bell Larkin, seemed to hold promise in each syllable. She'd whispered it and the name of the town over and over during the four-hour drive from Birmingham to Blue Moon, imagining all of the warmth, beauty and comfort that awaited them. And maybe, just maybe, Mae Bell Larkin and her drive-in would offer the solid foundation she'd desired all of her life.

"In a quarter mile, turn left onto 1522 Silver Stay Way," chimed a feminine voice from the GPS navigation system of the car's dashboard.

Kelly slowed the car, turned on her blinker and maneuvered the tight turn. "You got to admit, it's beautiful country out here. I saw an old-fashioned candy shop back there called Tully's Treats. Bet they have all kinds of sugary goodies." She glanced in the rearview mirror. "Whatcha think, guys?"

Daisy sucked her thumb in her booster seat and

smoothed her hand over her doll's ragged curls, her eyes drooping heavily. Todd, occupying the passenger seat, glared down at his cell phone, his fingers moving wildly over the screen as he played a video game, the steady pound of a heavy beat emanating from the earbuds stuffed in his ears.

She sighed. Todd had never been excited about living on a drive-in–theater lot. Though she'd been optimistic about the prospect of waking up to a huge silver screen full of happy endings each day, Daisy and Todd had remained mute. And rightfully so, it seemed, considering their new "homey living quarters" was a relic, the drive-in–theater lot had been neglected for years, and the owner had not only lied to her, but—

"She lives in a nursing home?" Todd yanked the earbuds from his ears and shot upright in the passenger seat. "You sure this is the right place?"

Mouth gaping, Kelly pulled into a parking space in front of a brick building with a wide front porch, long wheelchair ramp and wooden sign emblazoned with the words: *SILVER STAY. WELCOME TO BLUE MOON'S MOST PRESTIGIOUS SENIOR-LIVING GETAWAY!*

"I . . ." She dug in her pocket, withdrew a small piece of paper and read the address she'd scrawled hours earlier. "1522 Silver Stay Way." Her stomach churned. "Silver Stay." Oh, no. What had she gotten herself into? "Yes. This seems to be it."

Todd rolled his eyes. "At this point, it's obvious that you didn't ask enough questions about this job before accepting it."

Kelly squeezed her eyes shut and drummed her fingertips on the steering wheel. "Chances are, she probably owns this place, too." She opened her eyes and smiled despite the judgmental daggers in Todd's gaze. "Lots of people dabble in different occupations and she chooses to spend her days caring for others. That's a noble pursuit I admire." She opened her door. "Now, get out. We're going inside so I can have a chat with Mrs. Larkin."

By the time Kelly helped Daisy from her booster seat, took her warm hand in hers and started up the metal wheelchair ramp, Todd had already trudged into the lobby. The wood flooring of the front porch creaked under Kelly's feet, and she lingered for a moment, taking in its wide wicker chairs and wrought iron tables. There was a clear view of the inactive fountain and tiny shops to the left and the curvy road leading to the drive-in could be seen to the right, just beyond a field full of green grass and the last of dead winter brush.

"There's a decent view out here on the porch, but I bet those chairs are a bit stiff and"—Kelly wrinkled her nose—"those empty tables could use a little sprucing up. If someone took care of the drab seating area, it might cheer the residents up a bit. Whatcha think?"

Daisy blinked up at her and remained silent.

"You're right. That's not what we're here for." Kelly winked. "Thank you for keeping me on track."

Squeezing Daisy's hand, she opened the front door of the nursing home and joined Todd in the lobby. An unpleasant mix of odors (apple juice, urine and bleach, maybe?) wafted around the open room. Two elderly men sat in wheelchairs in front of a window, one of them eating what looked like yellow gelatin, most of which fell off his spoon onto his lap.

The other man scowled at them, banged his fist on the arm of his wheelchair and shouted, "Where's my root beer?"

"Where's the prestige?" Todd returned.

A nurse, seated at a table directly in front of him, hung up the phone, which immediately began to ring again, and blew her frazzled hair out of her face. "I'm sorry, son, what did you say?"

Todd pursed his lips. "Your sign says, 'Welcome to Blue

Moon's most prestigious senior-living getaway.' So, where's the prestige? And where's that guy's root beer? He's been shouting for it ever since I came in here, and you haven't even bothered to answer him. Not to mention the other guy's losing half his food. You could get off the phone and help him, you know."

The nurse's mouth tightened. "Excuse me?"

"Exactly." Todd scowled. "Excuse y—"

Kelly clamped her hand over Todd's mouth. Her face flamed. "I-I'm very sorry." She forced a nervous smile, released Todd's mouth and ruffled his hair. "He . . . well, he's a bit outspoken for his age."

"'Outspoken'?" The nurse glared at Todd. "I'd say he's in need of a good spanking. He's a right bossy butt if you ask me."

"I'm too old to be spanked." Todd's mouth twisted with disdain. "And 'bossy butt' is a disappointingly rudimentary insult for someone *your* age."

Root beer man guffawed. "Get her, kid. And while you're at it, get me out of here. This place is a dump with bad service. *Baaaaaad* service!" He wheeled himself toward the front door. "I'm getting the hell outta here."

"Wonderful! See what you've done?" The nurse took two steps around the counter, then hesitated as the phone continued ringing, her head swiveling back and forth between the phone and the man who struggled to open the front door. "I had him halfway calm until you"—she stabbed her finger at Todd—"started with your backtalk and criticism." Decision made, she abandoned the ringing phone and jogged over to the front door, took hold of the man's wheelchair and tugged him away from the door. "Mr. Haggart, I told you I'd bring you a root beer as soon as I had a free moment. We're short-staffed today and I'm doing the best I can."

"Ain't good enough." Mr. Haggart swatted her hand

away, wheeled back to the door and wrapped his palm tighter around the door handle. "*Baaaaaad* service! I want a root beer and a cigarette."

"You know cigarettes aren't allowed." The nurse pulled harder on his wheelchair. "And they're bad for you anyway."

He elbowed her. "This place is what's bad for me, woman!"

"Please, Mr. Haggart, your son will have a fit if you take off again. Remember how angry and afraid he was last time?"

"Don't care, woman."

The two continued struggling with the door, the wheelchair and each other.

Kelly squatted beside Todd and gripped his shoulders. "That was incredibly rude, what you just did. You've got to learn to control your temper. It's inappropriate to speak to adults that way."

He shrugged. "I was right."

"It doesn't matter whether you were right or not," Kelly said in a low tone. She eyed the two adults still struggling with the front door. "You can't just go around saying whatever you think, whenever you think it. It's not always polite or appropriate."

The nurse managed to unfurl Mr. Haggart's hand from the door handle, then wheeled him back to his former position by the window. Disappointment flooded the older man's features, the phone began ringing again and moisture gathered in the corners of the nurse's eyes.

Sympathy for both of them flooded through Kelly. She squeezed Todd's shoulders. "Just stay quiet and let me handle things from here."

The nurse jogged back to the counter and answered the ringing phone, held a brief conversation regarding the delayed delivery of supplies, then hung up and dragged a hand through her disheveled hair.

"Look, I'm . . ." Hesitantly Kelly approached the counter. "I really am sorry about this, and I can see you're overwhelmed right now, so I'll try to be brief. I'm looking for Mrs. Mae Bell Larkin."

The nurse sighed. "Are you family?"

"No. Mrs. Larkin's my new boss. Is she available to see me?"

A strange expression crossed the nurse's face. "Oh, she's available. New boss of what?"

"I'm a new hire for the Blue Moon Haven Drive-In." The nurse stared, so Kelly added, "You know, the one right outside of town?"

"I know where—and what—it is. It's a dumpy relic and the only blight on our otherwise-immaculate town. Folks have been trying to raze it for several years now. Mae Bell's the only one who refuses to see reason." She eyed Kelly a moment longer, then slid a clipboard across the counter and tapped her fingernail on the paper. "Print and sign your name here. Add the time and date here. And I'll need to see some identification."

Kelly did as directed, then tapped the pen on the bold heading of the paper. "'Visitors Log'?" She rubbed her temple, where a painful throbbing had begun. "Is Mrs. Larkin a patient?"

The nurse glanced at Todd, then smiled in smug satisfaction. "Yes. Your new boss lives in room twelve." She pointed at a hallway to Kelly's left. "Halfway down that hall."

Fighting back the urge to crumple into a heap on the slick linoleum floor, Kelly took Daisy's hand in hers again, headed down the wide hallway and motioned for Todd to follow her.

Their tennis shoes squeaked along the polished linoleum, jerking to a halt when sorrowful wails echoed against the closed door of a patient room on the right. A fluorescent light flickered overhead and muted sounds from a TV, peppered with sporadic coughs, pierced the air.

Daisy tugged Kelly's hand, pulling her to a stop, then pointed at a door where the number 12 was formed in metal letters.

"Yep. This must be it. Thank you, Daisy." Kelly hesitated briefly, then lifted her balled fist and knocked.

A feminine voice, light, airy and formal, responded from the other side of the door. "If you possess a sense of humor and a healthy dose of ingenuity, you may enter. If you lack either, turn about and depart, please."

Kelly fiddled with the seam of her capris. "I have a sense of humor," she called out.

Wishing for the umpteenth time she'd had the money and opportunity to attend community college sixteen years ago, she glanced up at the tiled ceiling and tried to recall where she'd left off in the old pocket dictionary she kept stuffed in the cramped glove compartment of her car. She'd bought it right after her visit with the school psychologist. The dictionary had cost her fifty cents at a flea market near the mobile home park where she and the kids had lived, and she'd carried it to her car in her palms, as though it were a twenty-five-ounce diamond, in hopes it would help bridge the communication gap between her and Todd.

Anomaly, bucolic, catharsis, dogma, ethereal . . . Her shoulders slumped. She'd memorized all of those and many more words, but she hadn't made it to the *I*'s yet. Or . . . good grief, maybe *ahn-gee-new-ity* started with an *A* instead?

The door swept open on a sweet burst of floral perfume. A tall woman, perhaps seventysomething, dressed in a silky leopard print pants suit, purple heels a mile high and an air of confidence, looked down at them. Diamond studs glinted in her earlobes beneath the fluorescent lights, and a midnight black scarf secured her long pearl-white hair away from her powdered face in an elegant bun. Piano music played beyond her, flowing from the room in soft, tinkling chimes.

"I have a sense of humor," Kelly repeated.

The woman—Mae Bell Larkin, Kelly presumed—raised one immaculately manicured eyebrow. "And ingenuity?"

Kelly rubbed her cheek, her skin hot against her fingertips. "Whatever it is, I got that, too."

Todd scoffed. "It means *intelligent* and *origina—*"

"What'd I tell you earlier?" Kelly asked through a tight smile.

"That it doesn't matter if I'm right or not," he recited dully. "That I can't go around saying whatever I think, whenever I think it. That it's not always polite or appropriate."

The scorching heat in Kelly's cheeks traveled down her neck. She took a deep breath and counted to ten.

The woman in front of them studied Todd, a slow smile lifting her wrinkled cheeks. "My dear, one should never stifle one's voice or dull one's mind, no matter the circumstances. And saying—and doing—what's right is always appropriate, as it's the only honorable way to live." She tapped Todd's chin gently with a polished fingernail. "Don't you agree?"

Something almost resembling a grin flashed across Todd's mouth. "I do." He cut his eyes toward Kelly. "I totally agree."

Kelly stiffened. "That's a nice idea, but it doesn't always work in real life."

The woman's attention returned to her. "That depends on how you define 'real life.' How do you define it?"

Kelly winced. "Work, bills, responsibilities."

"Obligations." Todd crossed his arms over his chest and frowned.

The woman lowered herself to Daisy's eye level. "And you, my dear? What's your definition of 'real life'?"

Daisy's wide gaze roved over the older woman's face. She lifted her hand, trailed her fingertips along the woman's headscarf and rubbed the silky material between her fingers. Then, absentmindedly it seemed, stuck the thumb of her other hand in her mouth.

"Ah, I see. You're a lady who knows what she wants and unabashedly pursues it. That's a great way to live, doll." The woman patted Daisy's fingers, then straightened, looked all three of them over and smiled. Her maroon-painted lips were a stark contrast with her bright teeth. "I think y'all will do just fine."

"Are you Mrs. Larkin?" Kelly asked.

"Call me Mae Bell, dear. I enjoy ceremony, but prefer informal address with my friends. As you are my new hire, I hope you and I will become good friends during our venture together." She held out her hand. "Kelly Jenkins, I presume? 'Ambitious, independent and seeking a fresh start, hard work and interesting challenges,' according to your résumé, if I adequately recall?"

Todd scoffed. "More like broke, unemployed and looking for a place to liv—"

Kelly clamped a hand over his mouth. "I need to talk to you, Mrs. Lar—er, Mae Bell. May I come in?" She slipped past Mae Bell, then steered Todd farther into the hallway with Daisy. "Wait there with Daisy and don't move until I come out, okay?"

Todd glared. "Stop sticking your hand over my m—"

Kelly shut the door and rested her forehead against the hard wood. She became intensely aware of Mae

Bell's presence at her back. "I'm sorry for Todd's behavior."

"The boy speaks his mind. There's nothing wrong with that."

"Except the majority of what he says is insulting and he's great at it. At ten, his IQ is higher than that of most adults."

Mae Bell made a sound of impressed approval. "How high?"

"I don't remember, but high enough to make me feel dumb." Kelly pushed away from the door and faced Mae Bell. "I didn't realize you lived in a nursing home."

Mae Bell's smile dimmed. "We all must live somewhere, my dear. And as luck would have it, this"—she gestured toward the walls and ceiling—"establishment is the location my stepdaughter chose for me."

"Your stepdaughter?"

"Yes. The daughter of my seventh husband and my only living *relative*—I use the term loosely."

"Y-you were married seven times?"

Mae Bell's smile returned. "Indeed. The first three marriages were youthful mistakes, the fourth, fifth, and sixth I thought were true love, and the seventh, well. . . " A wistful expression appeared on her face. "My decision to marry Chandler was driven more by lust than love, but we made each other very happy, and I was devastated when he passed so soon after our marriage." Her eyes closed as her fingertips drifted down her neck and over her collarbone. "We had an adventurous seven months together, full of passion."

Kelly cleared her throat. "Yeah, about us all having to live somewhere . . . ?" She waited until Mae Bell opened her eyes and refocused on her. "You said one of my duties as assistant manager was providing a private viewing each week at the drive-in for you and your friends. You can't possibly still expect that of me."

"Of course." She frowned. "Why not?"

"Do your friends live here with you, too?" At Mae Bell's nod, Kelly gestured around her. "Well, how am I supposed to do that when y'all live here under what I'm guessing—from what I witnessed earlier with another resident—are pretty tight regulations?"

"I assume you're referring to Jimmy Haggart and his most recent attempt to escape?" Mae Bell waved away the concern. "He's made it out several times without being caught, one such escape in the dead of night." She shrugged. "I'm sure you also possess the resourcefulness to smuggle us out of here."

Kelly huffed out a breath. "I wouldn't bet on that. And in the emails you sent me, you referenced 'homey living quarters.' I've been out to the drive-in–theater lot and there's no home out there. It's totally run-down and neglected. There's trash everywhere, one of the projection screens has holes and the other screen is half blocked by big tree limbs. It's obvious no one's touched the place in—"

"Ten years." Mae Bell lifted her chin. "That's when I had my little stroke. Small, though it was, it did enough damage that my stepdaughter took it upon herself to place me here, and it's where I've remained ever since."

"Oh. I'm sorry. I truly am. But the trailer—"

"Is in perfect condition. Did you look inside or just frown at its exterior?" Mae Bell studied Kelly's expression. "You are the lucky resident of a 1951 Spartan Royal Mansion, the entirety of which has been renovated over the years, while still retaining its original charm. It's a spacious double ender, too. Everything you need is inside that beautiful gem of a home."

"I'll admit I didn't go in, but it didn't look very promising from the outside."

"And that"—Mae Bell spread her arms—"is how most people miss the greatest treasures in life. By judging everything and everyone by appearance, financial gain, and practicality. They seek the illusion of security and predictability when life is everything but." She tilted her head. "And you?"

Kelly blinked. "What about me?"

"Something brought you out here. What are you seeking?"

"A job."

"To support your son and daughter financially?"

"They're not mine." Kelly entwined her fingers, squeezing them tightly, and focused on the pain in her fingertips rather than the welling of hot moisture along her lower lashes. "I'm just taking care of them."

Mae Bell grew quiet as her gaze drifted over Kelly from head to toe. "Where are their mother and father?"

"She passed away a year ago." Kelly stared out of the window to the quaint, quiet street that lay beyond. The kind she'd only ever dreamed of living on. "Breast cancer." Her skin prickled as Mae Bell continued to scrutinize her. "Laice—their mother—was my best friend. We'd known each other since we were kids. I promised her not long before she passed that I'd look after Todd and Daisy if something happened to their father." Her lip curled. Just the thought of that man was enough to turn her stomach. "Zane, their dad, dropped Todd and Daisy off at my apartment three months after Laice died. I haven't heard from him since."

Mae Bell remained silent.

Kelly rubbed her hands together. "I was living in Birmingham, things weren't working out and I needed a job, so I had no choice but to take a chance on this one."

"That's not true, my dear."

Frowning, Kelly faced her.

Mae Bell smiled. "We always have choices, no matter the circumstances. The options might not always be ideal or the ones we want, but they're always present nonetheless." Her smile widened. "And you chose this one."

Kelly shook her head. "The three of us won't fit in that trailer."

"You will. Comfortably."

"You said no experience was required for the assistant manager position. I assumed the manager would be on the premises with me. I have no experience and no help. There's no way I can renovate and revive that place alone."

"The only experience you need is a steel spine, and I wouldn't have hired you if I didn't get the impression you had it. Besides, I'll help you every step of the way."

"How? You're living here, not on the property. And that place is in total—"

"Decay," Mae Bell said sharply. "Do you know how easy it is for something—or someone—to fall apart when it's left alone with no one to love it? No one to care for it? To even acknowledge its existence?"

Kelly watched as Mae Bell closed her eyes briefly, then walked slowly across the small room to the twin bed in the corner, her legs visibly shaking.

Heart aching, Kelly crossed the room and cupped her hand under one of Mae Bell's thin elbows, helping her to sit on the edge of the bed. "I'm sorry. I didn't mean to offend you or to imply . . ."

Mae Bell took Kelly's hand in hers and squeezed. Her blue eyes, wounded, widened at Kelly, the crow's feet fanning out from the corners caked with powder. "Be honest, please. Out of all the paths you could've taken, why did you choose to come to Blue Moon?"

Kelly looked down and smoothed her thumb gently over the delicate skin covering a thick vein in Mae Bell's hand. "I came because I wanted a different 'real life.' I wanted to bring Todd and Daisy to a place that would help them heal and become excited about life again." She lifted her chin, meeting Mae Bell's direct gaze. "And I came because of me. I'm capable of more than I was entrusted with back in Birmingham. I have more to offer, and I want a chance to do work I'm proud of. I want to help people smile again. And because, as silly as some people may think I am . . . I still believe in happy endings."

Mae Bell squeezed her hand tighter. "I promise, you've come to the right place. That clear, wide-open sky out there isn't the only beautiful jewel in this country town. There's more sweet, healing magic here in Blue Moon for those two beautiful children than you could ever imagine." Her smile returned. "Stay a while. Give the Spartan Mansion a try and the drive-in renovation a trial run. I'll call the bank and have you added to my business account for restoration expenses and get you an advance first thing in the morning."

Kelly smiled. That lonely gaze and pleading tone made it impossible to say no. "Okay. I'll give it a trial run."

"Perfect! I left a trunk in the Mansion for you. Your first task on our priority list is to follow the instructions inside. How about you stop by tomorrow and we'll make a list of the rest of the priorities for the renovation?" Mae Bell's expression brightened. "Any time is fine." She gestured toward the room around her and smiled wide. "As you see, my schedule is open."

"Then I'll be by tomorrow, midmorning." Kelly glanced at the closed door; Todd was probably still fuming on the other side. "For now, I'm gonna get the kids settled. Is there a chain saw somewhere in those trash piles at the drive-in?"

Mae Bell raised one eyebrow. "Why?"

Kelly grinned. "The top of my priority list—before this trunk unveiling of yours—involves sweating off some stress."

CHAPTER 2

Seth Morgan had been blessed early in life. He'd grown up in a loving two-parent home, developed a close bond with his entertaining (but sometimes aggravating) little sister, earned an undergraduate degree in agriculture and a graduate degree specializing in plant pathology, married his first love at twenty-two and, one year later, had the most perfect daughter in existence.

Now, at thirty-eight, Seth had a rowdy mutt with an unnatural fondness for hot dogs, an isolated pecan orchard, an eerily empty house and a heart heavy with regret.

Each day and night dragged on so long, Seth sometimes wished he could do without them altogether, and, at times like this, he feared his insomnia had led him to the brink of insanity.

"Who's there?"

A flutter of movement on the far left side of his pecan orchard caught his eye. He tossed his lopping shears in the bed of his pickup truck and walked slowly across the tree-lined field toward the soft rustling in the distance.

Patch, the stray mongrel who had taken up residence at Seth's house five years ago, stuck to his right leg like static cling, his beefy and somewhat-clumsy body moving in tandem with Seth's.

"Who's there?" Seth repeated. "This is private property—signs are posted everywhere. You have no business here."

Leaves rustled. A low-hanging branch dipped, a small face peeked around the thick tree trunk and two blue eyes blinked up at him from a distance.

Seth jerked to a halt, a twig snapping beneath his work boot. His heart kicked hard against his ribs and a clammy chill crawled along the flesh of his upper back and arms. Heaven help him . . . he had finally gone insane.

"Rachel?" he called.

His hoarse voice echoed across the silent lot; then a swift breeze picked up, disturbing the still branches of trees that formed perfect rows. The sun hung low in the sky, its rays sharp between the thick tree trunks, but dim among the dense limbs. A small figure darted out from behind the tree trunk and sprinted away from him.

Seth's legs propelled him forward, striding over the thick grass of his orchard in pursuit of the young vision, while his mind struggled to put logic above irrational hope. He'd been scouting for pecan scab and ambrosia beetles along the bark of each pecan tree for nine hours, and four hours prior to that, he'd installed a rain cover and windbreak for his beehives in preparation for the early-spring storms forecasted on the morning news for Blue Moon.

His back ached, his hands throbbed and he'd finally achieved his preferred state of exhaustion: one that caused his eyelids to droop, his senses to dull and his emotions to numb. At this point, with the sun dipping toward the horizon and sunlight and shadow mingling over the grassy bed of the orchard, he'd begun drifting between a state of dogged alertness and a dreamlike fatigue that slowed his movements.

It was only natural that he'd mistaken the dip of a branch and the rustle of leaves for his daughter's presence. A presence he missed every second of every day. He couldn't bear the knowledge that he'd no longer be able to see, talk or laugh with her.

But . . . there she was again!

"Wait!"

The shape—a little girl dressed in capris and a T-shirt—darted between two large pecan trees, running away, her white tennis shoes flashing with an ethereal grace through tall green grass, wilted leaves and fallen twigs.

His throat constricted. "Rachel?" He began jogging. Wove between massive tree trunks, shoved aside low limbs. "Rachel, wait!"

But it couldn't be Rachel. She'd died eight years ago. He'd watched it happen, ten feet in front of him. He'd been unable to prevent her death then, and certainly couldn't change what was happening now.

But still . . .

His lungs seized and his heart hammered in his chest, each thunderous beat seeming to echo across his orchard into the neighboring lot, breaking the silence that had cloaked his property for years.

The girl ran faster across the grass, the thick blades slowly springing back as proof of her passing.

"Rachel!" He reached out, his heartbeat pounding in his ears and his fingertips grazing the soft sleeve of her T-shirt before she slipped farther away, running toward two figures positioned by a massive pecan tree that straddled his property line and that of the neighboring lot.

The tree, almost two hundred years old, with sprawling branches and ledges and knots sized perfectly for climbing, had been Rachel's favorite. Years ago, she'd hopped into his truck cab at daybreak every Saturday morning, sipped her juice while he drank his coffee and drove to the far side of the orchard, then bounded out of the truck and ran to her tree. She would climb to the largest branch she could reach, scoot to a comfortable dip in the limb, settle in and smile as the sun rose, chatting to him as he worked in the orchard.

The pounding of his heart grew louder. Morphed into a rhythmic hack. And there she stood. A young girl of Rachel's age—but definitely not Rachel—huddled beside a scowling preteen boy, several feet from a woman who hacked at a limb of Rachel's favorite pecan tree with strong swings of an ax.

Grief and anger knotted in his throat, causing his voice to emerge in a hoarse whisper. "What are you doing?"

The woman hadn't heard him. Her back to him and legs spread in a strong stance, she kept swinging the ax, the toned muscles in her arms contracting with each effort, her long ponytail swinging across her back in tandem with her movements.

Hands trembling, he forced his frozen legs to move and strode quickly across the property line, high weeds tangling around his shins with every step.

"Stop."

She kept swinging. His anger rose higher.

"I said, stop!" Reaching her side, he threw out his arm, curled his hand around the handle of the ax and yanked, halting her swing in midair. "Stop!"

She stared up at him, her brown eyes startled, mouth gaping open in shock. "Wha . . . Who are you?"

"This tree is mine. It's on my property. You're not to touch it."

"What're you talking about?" She puffed a strand of hair out of her face. "It's blocking half the projection screen."

Seth pointed with his free hand to the ground. "You're standing on the property line. Everything from this point forward—including this tree—is part of my orchard and, therefore, my property."

Her knuckles tightened around the handle of the ax. "The trunk of this tree may be on your property, but the limbs aren't." She tugged against his grip. "And this ax belongs to my boss, so get your hands off it."

"Your boss?" He frowned as his heels lifted and he tipped forward. She was strong. Much stronger than he'd guess for a woman of her stature. He had to grip the ax handle with both hands to keep from toppling over. "No one's worked or lived on this lot for years."

Seth, of all people, knew that for a fact. He'd haggled with Mae Bell Larkin for almost a decade in futile attempts to buy the run-down drive-in lot and expand his pecan orchard. She'd refused him on all but one occasion, which had occurred three months ago during his most recent visit to Silver Stay nursing home. Mae Bell had been indignant and reluctant as always, but she'd shown a softening by asking him to visit her again in six months. If nothing changed, she had said, he'd be welcome to buy the lot for a respectable price. That had been the first and only time he'd left with a ray of hope about acquiring the property.

Nothing had changed on the abandoned drive-in lot for years, and he'd had every reason to believe it never would.

Until the short stranger in front of him took an ax to Rachel's tree. Each of her swings had sent the ache in his chest deeper into his body.

"Well, someone's working and living here now." She pulled harder on the ax.

"Let it go," he gritted. Patch started barking. "Stop trying to strong-arm me."

"Strong-arm you?" A sarcastic laugh burst from her lips. "I'm not the one who barreled over the property line like a lunatic, started manhandling a woman and scared an innocent little girl!"

His eyes darted to the left, taking in the tear-streaked face of the little girl he'd mistaken for Rachel. Her wet cheeks were flushed and her tiny chin trembled. Each time Patch barked, her eyes widened even more.

"Would you please stop this tug-of-war and discuss this with me like an adult?" His attention returned to the woman. Dirt smudged her smooth forehead, and her lush eyebrows were a bit ruffled, but the firm look of determination in her dark eyes and the maturity in her quiet tone made him feel like a brute. "You're upsetting Daisy."

Seth's grip on the ax handle loosened, his torso swiveling in the girl's direction as a long-buried instinct to console and protect sent a wave of shame through him. "I-I didn't realize—"

A sharp pain reverberated through his left shin.

"Let go, you jerk!" A young boy, no more than twelve, drew his leg back, pointed his toe and kicked Seth's shin again. "Get your hands off her." He started swinging. One fist hit Seth's left ribs, the other landed smack-dab in the center of his gut.

"My hands aren't on her." Seth released the ax handle with one hand, held it up and stepped back in an attempt to ease the boy's temper. Another punch, right in his gut. Despite the pain, Seth grunted in grudging appreciation. The kid had as strong a swing as his mom.

"Get back, Todd." The woman nudged the boy with her hip. "Let me handle this."

"You're not handling it." Todd kicked Seth's shin again. "You let people walk all over you whenever they want."

Distracted, the woman eased her grip on the ax as she leaned to the side, trying to move the boy back. "Stop it, Todd. How many times have I told you—"

"Kick him!" the boy yelled, landing another punch to Seth's ribs. "Stand up for yourself and kick the bastar—"

"Watch your language!" Flustered, she released the ax just as Patch lunged toward Todd. She gasped and jumped in front of the boy.

"Sit." Seth grabbed the scruff of Patch's neck and tugged him away. "Quiet."

Patch did as commanded, huffed out a breath and ducked his head, surreptitiously eyeing the three strangers in front of him.

Seth, murmuring words of approval, rubbed Patch's ears, then faced the trio. Each one wore a different expression: fear, anger, and disapproval. Silence fell over the derelict drive-in lot amidst their stares, magnifying his discomfort.

His face flamed. "You're right," he said quietly, meeting the woman's direct gaze. As he shifted from one boot to the other, her eyes strangely seemed to peer past his skin right to his soul. "We should discuss this like adults, and all things considered, I don't think this is the right time."

Seth waited a moment, mulling over an apology, but after glancing at the girl he'd mistaken for Rachel, a renewed sting of grief heated his eyes. Throat tight, he stepped back over his property line, clucked his tongue and walked toward the welcome cover of his trees with Patch following in his wake.

* * *

Try as she might, Kelly couldn't pull her attention away from the burly man striding through the maze of trees. Her eyes traced the slumping curve of his wide shoulders and watched his blond head lower more with each step he took until his tall figure, trailed by his dog, disappeared into the late-afternoon shadows gathering among the trees.

He'd been rude, forceful and even a bit frightening. But there'd been something else about him. Something in his voice, the dip of his head, his defensive posture. He'd avoided her gaze for the most part, only meeting her eyes directly twice during the confrontation, and there'd been a wounded look about him.

Kelly narrowed her eyes and hugged Daisy, who still sniffled with fear, closer to her leg. "It's all right, sweet pea." Strange to think that a big man such as that, who'd barged his way onto someone else's property, startled Daisy, physically intruded on her task and clearly expected unquestionable obedience to his demands, would be . . . what? Vulnerable, maybe? "You're just a bit shaken up. That'll ease once we get settled in our new Royal Mansion."

"Why didn't you kick him? Punch him? Yell at him? Something!"

She turned away from the trees and faced Todd. He scowled at her, balled his fists at his sides and stamped his foot on the ground for good measure.

"Obviously, he had no right to come over here and behave the way he did," she said calmly, smoothing her palm over Daisy's long hair. "But that doesn't mean we have to behave even worse. Violence has a way of creating more violence, and that's not something we want."

"So you'd just let him rip that ax out of your hands, tell you what's what and make Daisy cry?" Todd scowled. "You should've laid him out."

Despite it all, Kelly grinned. "Oh, so ya think little ol'

weak, ignorant me could've wrangled that big dude to the ground?" She pressed her hand to her chest and batted her eyelashes. "I'm flattered."

His scowl deepened. "You know what I mean."

"Yes, but I also know that man—as wrong as he was—had a reason for doing what he did."

"Some people are just mean."

"Yeah. Sometimes that's true. But sometimes it's not, and I get the feeling that this situation is different." She gestured toward Daisy, who snuggled her cheek tighter against Kelly's thigh. "He's a lot bigger than us. He could've hurt you, Daisy or me at any point if he wanted to, but he didn't. In truth, he never even laid a hand on me."

Todd's mouth tightened. "That's a technicality."

"And he even looked kinda sorry there at the end."

Todd glared.

"Maybe he's broke and needs every penny he has," she continued, "including that tree I was chopping. Or maybe we scared him a little, seeing as how no one's lived or worked here for years. Maybe he heard us making noise, got nervous and came over here ready to chase down a trespasser. Emotions take over at times. There isn't always a logical explanation for everything."

"Of course, there is. He's just a jerk looking for a fight, and you should've given it to him. You should've slapped his face."

The fury behind Todd's eyes made Kelly's breath catch. His rigid frame seethed with anger, pain and disdain. He'd never been this vengeful before, not even before Laice died or after Zane abandoned him. But lately he'd grown more judgmental—and full of hatred every day.

Kelly eased Daisy away, knelt in front of Todd and cradled his face in her hands. "Oh, Todd." She searched his eyes. "How can I help you see the world differently?

How can I get you to understand that your heart knows more than your mind ever will?"

He jerked away and stalked off, slapping away weeds as he went.

Kelly dragged a hand over her face and shouted at his back. "While you're on the move, work your way to the car, be our butler and start unloading the bags. It'll be dark soon, so we need to start settling in."

He stomped through the weeds for a few more feet out of defiance, then veered to the left and trudged toward the car.

Kelly smiled and beckoned Daisy closer. "Whatcha say, babe? You ready to live like queens and move into our Royal Mansion?"

"It's an aluminum can." Todd rapped his knuckles against the door of the travel trailer situated on the back edge of Blue Moon Haven's Drive-In lot. "Hear that? It's like an empty soda can."

Kelly's gut sank. She rolled her lips together to keep from agreeing. It wouldn't improve Daisy's spirits to give any credence to Todd's pessimistic commentary right now.

After the unpleasant confrontation over the tree with their grumpy neighbor, Kelly and the kids had spent almost an hour unloading and sorting bags of clothes, bedsheets, towels and Daisy's toys. It had seemed like a simple task at the time, but once all of their meager belongings had been separated into three small piles, it had become painfully obvious to Kelly how little Todd and Daisy possessed . . . and how very much they were missing. She'd tried hard over the past several months to provide as best she could for them, buying inexpensive toys for Daisy whenever possible and a new video game for Todd once.

Neither of them had said much as they'd sorted their stuff and eyed the trailer. But eventually Daisy had sat down among the weeds beside her bag of clothes, clutching her favorite doll, Cassie, to her chest and sucking her thumb, her eyes and spirits sagging.

"I mean, that thing is straight-up *aluminum.*" Todd flopped into a dilapidated outdoor lounge chair, which sat under a blue canopy attached to the front of the travel trailer. It creaked with dry rot. "We'd be better off sleeping under a concrete overpass."

Rolling her shoulders, Kelly maneuvered her way past the bags of clothes and belongings Todd had dragged from the car and piled on the grass in front of the trailer. She stepped carefully up to the front door, examined the shiny silver surface, which, surprisingly, was free of blemishes, and trailed her palm along the smooth surface, pausing when her fingertips encountered a red-and-blue logo.

"Spartan Royal Mansion," she read. "Manufactured by Spartan Aircraft Company." Excitement spilled over her skin. "An aircraft company designed this. Do you know what this is? This isn't just a trailer." She smiled at Daisy, who sat, stared and continued sucking her thumb silently. Todd crossed his arms and slumped farther back in his dry-rotted chair. "This is the closest I've ever gotten to stepping inside an airplane."

Todd sneered. "It's not a plane. It's a seventy-year-old aluminum-bodied travel trailer stagnating in the middle of nowhere, most likely built by engineers who worked behind a desk. What you're saying makes no sense."

"Maybe not. But it was designed by an aircraft company, and when I was your age, I always dreamed I'd fly a jet or plane or anything, as long as it got off the ground." Kelly smiled wistfully at Daisy, then bent close to Todd's ear and whispered, "And given the fact that this is the closest I may ever come to an actual airplane and that—*most importantly*—we want Daisy to feel better, we're going to pretend that this aluminum trailer is a rare luxury and that this is the most fascinating adventure of our lives, okay?"

Todd rolled his eyes, but lost the sneer.

"Come on, baby girl." Kelly clapped her hands and smiled at Daisy. "Let's take a tour of this beauty, shall we?"

Daisy glanced at Todd, who stared mutely at the weedy lot, then stood and slowly joined Kelly at the entrance. They stood still for a few moments, taking in the entirety of the silver trailer, which had large windows in the front and back end. There were a few small dents and dings and a slight bit of surface rust along one edge of the frame, but otherwise, the exterior of the trailer was, Kelly had to admit, in excellent condition.

"Looks good on the outside," she said, taking Daisy's warm hand in hers. "Let's get a look inside."

Cautiously Kelly opened the outer door, only to find a screened wooden door on the inside. She opened that as well and drew Daisy inside.

A low whistle escaped Kelly as she twirled around the space slowly, kicking herself for her flippant dismissal of the trailer earlier that day. "Mae Bell might've been onto something."

Solid, handcrafted wood shelves and soft upholstered furniture created an inviting space in the living-room area, complete with a foldout sofa bed. And true to Mae Bell's word, a large wooden trunk sat at one corner of the couch, with her name written on a small card attached to the top.

A fully equipped kitchen, comprised of a stainless-steel refrigerator, small gas stovetop, microwave, coffeepot and sink with a drainboard, also boasted a built-in, padded booth, which would comfortably seat four people. The bathroom down the small hallway had been updated with a modernized shower, new toilet, sleek sink and spotless mirror. And the bedroom . . . oh, the bedroom!

Deep pink and rose-tinted light from the sunset outside spilled through the open blinds of the large windows and cast an opulent dreamlike quality over the flawless white bedding and handcrafted oak headboard.

Kelly glanced down at Daisy. Her thumb had fallen out of her mouth and her lips curved into a grin. "Whatcha say?" Kelly asked. "Wanna race me for it?"

Daisy giggled, shoved past Kelly and ran to the plush queen bed positioned in the center of the wide bedroom. She jumped onto the center of the bed, flopping against the thick quilt and snuggling her face into the massive pillows.

"From your reaction, I take it that the bed'll do?" Kelly flopped onto her back beside Daisy, and a sigh of pleasure rose from her chest. "Ah! This is what you call a bed fit for a mansion. That'll teach me not to judge something based on its age or looks."

"There's only one."

Kelly shoved to her elbows and smiled at Todd, who stood in the bedroom doorway. "One here, and one in the living room. The sofa folds out." She stretched, allowing herself the luxury of wallowing once more, then dragged herself off the opulent bed and motioned for Todd to take her place. "You and Daisy will sleep here tonight, and I'll use the sofa bed in the living room. After that, you and I will swap out once in a while so we'll all get a chance to enjoy this beauty." She patted the edge of the mattress. "Go on. Give it a try."

Todd eyed her warily, then looked at Daisy, who'd popped her thumb back in her mouth, closed her eyes and was all but snoring. Slowly he walked over, tested the mattress with the heel of his hand, then lay down. He stared at the ceiling for a few seconds until his eyelids grew heavy and slowly closed.

Kelly laughed. "Told ya, you'd like it."

He cracked one eye open and smirked. "It'll suffice, I guess."

"It's the cat's meow, boy! Admit it." She ruffled his hair playfully, then skipped to the hallway. "Take a breather with Daisy while I bring in our things and heat up some hot dogs for supper."

Giddy with excitement, Kelly channeled her new-found energy into hauling their bags in, unpacking necessities for the night and retrieving a pack of hot dogs, buns and condiments from the cooler she'd packed that morning for the drive down to Blue Moon. A quick investigation of the kitchen appliances assured her they were all in working order, and she popped several hot dogs in the microwave, warmed the buns and set the table with condiments and cold cans of soda.

"Come eat, kiddos," Kelly called as she fixed a plate for Daisy and piled one high with hot dogs for Todd (the ten-year-old human garbage disposal). "It ain't fancy, but it'll fill our bellies."

They emerged from the bedroom, drowsy-eyed and flushed, but once they were seated in the booth and got a whiff of warm hot dogs and bread, they dug into their food with gusto, pausing between bites long enough to guzzle down several gulps of the fizzy drinks.

Thank you, Daisy mouthed before chomping into the last bite of her hot dog, mustard dripping down her chin.

"You're welcome." Kelly wiped her face and grabbed Daisy's overnight bag. "How about we get you in the shower, then in bed for the night? Todd, when we're finished in the bathroom, it'll be your turn."

He frowned. "You're not going to eat?"

Kelly nodded. "Soon as I get Daisy settled. Think I'll sit outside while y'all get settled in bed. I want to check out the trunk Mae Bell left for me. Will you please start unpacking what you need for tonight while I help Daisy shower and change into her nightgown?"

Surprisingly, he complied with her request without complaint and even cleaned up his and Daisy's plates while she helped Daisy settle into bed. The shower was already running again by the time Kelly left Daisy sleeping in the bedroom.

Kelly smiled, hauled the large chest, which Mae Bell had left her, outside beneath the canopy attached to the trailer and flipped on the light. Todd, growing boy that he was, had eaten all but one hot dog, which she nuked again in the microwave, and, finding no buns left, carried the hot dog outside wrapped in a paper towel.

Settled in one of the patio chairs, Kelly took a bite of the warm hot dog, her stomach growling in appreciation. She chewed slowly, keenly aware the one bun-less frankfurter wouldn't go very far in filling her stomach.

Weeds rustled in the distance and the multicolored head of a dog emerged above the tall grass, a black nose sniffing closer and closer.

Kelly tensed and scooted to the edge of the chair, ready to bolt if necessary. "What's up, pup? You wanna show your face? You don't belong here and you're making me nervous."

As if it understood, the dog waddled out of the tall grass and hesitated at the edge of the dirt outside of the trailer. Its big, brawny face was mottled with various shades of beige, black, brown and white.

Kelly froze. "Oh, it's you." The dog that had accompanied the man. The one that had almost attacked Todd. "I'm surprised you moseyed over here after the way you and your owner behaved."

The dog ducked his head and blinked, looking suitably ashamed.

"Well, don't think you're gonna take up over here, okay? Not only would your owner probably start fussing at me again, but I'd be hard-pressed to trust you after what you and he did. I have no idea what you thought you'd gain by coming back over here."

The dog sniffed the air, then whimpered, his eyes widening as he stared.

Kelly followed his gaze to the hot dog clutched in her hand. "Oh, no. Forget it, bud. This is all I got. Todd ate the rest of them." She took another bite, relishing its taste.

The dog stretched out on the ground, rested his chin on his paws and blinked up at her soulfully.

Kelly rolled her eyes. "Oh, all right. But don't ever say I never took the high road." She nibbled one more bite of the frank, then tossed the rest on the ground in front of him.

He shot to his feet, gobbled it up, then barked and ran off into the high weeds.

"Nice. Not even a thank-you." She shook her head. "I get no respect nowadays."

Sighing, she pulled the chest Mae Bell had left her closer, peeled the envelope off the top and opened it. A set of keys fell out of the enclosed note into her palm.

Dear Ms. Kelly Jenkins,

I hope your trip to Blue Moon was comfortable and that you're ready to hit the ground running regarding restoration of the magnificent Blue Moon Haven Drive-In! You'll soon find it's a one-of-a-kind treasure that will pay off far more than you may ever expect . . . once it receives a little tender love and care.

Enclosed you'll find the keys to every nook and corner of the property, as well as what amounts to a comprehensive history of cinema, which will serve you well in your endeavor to restore majesty to Blue Moon Haven Drive-In. After all, one cannot lovingly restore a great establishment if one doesn't first appreciate—and admire—its origins. Blue Moon Haven Drive-In is more than a theater; it's a stage where families draw together to enjoy stirring stories of the human heart that transcend time, distance and cultural boundaries. Start at the beginning . . . and I hope, with your valued help, Blue Moon Haven Drive-In will never see its end.

Mae Bell Larkin

Inside the chest, dozens of VHS tapes were stacked in neat piles, bound with ribbon and tagged with dates ranging from the 1920s to the 1980s. Silent-film fare, romance, mystery, Westerns, science fiction, horror, film noir—every genre imaginable was included, along with detailed notes taped to each.

Kelly glanced up at the clear starry sky and struggled to smile. Where in the world would she find a VCR in this day and age? The moon, only a tiny sliver, shined brightly and seemed to promise so much. Sighing, she whispered, "Guess, I'll start at the beginning . . ."

CHAPTER 3

This had to end. Right now.

Seth turned into the parking lot of Silver Stay nursing home, parked his truck and cut the engine. For a Thursday afternoon, downtown Blue Moon was especially busy. More traffic than usual flowed down the recently paved streets, several people strolled along the sidewalks and the chatter of voices and steady *thunks* of car doors shutting could be heard in the distance.

But Seth barely noticed these things. Instead, his attention was almost immediately drawn back to the conflicting emotions roiling inside him. A restless ball of anger, resentment, grief and regret that had kept him tossing all night after his encounter with the woman next door. Emotions that had dragged him out of bed first thing this morning, propelled him to drive his truck to the property line of his orchard so he could see whether her car still remained on the old drive-in–theater lot.

Unfortunately, the car was still parked in the weed-eaten field, and judging from the recently opened windows of the trailer, he assumed she'd moved herself and her two kids in.

Well, not for long, if he had anything to do with it.

Seth retrieved a cold can of root beer from the glove compartment, exited the truck, stalked up the front steps of the nursing home and went inside. He paused briefly by a man who sat in a wheelchair beside the door and handed him the root beer.

"Thanks, Seth." Jimmy Haggart popped the tab, took a hefty swig and smiled. "A man can't get no decent root beer in this place. Shoot, a man can't get no decent nothing here. No cigarettes, no wome—"

"Mr. Haggart, you haven't eaten lunch yet." Kadence Powell, head nurse and former classmate of Seth's, rounded the wide counter in the lobby and clucked her tongue. "Seth, I've warned you about bringing him sugar this early in the day."

Jimmy growled something obscene under his breath. "Ain't enough sugar in here to sustain an ant, woman."

Seth shrugged. "It's just one root beer." And more than likely, the only one Jimmy would get for some time. He couldn't see the harm in offering the old man what he considered a luxury once in a while. "Can't you look the other way just this once?"

Kadence grinned. "I've looked the other way one time too many for you, Seth Morgan." Her gaze roved over him slowly. "Even when I haven't wanted to."

"Ha!" Jimmy gulped another swig of root beer and winked at Seth. "If I had your looks and age, boy . . . oh, the damage I'd do in this town."

Kadence stopped grinning, cleared her throat and straightened her uniform. "I assume you're here to see Mae Bell again?"

Seth nodded.

"She's not going to budge on that land you want." She leaned in and lowered her voice. "Just so you know, a woman came in just yesterday with a couple kids and said Mae Bell had hired her to—"

"Thank you, but I already know." He forced a polite smile. "I had the misfortune of meeting her yesterday when she invaded my property."

Kadence grimaced. "She seemed nice enough, and her daughter was as cute as an angel, but that boy of hers is a pure heathen."

Seth flexed his foot, his shin still sore from yesterday's altercation. "I'm aware of that, too."

Kadence gestured toward the hallway on her right. "Mae Bell's up and at 'em early this morning if you want to go on in and see her. Seems yesterday's guests got her all riled up again over reviving that trash heap of a drive-in of hers."

He thanked her and eased past, walked down the hall and stopped in front of Mae Bell's door, where he knocked once.

"Come in, Seth," Mae Bell called from inside.

Lips thinning, he opened the door and entered.

Mae Bell stood by the window, dressed in a ruby-red dress and high heels, her white hair curling loosely about her shoulders. "I saw you drive up and sit scowling in the parking lot for five minutes. Still, it's nice to see your handsome face again, my dear. I'm practically starved for an attractive male in this desolate establishment."

Seth frowned.

"Oh, don't be so dry and buttoned-up. It doesn't suit you." She waved a hand, then brushed a long curl over her shoulder. "Besides, a body has to hold on to a sense of passion and humor in a place like this, or die of boredom. Come have a seat and get comfortable. I assume you're here to resume our argument over why I won't sell my land to you?"

"I don't want to argue with you, Mae Bell. I'd just like

to remind you that my offer still stands. Not as is, though." He reached into the back pocket of his jeans and withdrew a checkbook. "I'm willing to write a check today for double the amount I offered last month."

Mae Bell's brows rose. "Interesting." A slow smile spread across her wrinkled face. "Tell me, have you met your new neighbors yet?"

"They're not my neighbors," he said tightly. "Twice, Mae Bell. I'm offering you more than twice what that patch of neglected land is worth. I'll even go so far as to skip the check, go to the bank now and return, bills in hand."

"And what would I do with a stack of hundreds? Gamble in the casino on the forward deck while I sip a martini?" She laughed. "At my age, money holds a very different meaning than it did decades ago."

"It'd get you out of here." Seth bit his lower lip, thinking he ought to stop and not stoop to such low measures to talk her out of her property. But this transaction meant more than saving a tree. There wasn't too great a price for a precious memory. "You could buy an apartment or small house downtown. Hire a live-in nurse and regain your privacy and freedom." He gestured toward her queen-size bed, reupholstered chairs and record player. "I'd help you pack, furnish your new home and pay for top-notch landscaping so you could enjoy your coffee and a glass of wine on a warm sunlit deck every morning and evening."

Her smile slipped. "If only your offer sprang from a genuine fondness for me as an individual, or even as a gesture of goodwill toward a former neighbor, I might consider accepting a fraction of what you offer and feel as though I received the better end of the deal." She spread her hands. "But you and I both know better, don't we?"

"I need my privacy, Mae Bell." He clamped his mouth

shut, his cheeks heating as he recalled his boorish behavior yesterday. The woman shouldn't have gone after his tree, but he shouldn't have frightened her daughter, either. "I . . . I like my privacy. I like my land quiet and protected. And I'd like to expand."

"Expand that wall around yourself, you mean?"

He walked over to the window and stood by her side, twisting the checkbook in his hands. "Why do you want to hang on to that drive-in so badly?"

She looked down and entwined her fingers, her thumbs tracing the delicate veins in the backs of her hands. "My memories are there."

His chest tightened. "So are mine."

"Then we are at an impasse, hmm?" Her voice softened, a hint of sympathy lacing her tone. "As we usually are."

A car door slammed outside, drawing Seth's eyes to the parking lot. And there they were, the woman with the ax and her two kids, ambling up the front steps into the nursing home, the woman with an extra spring in her step. She looked different in the morning light without the ax and frightened frown. Her wavy brown hair was loose, bouncing around her shoulders. Her brown eyes were bright with excitement and her smile wide.

"Ah, here they are now." Mae Bell perked up. "I'll have the opportunity to properly introduce you."

Seth shoved his hands in his pockets. "They're loud. Rambunctious. The little girl wandered across the property line."

"Young ones tend to explore," Mae Bell said quietly. "It's in their nature and no fault of their own." Her eyes met his with an expression uncomfortably close to pity. "Never the fault of anyone else, either."

Seth's jaw hardened.

"Seth—"

"I won't do this with you, Mae Bell. Or anyone else,

for that matter." He faced her then, the biting tone of his words foreign to him. "You'd be a fool to turn down my offer. You and I both know that lot's beyond repair. I'm willing to take it off your hands for far more than it's worth. No one else has any interest in that relic of a drive-in."

"I do."

Seth turned at the sound of the soft, feminine voice. There she stood, one hand holding the little girl's, the other propped on her sassy hip. The boy (Todd, if he remembered right) stood slightly behind the two of them, an angry gleam in his eye as he glared at Seth.

"I'm interested in the property and the drive-in," she repeated firmly. "What's more, I know you're aware we've moved in, so I think it's in poor taste of you to proposition Mae Bell in this way."

"'Proposition'?" His lip curled in spite of the ridiculous situation. "I didn't *proposition* her."

Her graceful neck flushed. "Take advantage, then."

"Not doing that, either. I'm offering her an obscene amount of money to take that lot off her hands and save her a whole lot of headaches dealing with you and that"—he stabbed a finger at Todd—"temperamental son of yours."

"He's not my son. He's—"

"She should've slapped your face!"

The woman shot Todd a stern look over her shoulder, and he transferred his glare from Seth to her.

"And I'm sick of you saying that," Todd spat. "Why don't you tell the whole world! Shout it right out of that window? Cuz, Lord knows, I don't want anyone thinking Daisy and I are yours! You're a wimp. You let that guy walk over you yesterday, and now, you're letting him bully Mae Bell. He deserves to have someone whoop his a—"

"Don't say it." She held up a finger. "I mean it."

Even Seth hesitated to speak. The woman might be small, but that strict tone of hers could stop a man in his tracks and force him to think twice.

"And you're behaving no better," she shot in Seth's direction. "Antagonizing Todd like that. Calling him names. Starting an argument right here in Mae Bell's room. He's a boy, but you're a grown man and should know better. You should be ashamed of yourselves. You're both behaving like, like . . . inst . . . inst-uh-ga . . ."

When she faltered, Seth narrowed his eyes. *"Instigators?"*

Todd harrumphed.

"Whatever." She waved away the correction. "I haven't made it to the *I*'s yet."

Seth frowned. "What?" She refused to elaborate, and those big brown eyes of hers looked up at him with intense disdain. Which was entirely new for him. No woman had ever looked at him like that before. Pride stung, he pursed his lips. "That kid deserves a spanking."

"Well, so do you."

Automatically his attention darted to her hands, his own neck burning at the image her words conveyed. She felt the same apparently, her wide eyes meeting his, then flicking away as she shifted uncomfortably from one foot to the other.

Seth cleared his throat and tugged at the collar of his T-shirt, which suddenly felt too tight around his hot skin.

"Well, what do you know?" Mae Bell glanced from Seth to Kelly and back, her tone gleeful. "You've just been taught lesson number one, Kelly, without the aid of one of my trunk tapes. Welcome to a real-life Blue Moon meet-cute."

*   *   *

Kelly froze, her pulse throbbing so loudly in her ears, she could barely hear her own thoughts, much less Mae Bell's words. A meet-cute? *Meet-cute*? Between her and this . . . this . . . Neanderthal?

"No." She returned Mae Bell's gleeful grin with a somber glare. "Nope. No way. That"—she gestured between herself and her Neanderthal neighbor—"is most definitely not what this is. *This* is an argument between two people who—"

"Have two completely different agendas and dispositions," the hunk—er, jerk—said. He glared at Mae Bell, too.

Undeterred, Mae Bell motioned toward the man. "Kelly, this is Seth Morgan, my neighbor for almost two decades. Seth, meet Kelly Jenkins, Blue Moon Haven Drive-In's new assistant manager, and her two guests, Todd and Daisy. I trust you'll both manage to tolerate each other's existence throughout the duration of our restoration project." She smiled wider. "Which brings me to my first question, Kelly. Have you had a chance to view any of the films I left in the trunk for you?"

"Uh, no . . . but I very much want to." Kelly shifted from one foot to the other. "It's just, well, I didn't bring a TV with us during the move, and there's not one in the trail—"

"Mansion, dear."

"Yes. Mansion. And I—"

"And have you grown fond of the Mansion now that you've had a chance to settle in?"

Kelly smiled. "I have. Very much, thank you." Movement caught her eye. Todd had made his way over to Mae Bell's record player and was thumbing through her collection of albums. "Todd, please don't rifle through Mae Bell's things."

"Oh, let him look. What harm can it do?" Mae Bell crossed the room, dragged out a second box of records and set them in front of Todd, who tackled them instantly.

He frowned. "What are they?"

Mae Bell laughed. "Gracious, what delights young ones have missed out on. These are records—vinyl discs, or just plain vinyl if you prefer to refer to them in a hipper manner. They're the physical equivalent of music as opposed to those abstract tracks you kids play in the clouds nowadays."

Todd looked even more confused. "Huh?"

"Music, dear. It's simply good, old-fashioned music with a soothing scratch in the background and nothing between you and the intimate croon of the performer's voice." She sighed wistfully. "Technology is a wonderful thing, but it does have a curious ability to steal as much beauty out of life as it gives."

Todd rifled through a few more albums. "I don't know any of these bands."

"Visit me more often and you will," Mae Bell said, opening the top drawer of her dresser and withdrawing a checkbook. She walked over to Kelly and placed it in her hand. "You'll find the balance is accurate—I checked with the bank this morning. The forms have been signed and filed and you are an authorized user of this account. I've already written you a check for groceries and a few odds and ends, and you'll find a list of priorities to follow after your first task of watching the films. Unfortunately, my stepdaughter threw out my TV and VCR." She made a face. "Seems she thought my vintage audiovisual devices were too vintage. Feel free to use another check to purchase a suitable TV and VHS player to view the films. That's still priority number one, okay?" Mae Bell glanced at Seth and lifted her chin. "You see, Seth? I have a checkbook of my own."

Seth dipped his head, an expression almost like embarrassment flickering over his expression. "More never hurt anyone," he said quietly, taking a wide berth around Kelly and Daisy to the door. "If you change your mind, you know where I am."

Daisy, watching Seth closely, hid behind Kelly's leg as he left. Then the child tugged Kelly's hand and pointed at the pile of records Todd was picking through.

"Go ahead, but please put things back where you got them," Kelly said.

She smiled as Daisy joined Todd to explore the records, then eased over to the window and watched as Seth hopped into his truck, cranked the engine and left. He spared one last hard glance at Mae Bell's window.

"How do you put up with that man?" she murmured.

Mae Bell's shoulder brushed Kelly's as she joined her at the window, her soft perfume settling around them both. "Oh, he's not that bad, dear, and he has his reasons." Her voice softened on her next words. "He has a story, as we all do. His is just more tragic than most."

"What happened to him?"

Mae Bell tugged a strand of her hair and smiled. "The best way to get accurate details and a straight-forward answer is to ask the source directly rather than a third party."

Kelly slumped against the window. As curious as she was, she knew there was no way in the world she would do that. She did, however, have another urgent matter pressing on her mind, and she supposed she should do as Mae Bell suggested and go right to the source for an answer.

"Mae Bell, about those VHS tapes . . ."

Four hours later, Kelly hadn't found a VCR player—not a single one. After leaving Mae Bell with a promise to start viewing the films she'd left in the trunk for her, Kelly had bundled the kids in the car, driven to Blue Moon's Main Street and started shopping for a TV and VCR player. The task had been far more difficult than Mae Bell had suggested earlier.

TVs were in abundance in both Al's Electronics and the larger big-box retailer she'd visited. But they'd all been high-definition TVs, with the only peripheral choices being DVD or Ultra HD players. There was no point in spending a couple hundred dollars or more of Mae Bell's money on an HDTV she couldn't use if she couldn't track down a VCR player. Even the bank teller at Blue Moon Investments, who'd verified her identity before cashing her generous advance check from Mae Bell, had answered Kelly's VCR questions with a healthy dose of sarcasm and skepticism.

"A VCR?" the teller had asked. "Restoring the drive-in?" He had counted out her money onto the counter with the tips of his fingers, as though the bills themselves had offended him. "The only hindrance to Blue Moon being recognized as Small Town of the Year in *Best Homes and Towns* magazine is that outdated blemish on Mrs. Larkin's property. Unfortunate as the truth may be, Blue Moon Drive-In's time has come and gone. I wish you well in your endeavor, but I can assure you, it will be fruitless."

Less hopeful than she'd been initially, Kelly had summoned up her last ounce of optimism and visited every store in Blue Moon, only to discover not a single one carried a VCR. She'd even enlisted Todd and Daisy's help in searching Bitsy's Antiques and Consignment Shop from top to bottom, hoping to come across one. But when she'd asked Bitsy, the very talkative owner, if one had ever been traded in, Bitsy had outright laughed, then walked away, leaving Kelly standing there empty-handed, with two very tired, grumpy kids.

"Can I get a triple burger, onion rings, a jumbo milk shake and a large order of fudge?" Todd, seated opposite Kelly in a window booth located in Tully's Treats, drummed his fingers on the table. "Hello? Kelly? Can I get a trip—"

"I heard you the first time." Kelly narrowed her eyes. "And after you eat, do you plan on walking out of here, or will you just lie down on the floor and wait for me and Daisy to roll you out of the door?"

His nose twitched. "I'm hungry. You made us walk five thousand miles today looking for that stupid VCK player, and we still didn't get one."

"VCR player," Kelly corrected.

"Or a TV." Todd slumped back in the booth and crossed his arms. "We still don't have a TV, so there'll be nothing to do when we get back to the trailer but sleep anyway. Besides, you said Daisy and I could get whatever we wanted for supper if we were patient all day."

Yep. She had said that.

"You promised," Todd stressed for good measure.

Kelly propped her elbows on the table and buried her face in her hands. Well, that's what she deserved for bribing kids with food: a sleepless night soothing a boy with a junk food–induced stomachache.

Daisy rose to her knees on the seat beside Kelly and whispered in her ear, "Can I get what Todd's getting, but with honey taffy instead of fudge?"

Make that soothing a boy *and* a girl with junk food–induced stomachaches. Not one to break her word, and somewhat soothed by the healthy wad of dollar bills in her pocket, Kelly lowered her forehead to the table and mumbled, "Sure."

"Everything okay here?"

Kelly rolled her head to the side and cracked one eye open. A waitress, tall with long blond hair and a kind smile, stood by the booth, studying Kelly with a concerned look on her face.

"Yeah." Kelly peeled her cheek off the table, sat up and plastered a smile on her face. She should at least try to look presentable for the kids' sake. "I think we're ready to order." She gestured weakly toward Todd. "Go ahead."

Her eyes glazed over as Todd rambled off his and Daisy's long order, certain the waitress must think she was the most negligent guardian in existence for letting two children eat such a greasy, sugar-laden spread for supper.

But the waitress only smiled wider. "Sounds like a celebration. Did something wonderful happen today?"

Todd made a sound of disgust. "We spent all day wasting time looking for a VCK."

"VCR," Kelly corrected. Todd was too smart to make such a careless mistake repeatedly. He was doing it on purpose to rub her the wrong way.

"Doesn't matter," he said. "No one has one anyway. And since we don't even have a TV, this will be the most exciting thing we do all day." He made a face at the waitress. "Which isn't saying much."

Mortified beyond words, Kelly dug a handful of quarters out of her pocket and tossed them on the table in front of Todd. "Pinball machine." She pointed at the unoccupied machine on the opposite side of the small restaurant. "Go. Now."

Todd hesitated briefly, then scooped up the quarters, hopped out of the booth and tugged Daisy along with him to the pinball machine. "Come on, Daisy."

Kelly winced at the waitress in apology. "I'm sorry about that."

"No problem." She laughed. "I love how honest kids are. They don't leave you guessing about their thoughts or intentions. I understand them a lot better than I do adults, most days."

"Ain't that the truth." Kelly shook her head as Seth Morgan's dark frown sprang to mind. "My new neighbor's like that. I don't even know the man, but he barged in on me yesterday and was just as rude to me again this morning, all because he wants the property I just moved onto. He didn't even bother to introduce himself before he jumped all over me. And worse"—she gestured toward Daisy, who stood by Todd's side, smiling as he played pinball—"he made sweet Daisy cry. Scared her half to death."

The waitress's smile dissipated. "Where is it you just moved to?"

"Just outside of town. Mae Bell Larkin hired me as the new assistant manager to help renovate and reopen the Blue Moon Haven Drive-In." Kelly glanced up at the waitress and braced herself. Goodness knows, outside of Mae Bell's welcome, she hadn't had many enthusiastic responses to her presence in Blue Moon. "I assume you know of it?"

The waitress nodded slowly. "I do."

"And do you know the guy who lives next door?"

"Seth Morgan?" At Kelly's nod, she said, "Yes."

"Then you know what I'm talking about, right? He's easy on the eyes—I'll give him that—but he comes across as a complete Neanderthal."

A look of empathy crossed the waitress's features. "I know he can be very difficult at times. I'm sorry he was rude to you."

Kelly almost sagged with relief, hot tears pricking at the back of her eyes. "Thank you. I mean, I tried to see his side of things, tried to come up with a reason for why he behaved the way he did, but I just couldn't think of a justifiable reason for his being so horrible. And things didn't go any better today. No one thinks Mae Bell and I should even try to get the drive-in back up and running, and Todd and Daisy aren't excited about it at all. I'm beginning to think I made a huge mistake coming here." She gestured toward the peaceful sidewalks outside of the window. "I love Blue Moon. It's beautiful. It's just . . . I'd hoped for a better welcome, you know?"

"Blue Moon is ordinarily a very welcoming community," the waitress said softly. "I wish we'd given you a better first impression." She held out her hand and smiled. "Please let me welcome you properly."

Kelly brushed the back of her hand across her eyes, then squeezed the other woman's hand, grateful to have met at least one friendly person who hadn't judged her. A person she could get to know better and possibly befriend.

"I'm Kelly Jenkins," she said. "Thank you so much for being kind to me. You're such a nice change from that awful man who lives next door to me."

The woman's smile faltered as she said, "I'm Tully Morris. Seth Morgan's sister."

CHAPTER 4

Seth slid a four-inch leather strap around the bottom of the elevated hive stand of a Langstroth beehive and looped it back over the top of the outer cover, securing the medium and deep supers together. The Langstroth beehive was one of four stationed in a neat row along the far side of his backyard nearest the orchard. Tending the hives had quickly become one of Seth's favorite tasks.

Having established his apiary several years ago, Seth had fed, protected and nurtured his nuclear colony meticulously and added additional colonies over the years. He'd discovered the side hustle of selling local honey had not only been a profitable business in its own right, but it also complemented his pecan business.

Seth wrapped a second leather strap around the Langstroth beehive, then drove two thin metal posts into the ground on both sides of the beehive to anchor it. He used additional leather straps to tie the beehive to the posts for extra support and protection against rough weather.

His task finished, Seth straightened, tilted his head back and studied the dark clouds milling overhead. During his drive back from visiting Mae Bell in the nursing home yesterday, he'd managed to shove aside his frustrations long enough to focus on the weather report droning from the satellite radio in his truck. Spring was on the way, the weatherman had announced, and the first round of March storms would be rolling in the next day.

And just as the weatherman had predicted, the wind had strengthened overnight, rattling branches in the orchard and whistling along the eaves of Seth's house as he'd hopped in his truck to tend to his orchard at dawn. By lunchtime, the storm clouds had piled up enough to alert him that the spring storms predicted on the news were well on their way and that his hives would benefit from additional protection.

He wiped his sweaty brow and neck with the hem of his T-shirt, propped his fists on his lower back and stretched, exhaling with satisfaction at the slight ache in his muscles.

"Nothing like a good day's work, huh?"

His mouth curved into a small smile, his chest warming at the cheery voice. "It certainly offers a nice sense of accomplishment." He straightened and turned to find his sister standing a few feet away in his backyard, her arms holding a box of empty glass jars. "Back for a refill already?"

Tully grinned. "What can I say? My customers love your honey. They ask for a dab of it on everything—ice cream, pie, toast, you name it. They 'bout eat me out of house and home up there, thank goodness!"

And that was to be expected. For as far back as Seth could remember, Tully had loved to cook. His mom used to keep a step stool by the stove so his little sister could reach the counters and mix cake batter or create a new confection. Tully, now thirty-three years old, had a flair for creating delicious candies and baked goods, as well as main courses, so it was no surprise to Seth when her restaurant and candy shop, Tully's Treats, became a Blue Moon overnight success more than a decade ago.

He walked over and took the box of jars from her. "It'll be tomorrow before I can fill these. I just tied the hives down in preparation for the storm that's coming."

A gust of wind lifted her long hair and splayed it over her shoulders. She shoved it back and glanced at the sky. "Yeah, I heard it was headed our way, and no rush on the honey. Just thought I'd get a jump start on this refill, since I've had a surge of interest in my honey taffy."

He carried the box of glass jars toward his house, asking over his shoulder, "Oh, yeah?"

"Yep." Tully followed him to the front steps, and Patch, who'd been napping on the front porch, sprang up and clambered down the steps to rub against her legs. "Hey, ol' Patch." She scratched his head, then said softly, "The little girl who's moved in next door . . . named Daisy, I think? She took quite a liking to it yesterday evening when she and her brother stopped in for supper."

Seth froze midstep, one boot on the porch landing and the other on a lower step. The girl's name drew forth a fresh welling of guilt within him. He'd been unable to shake the memory of her frightened expression and tearstained face . . . or the realization of how badly he'd behaved in front of her.

"They weren't alone." Tully's voice drew nearer to his back as she ascended the steps behind him. "A woman was with them. Her name's Kelly Jenkins. She mentioned you two may have already met?"

He closed his eyes, a chill creeping over his skin that

had nothing to do with the cool whip of spring wind. Great. Just great. No telling what Kelly had already told Tully about their encounter. Whatever Kelly had said, given the tone of Tully's voice, he imagined it hadn't shown him in the best light.

Huffing out a breath, he walked across the porch, entered the house and headed for the kitchen.

Tully continued to follow him into the kitchen, with Patch padding along behind her. "*Have* you met her?"

"Yeah."

"And how did it go?"

Seth dropped the box on the counter. The glass jars clanged together, rattling the peaceful stillness of the house. "I'm guessing you already know how it went."

"Not well, from what she said."

"Then why are you asking?"

"Because if I don't ask, you'll never tell me." She released a heavy sigh behind him. "You never tell me anything anymore. We never talk. I miss you. I hardly see you, and I'm running out of excuses to swing by and check on you without the risk of exposing myself to one of your lectures on giving you space and not prying."

He started removing the glass jars, one at a time, and setting each on the table with a thud. "Then don't. I'm fine and don't need checking up on."

"Kelly said you were rude. That you made Daisy cry."

He ducked his head and continued removing the glass jars from the box.

"Did you?" At his silence, her voice grew quiet. "That's not like you—"

"I saw Daisy running through the orchard and thought she was Rachel." He slammed the last jar on the counter and spun around to face her. "I actually thought, for just a moment, that it was her. No matter how desperate or illogical or crazy that sounds. I was okay with finally breaking with reality as long as it meant I could see her again." His chest heaved and he stopped to catch his breath. "And when I caught up with her, I saw Kelly cutting down Rachel's tree." His chin quivered and he looked away, clenching his jaw. "So I lost my temper. I offended Kelly, ticked off that temperamental boy of hers and, yes, I made Daisy cry."

The kitchen was silent for a moment; then Tully's shoes shuffled across the floor, and she touched his arm. "Seth . . . there's nothing wrong with asking for help, you know? I'm a good listener. I could come stay with you for a while if—"

"I'm not a kid, Tully." Swallowing hard, he forced himself to face her. "I'm perfectly capable of taking care of myself. I just have bad days now and then." He gently nudged her chin with his knuckle and managed a small smile. "Besides, what would Cal say if I took his wife away from him just to come baby her big brother?"

"Cal would be just fine." Her expression brightened. "Maybe he'd learn to do his own laundry while I'm away."

"Thank you for the offer—I mean that—but I'm okay."

She reached up, took his hand in hers and squeezed. "You'll call me if you aren't, won't you? You'll tell me if you need me? Promise?"

"I promise." He kissed her forehead, turned back to the table and started removing the lids from the glass jars. "You better head home before it gets dark. The storm will be here before you know it."

She hesitated, but after a moment, she patted Patch's head once more, then walked toward the front door and paused on the threshold. "You know, I drove past Mae Bell's lot on the way here. I didn't realize Kelly and the kids were staying in the trailer. From the road, it certainly doesn't look as though it'd weather tornado winds if they spring up. And here you are in this great big house with all this extra space . . ."

Seth looked over his shoulder. "What are you suggesting?"

"That you should consider inviting Kelly, Daisy and Todd to sit out the storm here."

He scoffed. "It's supposed to last all night and into the morning hours."

"All the more reason for you to be neighborly and extend the invitation. Prove you're a considerate, mature man and not a temperamental kid." Tully grinned. "Oh, and Kelly, by the way, might have a teeny tiny soft spot for you somewhere deep down inside, considering she did say you were easy on the eyes."

If *mortification* had a picture in the dictionary, Kelly felt sure her face would be the accompanying illustration.

She leaned back against the sofa cushion in the trailer, turned on the built-in wall lamp and flipped to section *M* in her pocket dictionary. *Ma, me, mo . . .* There it was: *mortification.* She read the definition and variations, then slapped the book shut.

Mortified. Yep, that's exactly how she felt after wasting an entire day yesterday scouring Blue Moon for a device that had ceased being manufactured around six years ago (according to Todd's research on his cell phone), making no progress whatsoever on Mae Bell's priority list and insulting the first kind person she'd encountered in Blue Moon—completely mortified.

After her complete boneheaded blunder with Seth's sister in Tully's Treats yesterday, she'd been so taken aback by Tully's admission that she'd had no idea how to respond. All she could focus on was what she'd said about Seth. What was it she had called him? A Neanderthal? Rude? Horrible?

Oh, good grief! She buried her face in her hands. Why couldn't she have just kept her mouth shut? It didn't matter how poorly Seth had behaved. Hadn't she just recently chastised Todd for his insults regarding Seth? And then, there she'd gone, running off her mouth to his sister simply because she'd had a bad day. There was no telling if Tully would decide to share what she'd said with Seth.

Last night, after the kids had finished eating their mountain of junk food, it had taken all she had to walk up to the register, seek out Tully and apologize for insulting her brother. Tully had been very gracious about it all—had even given them a discount on their meal—but for some reason, Tully's additional kindness had only made her feel worse.

On top of it all, she'd spent the majority of last night consoling Daisy, who'd developed a honey taffy bellyache, as Kelly had anticipated. Todd and his cast-iron stomach, however, had slept soundly—had even snored—the entire night. After spending the night nursing Daisy, Kelly had overslept this morning, then spent most of the day on the phone attempting to enroll Todd and Daisy in the local school and have their records transferred from their previous school in Birmingham.

After scheduling an appointment to bring Todd and Daisy to Blue Moon Central (the only school and K–12 campus in the small town) and enroll them officially on Monday, she'd spent the rest of the afternoon unpacking, washing clothes and cleaning up the car. And as the sky had grown darker each hour, she'd been more and more tempted to curl up on the sofa and take a nap . . . which had been difficult to do, with Todd blasting music from his phone and Daisy attempting to climb every surface in the trailer.

A rumble of thunder rolled over the Mansion, shaking the sofa beneath Kelly.

Daisy sprang onto the sofa beside Kelly, poked her toes into Kelly's belly and climbed over her shoulders to reach the blinds above the sofa.

"Ow!" Kelly lifted Daisy by the waist as the blinds clacked behind her head. "Daisy, please stop climbing on everything—including me, okay? You barely weigh as much as a feather, but your toes are like daggers."

Daisy climbed down and whispered in Kelly's ear, "Lightning outside."

A second boom of thunder sounded, and Daisy jumped into Kelly's lap and buried her face in her T-shirt. Fat raindrops pelted the roof of the trailer, the low-toned dings echoing throughout the living room and kitchen space.

"This thing's made out of aluminum, you know," said Todd over the steady pulse of his music as he removed his earbuds. A devilish grin appeared as he stared at Daisy. "All it'd take is one good strike and *pop, sizzle, fry,* baby! We'd be like strips of bacon on a frying pan."

Kelly shuddered and cuddled Daisy closer. "Stop it, Todd. That's not true, and you know it."

He frowned. "How do you know it's not true?"

"Because of that . . . that . . ."—she snapped her fingers as the words came to her—"cage effect. I forget the guy's name—it started with an *F*. But he says aluminum roofs and frames will protect you just fine from lightning, like cars. There's that cage effect thing. I got an A in high school science, so I know that much, and if I know it, then I know you know it."

Todd made a face. "Technically, Benjamin Franklin came up with the idea first. Michael Faraday just honed it."

Kelly smiled. "But I was right that time, wasn't I?"

Todd turned his music back up and stuck his earbuds in his ears.

Another booming clap of thunder rattled the trailer, and the rain drummed the roof more heavily.

Daisy whimpered, huddling closer, but grew still when a heavy knock sounded on the door. She stared at the door, then looked up at Kelly with a questioning expression.

"I don't know who it is, sweet pea." Frowning, Kelly eased Daisy off her lap and onto the sofa cushion beside her. "Wait here while I find out."

Todd, eyes closed and nodding to the beat of his music, was completely oblivious.

Shaking her head, Kelly walked to the door, turned on the outdoor light and peeked through the round window. All she could see was a lean, muscular male back encased in a black T-shirt. *Please, Lord, don't let it be an ax murderer.* With the past few days she'd just had, she didn't have the energy to fight one off.

"Who is it?" she called.

The male back turned, a broad chest dipped and Seth Morgan's face appeared in the window. His blond hair was slicked to his skull with rain, bringing his sculpted cheekbones and strong jaw into stark relief. "Your neighbor."

She met his eyes, her pulse kicking up a notch at the sight of him. *It's better him than an ax murderer,* she supposed. "That would sound a lot less intimidating if you smiled when you said it."

He returned her stare, then slowly . . . ever so slowly . . . his sensual lips stretched into a small, somewhat-insincere smile. "I'm your neighbor."

The smile was kinda charming, even if it was fake. "Thanks, I guess." Kelly bit her lip. "What do you want?"

He held up a clear jar filled with something gooey

and raised his voice over the increasing pound of rain. "I brought Daisy a gift. And I"—his lean cheeks flushed— "came to apologize for the other day."

Kelly's jaw dropped. "In the storm? You came with a gift in the storm?"

He gave a jerky nod. "Well . . . there's another reason I'm here. You mind if I come in for a minute? It's pouring out here."

She narrowed her eyes. "You promise to behave in a civilized manner?"

He stopped smiling. Even looked a bit ashamed. "I promise. Now, do you mind opening this door before I get struck by lightning?"

"Oh, yeah. Yes"—she fumbled with the lock—"sure. Come on in." She opened the door and stepped back, allowing him inside.

She'd forgotten how tall he was. So tall he had to dip his head slightly to fit inside the trailer. Water dripped from the hem of his T-shirt and jeans, creating a soggy puddle on the faux-hardwood vinyl floor.

He lingered by the door, glanced around the room and issued another tight smile. "This is nice. Much nicer than the last time I visited Mae Bell here. She told me she had it renovated recently."

She followed his gaze, then hesitantly returned his smile. "Thank you."

"This model trailer is incredibly rare in today's market." He met her eyes, his smile widening a fraction more. "It'd be worth over, say, three hundred thousand."

Kelly took in her surroundings again, her eyes widening. Sure, the trailer had impressed her far more than she'd expected when she'd first entered, but three hundred thousand dollars? Who'd have thought this thing would be worth that amount of money?

"Really?" Her smile grew, too, as she looked at the kids. Todd, having removed his earbuds, glared up at Seth from his booth seat, and Daisy had scooted to the farthest edge of the couch, her eyes following each of Seth's movements. "Well, what do ya know, guys? We actually do live in a mansion."

Seth nodded. "It's a retro classic. You could get more than that for it, if you played your cards right."

Kelly's gaze snapped back to his as she glared. "I'm not selling Mae Bell's trailer. And if that's why you came—"

He held up a hand. "It's not, I promise." He looked down and dragged the toe of his right boot across the floor. "It was just an observation."

She crossed her arms over her chest. "Well, observe something else."

He looked down at her, his deep green eyes traveling over her face and lingering on her mouth before he jerked away from her and faced Daisy.

Daisy's wide eyes blinked up at him, and he shifted awkwardly from one boot to the other, then lifted the jar in his hand.

"This is for you," he said, stepping toward her hesitantly.

Todd scrambled off the booth, stalked across the room, sat beside Daisy and threw an arm around her shoulders. "We don't want anything from you."

Seth stilled, holding Todd's stare. "Look. I'm sorry about the way I approached y'all the other day. It wasn't my best moment and I'm . . ." He rubbed the back of his neck. "I'm trying to make it right, okay?"

Todd remained unimpressed. Daisy, however, eyed the jar with interest.

Seth lifted it closer to her. "It's honey. My sister owns Tully's Treats downtown. She said y'all stopped by the other night and that you took a liking to the honey taffy. She uses the honey my bees produce to make it, so I thought you might like the actual honey, too."

Kelly cringed. So his sister had mentioned she'd met them. How much of what she had said had Tully told him?

"You have bees?" Todd asked, a tiny hint of interest entering his tone.

"Yeah. I have several hives." Seth lowered himself to his haunches, meeting Daisy at eye level, and said gently, "I'm sorry for scaring you the other day, Daisy, and I'm very sorry I made you cry."

Daisy studied Seth's expression, then the jar of honey. She licked her lips as she focused on the honey, reached out slowly then, apparently thinking better of it, drew her hand back and stuck her thumb in her mouth.

"It's okay, sweetheart," Seth murmured, easing closer and setting the jar on the sofa beside her. "I understand. I'll just put it here for you, okay?"

Kelly held her breath, the warm soothing tone of Seth's voice stirring unexpected flutters of pleasure in her middle. For such a brawny man, he could be surprisingly gentle . . . and tender, even.

Daisy eyed the jar of honey for a minute. Then she picked up the jar, clutched it to her chest and rose on her knees to whisper something in Todd's ear.

Todd's lip curled, but he nodded, then pursed his lips at Seth. "She said thank you."

Seth grinned at Daisy, the action brightening his features. "You're welcome." Rubbing his hands over his thighs, he stood slowly and turned back to Kelly. A boom of thunder rattled the windows of the trailer and he grimaced. "That's the other reason I came. According to the weather report, this storm's gonna get worse tonight, and this time of year, it's always hard to tell exactly what we're in for. It could be just another spring thunderstorm, or it could be worse." He glanced back at Daisy and Todd. "Thing is, I have extra bedrooms and plenty of space, if you'd like to bring the kids over and hunker down at my place until it passes."

"Hunker down"? Kelly's gaze roved over the wet clothes clinging to his muscular frame. *At his place?* She rubbed her arms to still the completely unwelcome shivers of excitement coursing through her. "I don't think that's a g—"

"You got a TV?" Todd asked, his glare easing just a bit.

Seth nodded. "Two of them."

"And internet access?"

"Yep."

Todd sprang off the couch. "Let's go."

"Wait a minute." Kelly frowned as Todd jogged to the bedroom, grabbed a bag and started throwing clothes in it. "What do you think you're doing?"

"Going to his place." Todd headed for the bathroom. "I'll grab y'all's toothbrushes."

"Wait, Todd!" Kelly glanced at Seth and lowered her tone. "Excuse me, please." She race-walked down the hall and squeezed into the small bathroom with Todd. "I haven't accepted his offer yet, and whatever happened to your outraged indignation on behalf of my and Daisy's honor? Your demands that I kick his shins and slap his face? All that no longer matters because he has a TV?"

Todd tossed three toothbrushes and a tube of toothpaste in an overnight bag, then smirked. "A TV *and* internet access."

CHAPTER 5

Seth flipped his windshield wipers on high, slowed down his truck and carefully maneuvered the curving dirt driveway to his house. During the ten minutes it had taken for Kelly to pack a few necessities, lock up her trailer and bundle Todd and Daisy into his truck, the storm had settled in, dumping heavy rain and flashing bright bolts of lightning across the black sky.

"How fast is your internet?" Todd asked from the backseat of the extended cab. "Do you have fiber? Gigabit?"

Seth glanced in the rearview mirror. Daisy sat in the booster seat Kelly had transferred from her car to his truck, sucking her thumb and clutching her jar of honey. Todd met his eyes in the rearview mirror and frowned.

"You don't have one of those slow, choppy services that drops signals, do you?" Todd prompted.

"Todd." Kelly, seated in the passenger seat beside Seth, swiveled in her seat to face Todd, a note of warning in her tone. "Don't be rude."

"I'm not being rude," he shot back. "It's a legitimate question. And besides, anything he has will be better than the nothing we have right now at the trailer."

Seth eased his truck to a stop in front of his house and cleared his throat, not eager for another round of Todd and Kelly bickering. "I'm not big into Gigabits or tech stuff, but it serves its purpose, and I have no problems submitting business reports and videoconferencing."

Todd made a small sound of approval. "Decent, then."

"More than decent," Kelly whispered from the passenger seat.

Seth followed her line of sight to his house and studied the building as a stranger might. His truck's headlights cut through the heavy curtains of rain, highlighting the wide front steps leading to a wraparound rocking-chair front porch flanked by thick wood columns. The white siding, black porch lights and red metal roof added a rustic elegance to the two-story home.

A small surge of pride lifted Seth's chest. It'd been eight years since he'd stopped long enough to admire what had taken him almost a year to build with the aid of a local construction crew. He'd designed every detail himself, right down to the landscaping, which included lush green hedges lining the foundation of the front porch and red knockout roses bordering both sides of the house. The house, like his family, had seemed a dream come true when he'd stood in front of it with Madeline on their wedding day. They'd both been all smiles and eager anticipation at the thought of the beautiful future that awaited them.

He turned off the engine and slumped back in his seat. The dream hadn't lasted for long. Eight years later, just days after his thirtieth birthday, he and Madeline had stood by a grave and said goodbye to Rachel, the child-size casket a painful reminder of how much life Rachel had lost . . . and how much joy he and Madeline would never have again.

One year after that, Madeline had packed her bags, driven away and, a few days after that, Seth had received a letter in the mail, notifying him that Madeline had filed for divorce. He had known it would come, but the reality had still stung. So much so, he'd sat on the front porch of his now-empty home, contemplating his empty life for two days. He drank from a bottle of scotch, watching the sun rise and the stars descend, wondering, if he asked long enough, would the good Lord see fit to take him earlier than planned?

But it hadn't worked out the way he'd hoped. Instead, the sun had continued to rise, the stars had continued to descend above his head and he finally had been forced to accept that there would be no divine intervention. He'd be left to deal with the grief and pain that filled his heart on his own.

" . . . absolutely beautiful," Kelly was saying now from the passenger seat. "Would you mind turning your high beams on so I can get a better look?"

Shrugging, Seth did as she asked and waited as she ducked her head, leaned closer to the windshield and peered through the dense rain at his house.

"Is . . . is that a red roof?" she asked quietly.

"Yeah." He gestured toward the structure. "I thought it made for a good contrast with the white siding. A traditional, homey look, so to speak. Seemed to fit the surroundings at the time."

Kelly eased back into her seat and faced him, her big brown eyes clinging to his. "It does. Was it like that when you bought it, or did you change it later?"

"I designed it."

She blinked, then glanced at each of his arms. "And built it?"

Seth jerked his head in affirmation, then cut the lights and thrust the driver's-side door open. "We'd best go in. It's starting to rain harder," he yelled over the sound of rain echoing inside the cab. "I got an umbrella in the backseat. I'll grab it, come around and hold it so you can carry Daisy out without the two of you getting drenched."

He hopped out without waiting for agreement, retrieved the umbrella, then hustled around to the passenger side and opened the door. She joined him under the umbrella, and he held it over her while she unbuckled Daisy from the booster seat and lifted her into her arms, remaining acutely aware of her soft warmth brushing his side with each of her movements.

Face heating with embarrassment that he'd even noticed such a thing, Seth focused on Todd. "If you wait here, I'll come back with the umbrella after I help them to the porch. That way, you won't get drenched."

Todd stared at him, his eyes examining Seth's face, then shifting to Kelly, who continued helping Daisy into her arms beside him. "Forget it. I'll be fine."

Seth shook his head as Todd shoved his door open, jumped from the cab and ran through the downpour and up the front porch steps.

"That's the most hardheaded kid on the planet," Kelly muttered beside him, her smooth cheek brushing the exposed skin of his neck as she straightened with Daisy in her arms and huddled closer under the umbrella. "Angry at the world." She glanced up at him, her face barely visible in the dark cover of night and storm. "Please don't take it personally."

Maybe it was the kindness in her voice, the soft tickle of her hair as the rain and wind lifted it against his bare arm or the way she leaned slightly toward him, prompting thoughts of how her arms might feel around him in another place, at another time, that made his breath catch and his chest tingle.

No matter what the cause, she stirred emotions inside him that he hadn't felt in years . . . at the most inappropriate and unexpected time.

"Stay close and jog," he said, his voice emerging in a gruff rasp.

Without waiting for a response, he began sprinting toward the front steps, taking care to keep pace with her shorter stride. They reached the steps, and with no better option to prevent her slipping with Daisy in her arms, he curved his arm around her shoulders and guided her steps until they reached the front door.

"Whew! That'll wake a person up." She lowered Daisy to the porch floor, shook out her T-shirt and ran her fingers through the damp ends of her hair, not meeting his eyes. "Thank you for your help."

He didn't respond. Instead, he focused on unlocking the door and avoiding Todd's skeptical gaze from the rocking chair he'd plopped down on as soon as he'd reached the porch.

Patch barked from the other side of the door and barreled into Seth's shins the moment he opened it.

"Hold up there, buddy." Seth rubbed the dog's ears and patted his back. "We've got guests. Be on your best behavior, okay?"

He dragged his hand over his face and stepped back, reminding himself to do the same as he motioned for Kelly and the kids to precede him inside.

"Will he bite?" Kelly asked as she tucked Daisy and Todd behind her with both hands.

"Nah." Seth smiled. "He just puts on a good show. Worst he'll do is knock you down and lick you to death."

She scoffed. "Was that what he was trying to do to Todd the other day?"

Seth tossed his keys from one hand to the other and

shrugged. "Todd startled him. He was just being protective. But even if he'd managed to get ahold of him, the worst damage he'd have done was to stand on Todd for a while."

She didn't look reassured, but she eased her hold on the kids and led the way inside the house.

Patch backed up a bit, eyeing the trio from head to toe, then wagged his tail and padded closer to sniff their hands.

Surprisingly, Daisy grinned and held out her hand, splaying her fingers. Patch took her up on the invitation, lapping his tongue between her fingers with friendly gusto.

"Ugh. The germs, Daisy." Kelly tugged Daisy's hand away from Patch and looked at Seth. "Do you mind if I wash her hands?"

"Go ahead." He pointed to her right. "The kitchen's right through there, and the soap's on the sink."

She thanked him and crossed the foyer hesitantly, glancing around. Her steps slowed as she passed the wide staircase that led to the second floor, and she stopped once to glance into the living room across the hall.

"You have a beautiful home," she said softly. "Thank you for letting us stay here."

Seth tossed his keys on the foyer table, shoved his hands in his pockets and stared at the polished hardwood floor beneath his boots. The wood planks always stayed clean and shiny. He rarely had company and there was never anyone but him and Patch to track in and out of the front entrance. "No problem."

"Where's the TV?" Standing by the staircase, with his arms folded across his chest and sporting an impatient look, Todd didn't waste time on polite exchanges.

Ten minutes later, he was comfortably settled on one side of the massive sectional, which occupied the center of Seth's living room. He held a remote in one hand

and a glass of soda in the other. "How do you work the guide on this thing?"

"Todd," Kelly prompted quietly from the seat beside him.

"What?"

She eyed him, her mouth tightening. "Isn't there something you'd like to tell Seth?"

Todd blinked, a perplexed expression on his face, then sighed. "Oh, yeah." He looked at Seth. "Thank you. You know . . . for the TV, the soda and the invitation and all. Now, how do you work the guide on the TV, please?"

Kelly scowled. "Todd."

"What?" He glared. "I said thank you."

"Yes, but you did it without true sincerity. Seth would've appreciated it much more if it'd been from the heart."

"The *heart?*" Todd laughed. "It's a TV, not a birthright."

Seth rolled his lips, stifling a smile. The kid was a pain in the butt, for sure, but he seemed to be a rather smart pain with a dry sense of humor.

"It's more TV than you had access to just a little while ago," Kelly said tightly. She stood, put her hands on her hips and looked at the boy sternly. "You have a cold soda in your hand, which Seth gave you from his kitchen without a request for payment, you've been given a very comfy seat on a beautiful sofa under a sturdy roof during a rainstorm and you have freedom to watch whatever you want on what I can only say is a state-of-the-art entertainment system."

She froze, her eyes glued to something below the large HDTV positioned on a wooden TV stand in the front of his living room. A squeal burst from her lips and she dropped to her hands and knees on the hardwood floor.

"What?" Seth rounded the sectional, scouring the floor around her hands and knees for an unwelcome roach or vermin. "You see a rat or something?"

"No." She leaned closer to his entertainment center, lifted one hand and trailed her fingers over an electronic device on the second shelf. "You have a VCR." She looked up at him and smiled, a tone of reverence in her words. "An honest-to-goodness, I-pray-it-works VCR."

Seth rubbed the back of his neck and glanced at Todd and Daisy. They continued to sit silently on the sectional, Todd raising one eyebrow and sipping his soda, while Daisy sucked her thumb and cradled her jar of honey.

"Well, technically," Seth said, "it's a DVD/VCR combo." And he'd hoped she wouldn't have noticed it. He recalled Mae Bell mentioning in the nursing home that Kelly would need one to play her tapes and at the time he hadn't offered the use of his since, Lord knew, that would only intensify Kelly's intrusion into his routine. "As to whether or not it works, I have no idea. No one's touched it in at least eight years."

Hope filled Kelly's big brown eyes. "May I try turning it on, please?" she whispered.

Seth closed his eyes briefly and shook his head. "Sure."

Kelly pressed the power button gently, stilled, then whooped out loud when the device whirred and a white light blinked on. "It works! It powered right up. Oh, please, please, please tell me I can use it!"

Seth stiffened as she blinked up at him, eager excitement in her eyes. "I . . ." He glanced at the kids, who remained seated in the exact same position as before, as if this strange behavior was a regular occurrence. "Sure." He gestured toward the device. "Have at it. I don't have any discs or tapes though. All of those—"

He clamped his mouth shut, keeping the rest of that thought to himself. *All of those belonged to my ex-wife, and I threw them out.*

"Doesn't matter." Kelly scrambled to her feet. "Thank you, thank you, thank you! I'll bring the trunk over Monday morning after my meeting at the school with the kids, and I'll get started right away if that's okay with you?"

"Wait." Seth shook his head. "What trunk? And what about Monday?"

"She's talking about the trunk Mae Bell left her," Todd said dryly. "And unfortunately, she's dumping us off at school Monday."

Kelly propped her hands on her hips. "I'm not dumping you anywhere. I'm enrolling you in an educational institution to further your knowledge. Something that's required by law, by the way."

Todd rolled his eyes, then sipped his soda and said, "The trunk she's talking about is full of stinky old movies Mae Bell said she has to watch, but we couldn't find a VCR to play them on. No one makes them anymore."

"But Monday?" Seth held up a hand. "I thought you meant you wanted to use it tonight while you're here during the storm. When I invited y'all here, I didn't mean it to be a regular thing. It was just supposed to be for one night because of the storm, and once that's over, y'all can go back to your trailer and I stay here." He eyed Kelly and stated slowly, "Alone."

"Yes, but this is extremely important," she said. "And I promise I won't get in the way. You won't even know I'm here. I'll just slip in after I drop the kids off at school and set myself down right where Todd is. I won't move except to change the tape every couple hours. You won't even know I'm here most days."

"*Days?*" Seth held up both hands. "As in plural? No

way. Nope. I told Tully I'd invite y'all over for the night to help you out during the storm, but that's all. I didn't agree to anything more than that."

Kelly stepped back. She looked him over slowly, an expression of displeasure appearing. "So you only invited us over here because Tully told you to? Not because you were genuinely concerned for our safety, wanted to apologize for your behavior and truly wanted to be a good neighbor?"

Oh, crap. He'd walked right into that one without even realizing it.

"No. That's not what I meant. I just meant that, well, I hadn't thought of anything beyond the storm tonight. That's all."

She crossed her arms over her chest. "Then please"—she tapped her foot slowly—"think about it now. Mull over whether apologizing to Daisy was actually your idea or Tully's, and then consider whether you're actually trying to be a good neighbor to us or just going through the motions to get your—very nice and totally-unlike-you—sister off your back."

Seth sighed, his shoulders slumping. Yep. He'd created this mess all by himself.

He glanced at the kids, who continued staring at him from the sectional, swallowed hard and asked, "Just you, right? While the kids are in school? No noise or intrusions on my work?"

Seemingly pleased with herself, Kelly smiled. "You won't even know I'm here."

Though it had been sixteen years since she'd sat in a public school principal's office, Kelly still fought a sense of panic as she faced the principal across a wide mahogany desk.

"And how did he adjust to skipping two grades?"

Dr. Sandra Helm, Blue Moon Central's principal, adjusted her reading glasses and peered closer at Todd's file, which she had spread out on her desk.

Kelly placed a hand on her thigh and pressed down in an attempt to still her bouncing knee. "He, uh . . . Well, it wasn't exactly an uneventful transition."

That was putting it lightly. Kelly bit her lip and folded her hands together in her lap, whispering a silent plea that Dr. Helm wouldn't ask for details.

Dr. Helm removed her reading glasses, set them on the desk and tilted her head. "In what way?"

Uh-oh. "Well, it took a little time for him to adjust to being in new classes with new teachers and older students. He had to learn to . . ." Kelly glanced up at the ceiling, her gaze tracing the outline of each ceiling tile as she struggled to find the right words. "He had to learn to get along with others who might not be quite as advanced as he is." She smiled brightly at Dr. Helm. "He's very smart. Really intelligent. The psychologist and counselor at his former school told me he was unusually bright—"

"Yes, I've read his file and he certainly shines intellectually." Dr. Helm clicked the top of the pen she held twice as though in thought, then leaned her elbows on the desk. "What I'm more interested in is how did Todd get along with the older students? Did he make friends easily? Connect with them and his teachers on a mature level?"

Did maturity involve cussing out a teacher, throwing his laptop out of the window and demanding the principal ask for a teacher's resignation? Kelly pondered this for a moment and her knee started bouncing again.

She glanced down at her tennis shoes, still scuffed with grime from her sprint through the mud with Seth into his house during the storm a couple days ago.

Quite frankly, given a choice between discussing Todd's disruptive behavior or sloshing through mud again, she'd definitely choose the latter.

Though she had to admit, Todd had behaved exceptionally well since the night they'd rode out the storm at Seth's house. He hadn't argued too much when she'd piled him and Daisy in the car for another shopping trip on Saturday to acquire cleaning supplies, tools and a couple cheap new outdoor chairs to replace the dry rotted ones outside of the trailer. And he'd even sat quietly when Kelly had dragged him and Daisy out yet again on Sunday to a local clothing store to buy a couple new pairs of outfits and school supplies for both of them.

Last night, however, Kelly had heard Todd toss and turn every hour or so in the bedroom and get up several times to use the bathroom and take a drink of water. She'd tried not to pry, but sleeping on the sofa only five feet away from the kitchen sink, she really couldn't ignore his sleepless night. When she'd asked what was bothering him, he'd simply shrugged and gone back to bed without comment.

"Todd had a little difficulty at his previous school," she said. "Mainly with his teachers and fitting in with the other kids. He has a bit of a temper when other people can't keep up with him." She forced a laugh, her face heating as she glanced at the closed door of the principal's office; Todd and Daisy sat waiting on the other side. "Like me. He and I are always butting heads because he's always light-years ahead of me in an academic sense. But Todd means well—he always means well. He's a great kid and he has a very strong sense of what's right. He just doesn't put much thought into whether or not what he does to set things right might offend others."

Dr. Helm tapped her pen on the open file splayed across her desk. "It says here that he damaged school equipment at his prior school?"

Kelly laughed awkwardly again. "Oh, that. He, uh, he got a little mad about his teacher making a math error, so he threw his laptop out of the window. But it was okay in the end. I paid for a new LCD screen and scrubbed the mud off it. It had rained that morning, you see."

Dr. Helm studied her silently.

Kelly smiled wider. So wide her cheeks ached.

"Do you do that often?" Dr. Helm asked.

"What?"

"Clean up Todd's messes?" she clarified quietly.

Kelly's smile fell. "Sometimes. I couldn't help but do so after Laice—his mom—passed. He was very angry. Very sad. I didn't quite know what to do." Her chin quivered, an unexpected wave of emotion rolling through her, stinging her eyes and tightening her throat. She stared at the framed degree hanging on the wall over Dr. Helm's right shoulder, blinked hard and drew in a deep breath. "I still don't know what to do for him sometimes."

Dr. Helm put down her pen, closed the file and smiled gently. "Ms. Jenkins, I don't mean to imply that you're not doing a good job as guardian. As a matter of fact, everything in this file and the conversations I've had with officials from his prior school indicate you've done an outstanding job caring for Todd and his sister after their mother's death. Please don't think I'm suggesting otherwise."

"Oh, no. I didn't think you were." Kelly pushed her hair back and quickly wiped her eyes. "But I know that I fall short sometimes. Most times, actually. I'm nowhere near as good a parent to Todd and Daisy as Laice was."

"Maybe not," Dr. Helm said. "But as I didn't know

Todd and Daisy's mother, I can only speak in regard to my impression of you. I see that you care very deeply for both Todd and Daisy and are critical of yourself as their caretaker. Both are traits that I find are usually displayed by loving parents."

Kelly's throat closed and she managed a smile. "Thank you. I . . . I can't tell you how much I appreciate you saying that."

"Please don't worry about Todd and Daisy," Dr. Helm said, standing and extending her hand. "We'll take great care of them, and I'll be sure Todd is enrolled in classes with patient, understanding teachers and that they're given an in-depth explanation of his needs, both academic and social. We're very happy to have you, Todd and Daisy join our community."

Kelly stood and shook her hand eagerly. "Thank you, Dr. Helm."

"You're welcome." She smiled as she escorted Kelly to the door. "And what will you do with your day, now that you'll be child-free until three this afternoon? Will you begin work on Mrs. Larkin's drive-in?" She paused by the door, smiling good-naturedly. "I hope you don't mind my asking. Word travels fast in Blue Moon, and Tully Morris told me yesterday that you were her brother's new neighbor." She leaned in and whispered with excitement, "I would love to be at your grand opening. My twins are turning six this summer and I know they'd just love it, and my husband and I are hoping to schedule a date night for ourselves, too."

Kelly smiled, feeling her spirits lift. Their meeting had gone better than expected and she was looking forward to viewing the films Mae Bell had left her. "When we have a grand-opening date, you'll be the first I tell."

Outside of the office, Dr. Helm welcomed Todd and Daisy to school and waited patiently while Kelly said goodbye.

"Are you coming back?" Daisy whispered in Kelly's ear as she hugged her tightly.

"Of course." Kelly lifted Daisy's wrist and tapped her pink watch. "When you see three o'clock, I'll be sitting right outside waiting to pick you up."

Daisy smiled, though it was weak, took Dr. Helm's hand and began walking down the hall toward class.

"Todd?" Kelly called, waiting for him to turn and face her. "Have a good day, okay?"

"Yeah, okay." He didn't look enthusiastic.

"I'll miss you," Kelly added, but he'd already stuffed his earbuds back in his ears and didn't respond.

Oh, well. Maybe a long, intellectually challenging day at school would tire him out enough to be civil when she picked him up this afternoon. But for now, Kelly thought, rubbing her hands together, it was time to start on Mae Bell's priority list.

And if she were being honest with herself, she was eager to get another look at that beautiful house Seth had built. The place had really surprised her because Seth didn't seem to have an interest in (what had he called it? Oh, yeah . . .) *homey*-type things. That side of him had been as surprising as his gentle apology to Daisy.

Kelly ran her shaky palms over her jean shorts, shouted one last goodbye to Todd and Daisy as they rounded a corner out of view and headed to the parking lot. Her excitement about the next few hours had everything to do with getting another peek at that beautiful red roof and taking care of priority number one on Mae Bell's list. It had absolutely nothing to do with her curiosity as to which Seth Morgan she'd run into today: The rude Neanderthal she'd first met? Or the kind, good-natured gentleman who'd offered a heartfelt apology to Daisy and protected her from the rain?

* * *

Seth inspected the leaves and twigs on one of the pecan trees in his orchard for black lesions indicative of pecan scab. He wrote notes on his notepad, tucked it and his pen in the back pocket of his jeans and walked to the next tree in the row. Patch followed him, as always, sniffing the grassy lawn as he padded along.

He glanced at the dirt driveway curving toward his house beyond the tree line, but there was no sign of Kelly's car yet.

"Get ahold of yourself," he muttered to himself as he examined the leaves of the next tree with trembling hands.

It was absolutely juvenile to be so nervous about having a guest. He'd entertained before. As a matter of fact, when he was married, he and Madeline had friends over almost every weekend to hang out, grill steaks and share a few laughs. That, of course, had changed to involve more couples and kids after Rachel had been born, but the house had always welcomed lively guests of some sort almost every other weekend.

That had all ended eight years ago when they'd lost Rachel. The more angry, regretful and grief-stricken Seth had become, the less frequently anyone had visited, leaving him free to wrap himself in a cloak of comforting silent isolation. In the end, even Madeline had been unable to endure his temper. She'd cried for hours the night she'd made the decision to leave him, had even apologized for considering it. Madeline, like Seth, had thought they would be together forever. That the vows they'd made had been unbreakable and that happy endings actually did come for good, honest people who worked hard.

But Seth couldn't be that type of person. If he had been a good man deserving of a happy ending, Rachel wouldn't have been taken from him, and Madeline wouldn't have followed.

No, happy endings didn't exist, and Seth was content with the current status quo of quiet predictability at his house. Which made his nervous, somewhat-eager anticipation of Kelly's arrival all the more surprising to him.

Patch barked and sprinted off, kicking up blades of grass behind him.

"Patch!" Seth stopped inspecting the tree, returned his notepad to his back pocket and walked toward the driveway just as Kelly's compact car rounded the curve.

Patch chased the car until it parked in front of Seth's house; then the dog started jumping and barking at the driver's-side door, his tongue lolling out of his mouth with giddy excitement.

"Back, Patch." Seth strode quickly up to the car and tugged at Patch's collar, his heart kicking anxiously in his chest at the sight of Kelly waving at him through the window.

Seth stepped back from the car and pulled Patch with him, stealing a moment to brush the dirt from the front of his T-shirt. "I've got him," he called out to her through the window. "It's safe to come out. Like I said the other day, the worst he'll do is . . ."

Kelly opened the driver's-side door, stepped out and smiled. She wore simple jean shorts and a cotton T-shirt, ordinary everyday clothing that shouldn't draw attention, but the soft cling of the fabrics along her curves made her look welcoming . . . like a soft place to land after a hard day of work. And she'd left her hair loose today. The wavy strands framed her cute features, highlighting the soft curve of her cheekbones and the tempting pink shade of her mouth.

". . . lick you to death." Seth finished his sentence on an unconscious whisper.

She frowned. "What?"

Oh, Lord. Scorching heat coursed up his neck and flooded Seth's face. He coughed and stood straighter, tugging Patch closer to his legs. "I said, you're safe around Patch. The worst he'll do is lick you to death."

"Oh." She smiled, the action drawing attention to her bright, even teeth. "Thanks again for letting me use your VCR." She popped her trunk and hauled out a large wooden trunk. "I can't tell you how much I appreciate it."

"Here, let me get that." Seth released Patch and joined her at the car, relieving her of the wooden trunk. "Time to start Mae Bell's movie marathon, huh?"

"Yep." Smiling wider, she dropped to her haunches as Patch sprinted over and butted her shins. "Oh, so I get an actual hello this time?" She laughed as Patch rose on his back legs, propped his front paws on her shoulders and started licking her cheeks. "You were right. He'll definitely lick you to death." Still laughing, she patted Patch's head, then stood. "Sorry, I don't have any hot dogs today, buddy." She held up a finger, then hauled a small cooler from the backseat of her car. "But I did bring my own lunch."

Seth lifted the wooden trunk higher in his arms and shrugged his shoulders. "You didn't have to do that."

"I didn't want to mooch off you." She thought for a moment, and her smile turned self-conscious. "Well, any more than I already am, I guess."

"And how did you know Patch likes hot dogs?"

"Oh, he paid me a visit the night we moved into the trailer. I was savoring the one and only hot dog Todd left me, but Patch seemed to want it more than me, so I handed it over."

"Then I owe you one."

"No worries," she said, lifting her cooler. "I brought everything I need."

Ten minutes later, Kelly had unloaded the VHS tapes

and DVDs from the wooden trunk Seth had carried in for her, sorted them in piles according to the year they were made and sat in the middle of them on the floor, rubbing her hands with excitement. Patch lay by her side, stretching out on the hardwood floor and resting his chin on his paws.

"I don't want to disappoint you," Seth said as she pulled the first VHS tape out of its sleeve. "But that thing hasn't been used in years. It may not even work properly."

Kelly leaned close to the entertainment stand and powered up the VCR and DVD combination player. "Have faith." She paused, glancing up at him from her seated position on the floor. "Do you believe in things happening for a reason?"

He shoved his hands in his pockets. "I don't know. Maybe, maybe not." His gaze moved beyond her, seeking out a framed picture that sat on an end table at one end of the sectional. An ache spread through him. "Sometimes I think things just happen for no reason."

She remained silent, staring up at him, then said, "That could be. But I think there's more to it than that. I mean, the kids and I had next to nothing a few days ago and now"—she laughed—"we live in a Royal Mansion on a piece of property where dreams come true every night. And then, here you are, our neighbor, offering us shelter from the storm and you just so happened to have a VCR, which we desperately needed." She raised an eyebrow. "I just don't think things like that happen unless there's a reason. And having faith in that"—she slid the VHS tape into the player and looked up at the large HDTV expectantly—"I'm betting this thing'll work."

Sure enough, the VHS player whirred, the TV blinked on and the tape started playing.

"Woo-hoo!" Overjoyed, Kelly clapped her hands and started bouncing. "Look at that. We're in business, honey bun. What'd I tell you?"

Seth smiled. "Honey bun?"

She stopped bouncing and her cheeks turned red. "It's just an expression. Though . . ." A flirtatious gleam lit her eyes. "You do make honey."

Despite the awkward exchange, Seth smiled.

"And . . ." Her blush deepened as her attention lingered on his mouth. "You have a nice smile."

His smile widened at the hint of appreciation in her gaze. The woman had a silly excitement about life and those around her. An almost childlike, gleeful sense of humor, and he got the impression she'd never met a stranger and might strike up a conversation with anyone who'd be willing to listen. All of these traits were completely at odds with his staid, levelheaded, predictable existence. And yet, strangely . . . the sight of her lounging on his floor with Patch leaning against her struck him as familiar. As though she fit in right there where she sat in his living room and should've been there forever.

The odd thought was enough to startle him. "I'll leave you to it."

"But—"

He whistled for Patch to join him, more grateful than ever for the silence of the orchard.

CHAPTER 6

Four hours later, Kelly scribbled notes furiously in a notebook she'd brought with her as she stuffed a ham and cheese sandwich in her mouth with her other hand.

"'Bout through watching for the day?"

Startled, she shot upright on the sectional, her pen making a stray mark on the paper, and blinked her dry eyes up at Seth, who stood on the threshold of the living room. "Not yet." She smiled apologetically. "I hope you don't mind? I planned to stay until around two-thirty, when I have to go pick up Todd and Daisy from school. I've made it through three silent films, one from the year 1919, another from 1920 and the third from 1921, but I still have a *looooong* way to go."

And that was an understatement. She took another bite of her sandwich and chewed furiously as she studied the piles of VHS tapes and DVDs on the floor of Seth's living room. There was one more small stack of silent films ranging in date from 1922 to 1924, one stack of films that spanned the 1930s and 1940s and a various assortment of other films ranging from the 1950s to the 1980s. There were hours upon hours of viewing ahead of her; she'd barely made a dent today.

"You're welcome to use the TV as long as you need," Seth said, crossing the living room and walking into the adjacent kitchen. "I rarely watch it anyway."

Kelly set her notebook aside and swiveled around on the sectional, propping her chin on her hands on the back of the seat and watching Seth's movements. He opened the refrigerator, withdrew a pitcher of tea, grabbed a glass from an overhead cabinet and poured himself a generous serving over ice.

"You want one?" he asked over his shoulder.

"No, thanks. I brought some soda." She pointed to the large island at his back, where she'd placed a plastic bag for him ten minutes ago, aware from his silent comings and goings the past few hours that he'd be in for a drink soon. "I made you a sandwich. It's on the table there whenever you're ready for it."

The cushion beside her bounced, jostling her as Patch jumped onto the sectional and head-butted her ribs.

Smiling, she patted his head. "Don't worry, I didn't forget you." She gestured toward a second plastic bag she'd placed on the island. "That bag with just the meat in it is for Patch. I wasn't sure if he liked ham, but considering how much he likes hot dogs, I thought I'd save some for him just in case."

Seth set his glass of sweet tea on the island and opened the plastic bag with his sandwich. He took a bite, chewed several times and a look of pleasure crossed his face. "Thank you. This is delicious."

Kelly grinned. She'd spent extra time on his sandwich when she'd made one each for Todd and Daisy to take to school for lunch, stacking thick tomatoes, lots of lettuce, provolone cheese and slathering mayonnaise on both slices of bread. "I hoped you'd like it. It's the way the kids and I like ours."

He chewed his second bite and nodded. "It's perfect, and much appreciated."

It seemed to be, given the way he bit into it, holding it with both hands and sighing in contentment. He'd spent the majority of the past four hours working outside in the warm spring sun, only coming inside occasionally for a drink of water or tea. Each time he'd come in, his lean cheeks seemed to have tanned a bit more, his blond hair had been slightly damper and the small sweat stains around his collar and underarms had darkened a little more.

Clearly, he worked hard, and she hoped having a ready-made lunch waiting for him would help, in some small way, to repay him for allowing her to use his TV.

He chewed another bite, swallowed, then motioned toward her. "I didn't mean to interrupt."

"You're not interrupting," she said, holding up her half-eaten sandwich and taking another bite, too. "You wanna join me for a few minutes?" she mumbled around a mouthful of sandwich. "There's another sandwich in the fridge for you, in case you're extra hungry. Why don't you grab it and take a load off?"

He hesitated, finishing off the last of his sandwich and eyeing the bag of ham on the island, then looking at Patch, who stared at the sandwich in her hand and panted. "All right. It's lunchtime anyway, so it won't hurt to take a break."

Grinning, Kelly swiveled back around on the sectional and faced the TV, while Seth grabbed the second sandwich from the fridge and brought it and the extra helping of ham to the living room. He sat on the opposite end of the sectional and patted the sofa next to him.

"Come here, Patch."

The dog sniffed the air, then did as he was bid, leaving Kelly's side and scrambling across the leather cushions to Seth's side. Seth opened the plastic bag and tossed a slice of ham in the air. Patch jerked his chin in the air and caught it in his jaws, gobbling it up with enthusiasm and a low doggy moan of approval.

"You've made a friend for life," Seth said, smiling at her.

Kelly, knowing he meant Patch, but delighting in his warm look, cradled her sandwich to her chest and pointed at the silent film playing on the TV. "This is a good one. Not that the others haven't been great—it's just that this one's a bit more stylish."

He bit into his second sandwich and watched the silent film play out on the TV for a few minutes. One clip showed a family setting the table for dinner in black-and-white images that jerked and blurred; the next clip showed text in a frame that read: *The guest arrives.* Next a clip showed the family again, welcoming their guest to dinner with flourishing motions and wide smiles.

Frowning, Seth shifted uncomfortably before tossing another piece of ham to Patch. "I know these are silent films, but I thought there was at least some music that accompanied them. There's no music, either?"

Kelly shook her head. "Not with these earliest ones. Mae Bell included notes on most of the VHS covers and a few of them had some research noted as well. The notes mentioned that these earliest films were played in theaters where music was played on a phonograph, or someone played a piano. At the fanciest events, a live orchestra performed." She finished off her sandwich and sipped her soda. "The few I watched are from that era."

She glanced at Seth, who tossed another piece of ham to Patch. His frown deepened as he watched.

"It's odd, huh?" he asked. "Kinda strange with no sound and the old footage blinking in and out and blurring from time to time."

Kelly nodded, but added quietly, "Give it a few minutes. It grows on you."

They sat silently for a while, watching the story play out. It turned out that the guest didn't fit in with the dinner party very well, and after several heated debates, the father and head of the family decked him.

Seth grinned. "Whoa. That was a sucker punch if I ever saw one." He lifted the last bite of his sandwich, then popped it in his mouth, mumbling, "It's not exactly good sportsmanship to punch a man while he's eating ham."

A black screen with the words *Enemy vanquished* appeared and Kelly laughed. "Seems his poor table manners made it acceptable." She sipped her soda, adding, "That's the thing with these movies. It's the mixture of comedy, romance, adventure and ironic violations of social norms that makes them so interesting."

The screen changed to a new scene of two boys standing at the top of a staircase, trying their best to slide down the banister, only for their younger sister to beat them to it.

"So much revolves around family and fun and just . . . I don't know, enjoying life," Kelly continued. "And there's an intimacy with these silent films that you don't find in today's movies with all their booms, bangs and special effects. There are just images, the written word and silence between you and the story."

He watched the film for a few more minutes, his lips lifting a time or two as an elderly man in a fancy suit and handlebar mustache tried his best to chat up several elegantly dressed matrons. When each one smacked him in the mouth with her purse, he gave up and lay down in the street, waving at people as they stepped over him.

"And what you make of it," he said.

Kelly glanced at him. "What?"

"'There are just images, the written word and silence between you' and what you make of the story," he clarified. "For instance, what did you make of that scene?"

She smiled. "That a lecherous man up to no good got his well-deserved comeuppance. Classic slapstick comedy."

"Or," he suggested, "comedic tragedy. Could be that guy spent all day putting on his Sunday best, desperate for companionship, only to be shot down ruthlessly by a string of women who thought they were too good for him. And then, when he's at his lowest, a bunch of strangers just step right over him and continue on as though he doesn't exist." He looked at Kelly, a rueful expression on his face. "Could be, he just figured out that he'd missed his final shot at happiness and life was never going to go the way he wanted or planned."

Her smile faded.

"I'm just saying," Seth added, standing, "without the accompanying music, the intended meaning's up for debate." He clucked his tongue and Patch hopped off the couch and followed him toward the front door. "Thanks again for the sandwich."

"You're welcome," Kelly whispered.

When the door shut, she paused the movie, strolled quietly to the front door and peered out of the window. She watched him amble across the sunny front lawn and into his orchard, Patch shadowing his movements, and wondered what shot at happiness he'd missed. . . . and how long he'd been alone.

* * *

Later that afternoon, Seth dragged the back of his forearm across his sweaty forehead and left the orchard. Patch followed, as always, and Seth stopped twice to pat his head and rub his back. He passed the empty spot where Kelly's car had been parked earlier and caught himself glancing at it more than once with a pang.

"Finally," he said on a heavy exhale as he tipped his head back and smiled serenely at the clear blue sky. "Some peace and solitude."

Patch butted his head against Seth's thigh and wagged his tail.

"Come on. Let's get cleaned up and have a beer."

After going inside, Seth went upstairs, stripped down and stood beneath the lukewarm blast of the shower-head, savoring the relaxation coursing through his sore muscles as water rippled over his skin. Nothing quite compared to a cool, comfortable shower after a long day of hot, sweaty work outdoors.

He toweled off, put his dirty clothes in the hamper, dragged on a pair of clean jeans and padded barefoot down the staircase in anticipation of a cold beer and another sleepless night spent contemplating the stars.

". . . teacher doesn't know what he's doing, and the classes are so small, everyone already knows everyone else and doesn't care about getting to know someone new."

Seth jerked to a halt at the threshold of the living room and covered his bare chest with his hands. Kelly stood in his kitchen, unpacking several to-go containers that released the tantalizing scent of fried chicken, mashed potatoes, green beans, and . . . was that the aroma of buttered biscuits, too?

"You've got to stop judging people before you have a chance to get to know them," Kelly was saying as she propped her hands on her hips and leveled a stern look at Todd. "Give the place a chance. You never know, you might meet one of the best friends you've ever had at Blue Moon Central and forget how much you think you hate school."

Seth clenched his jaw. "What's going on?"

Kelly started, a pack of plastic silverware spilling from her hands onto the island. "I . . . well, I—" Her eyes drifted over his bare chest, unbuttoned jeans and bare feet. "You're half-naked," she whispered. Tearing her gaze away, she pulled Daisy, who stood by her side, close and plastered her hands over the little girl's eyes. "You're half-naked," she repeated, this time in an accusatory tone.

"Yeah, well, this is my house." Seth hugged his arms tighter across his chest. "And you left an hour ago. Why are you back? And why are they here?"

She, at least, had the good grace to blush. "School ends at three, so I picked Todd and Daisy up and grabbed some to-go supper. I thought I'd surprise you with another free meal."

"I do have food in the refrigerator," he said tightly.

"I know." She smiled, but it looked forced. "But I bet you don't have fabulous crispy fried chicken."

Nope, and he had to admit, if he went by the deep growl of his gut at the delectable smell, it'd be a welcome change from the can of soup he usually had every night.

"And," she added shyly, "I need to watch some more movies tonight, if that's okay?"

She stared at him expectantly. As did Todd and Daisy, who'd made a peephole between Kelly's fingers.

Seth's right eye twitched.

"The kids are gonna eat and do their homework quietly," she said. "I'll fix us both a plate and I'll sit right where I sat earlier today, watching movies, and you won't hear a peep out of me until the door shuts as we leave in a couple hours." She lifted one hand from Daisy's face and made a cross over her heart. "I promise."

Seth sighed. "All right. I'll go grab a shirt." He rubbed his bare arms and headed for the stairs, then paused, calling over his shoulder, "But I'll have you know it takes more than a bucket of chicken to buy me."

Thirty minutes later, they were all seated on the sectional. Seth occupied one end, reclining with his feet up and a hefty plate of fried chicken, mashed potatoes, green beans and a buttered biscuit in his lap, and Kelly sat on the other end, the same food in smaller portions on the plate in her lap. In between them, Todd and Daisy dug into their chicken happily, tossing a piece, now and then, to Patch, who sat on the floor in front of them.

"This one is called *A Starry Romance,*" Kelly said, holding up the remote and pressing play.

Daisy smiled around a spoonful of mashed potatoes. Todd gagged.

"How lame is that?" Todd asked, sneering at the TV. "*A Starry Romance?* Why can't we watch a Western or something?"

Seth bit back a smile. "I have to agree with Todd on this one. Any Western sounds like it'd be a welcome alternative to what you just announced."

"Daisy and I would like to enjoy a soothing romantic film before we go back to the trailer and turn in for the night, wouldn't we, Daisy?" At the little girl's nod, Kelly continued. "This film is about a poor country man who falls in love with a rich movie star who's come to the countryside to visit her uncle. He sacrifices everything to win her heart—his family, friends, business, what little money he has—but she takes total advantage of him, then walks away. It's supposed to be one of the finest examples of early silent cinema."

"Silent?" Todd's expression was full of disgust. "You mean there's no sound, either?"

"Suck it up, kid." Kelly shushed him as the opening credits flashed on the screen. "It's starting."

And start, it did. Todd, who'd adamantly resisted watching the film, looked horrified for the first five minutes, his expression shifting between confusion, irritation and frustration as the silent black-and-white images flickered across the TV. Daisy, however, continued smiling with delight and eating her mashed potatoes, pausing once in a while to give Patch another piece of chicken.

"I can't stand it," Todd complained. "This is weird. Why can't we watch something with sound?"

Kelly, clearly exasperated, couldn't respond because her mouth was full.

Maybe it was the savory taste of crispy fried chicken on his tongue, or maybe it was the way his body seemed to settle more comfortably into the soft cushions with every bite he took, but Seth felt a surprising urge to help Kelly out with Todd . . . just this once, of course.

"That's what I thought at first," he said, sipping his tea, then replacing the glass on the side table. "But give it a few more minutes. It'll grow on you."

Todd frowned. "How?"

"The silence." Seth motioned around the living room. "Just let it fill the void for a little while. Absorb the images, focus on the story and let your mind wander." He shrugged. "Kelly suckered me into watching one earlier this afternoon, and I have to admit, I found it kind of relaxing."

Todd remained skeptical, but faced the TV again and stared at the screen, a pensive look appearing on his face. After a while, Seth glanced at him and noticed he'd settled into his seat and his pensive expression had changed to one of reluctant interest. He still scoffed at the corniest jokes and slapstick comedy, but he seemed genuinely intrigued by a medium that had previously been foreign to him.

Daisy, too, found comfort in the film, hugging Patch, who still sat beside her on the sectional.

And Kelly . . . well, Kelly was all in. Her eyes filled with tears at the romantic moments, her chin trembled at the tragic ones and a soft smile curved her lips at the tender scenes. At one point, when the heroine broke the hero's heart, telling him she only wanted to be friends and that she could never be happy with a man as simple or poor as him, a sob escaped Kelly.

She watched, her mouth halfway open and tears coursing down her cheeks, as the hero's response flashed across the screen while he backed away, crushed, having gambled everything that was meaningful to him on someone who would never love him back: *I don't want to be your friend. I wanted to be your everything.*

Seth rolled his eyes at the corny dialogue, smiling as he realized he could appreciate Todd's disdain for some parts of the film. But Todd didn't seem to mind too much at the moment. He even looked a bit sad for the hero.

"Growing on you, huh?" Seth asked Todd softly, hesitant to spoil the peaceful atmosphere.

Todd glanced at him, reluctance in his eyes. "I guess. It's different from anything I've seen before. It's beyond old." His upper lip curled with irritation, but he refocused on the TV and began eagerly watching again.

Kelly met Seth's eyes over Todd's head and grinned, then mouthed the words *Thank you.*

Seth dipped his head, an unexpected warmth coursing through him at her appreciative gaze. *You're welcome*, he mouthed back.

Seth turned his attention back to the TV and began watching again, but a few minutes later, his eyes grew heavy and he caught himself drifting off a time or two before he set his empty plate aside and refocused on the film. Try as he might, though, the combination of silence and Kelly, Todd and Daisy's quiet breathing lulled him further into relaxation. He yawned again, his eyes growing heavier by the second, and one more thought drifted softly through his mind, making him smile just before he drifted off to a deep sleep.

Maybe I can be bought with a bucket of chicken after all . . .

CHAPTER 7

Sleeping, undisturbed, through an entire night was not something Seth was accustomed to. So, after he awoke, it took several minutes for him to get his bearings.

He blinked, groggily taking in his surroundings. The TV was off, the end of the sectional where Kelly, Todd and Daisy had sat the night before was empty and the aromas of dinner had dissipated. Sunlight trickled in through the partially opened blinds and slanted warmly over the soft throw that someone—Kelly?—had draped over him the night before. Patch had settled over Seth's outstretched legs on the reclining seat of the sectional at some point during the night, his large head resting on Seth's knees, and he still snored with contentment.

"Patch," Seth called softly. "Hey, Patch. It's morning."

The dog stirred, lifted his head and blinked up at Seth twice before lowering his head again and closing his eyes.

Seth smiled. "I know the feeling." He stretched his

arms overhead and pointed his toes, jostling Patch into alertness again. "I think it's past time for us to get up."

And Seth was okay with that. More than okay, actually. He nudged Patch off his legs, lowered the footrest and stood. Muscles sore from the day before stretched easily, and his skin tingled just a bit with a pleasurable sense of well-rested contentment that he hadn't experienced in years.

Slowly he made his way into the kitchen to find all of the dishes washed and stacked neatly in the drainboard. Leftovers had been put away and he couldn't help but smile at the sight of another dinner's worth of fried chicken in his refrigerator. Kelly had even locked the front door behind her when she'd left last night, and the thought of her considering his safety only made him smile more.

Seth started a pot of coffee, fed Patch, then filled a thermos with the hot coffee he'd prepared, sipping the hot black liquid, while Patch ate more slowly than usual.

"Are you a lazybones, too, this morning?" Seth asked.

Patch finished eating, licked his chops and padded at a snail's pace toward the front door.

"Yeah," Seth said, following him. "I feel ya. We haven't had a night's sleep that good in ages."

He ambled out onto the front porch with Patch, tipped his head back and closed his eyes, soaking up the warm rays of the morning sun. After a few minutes, he grew alert enough to feel up to tackling the day's chores and headed to the orchard with Patch to begin the morning rounds, checking for pests and ensuring all was well on his property.

Usually, he welcomed the solitude of his daily tasks, content with only Patch for company. But today, for some reason, he caught himself glancing at the empty spot in his driveway where Kelly had parked yesterday, and then down the lane, hoping to see her small car cruising around the curve again. She had stacks of movies left in his living room to watch, so he felt sure she'd return, but his disappointment grew with each passing hour that she didn't arrive.

When he reached the line of trees on the border between his property and Mae Bell's, he noticed Kelly's car was gone. He checked his watch, noting the time. It was already ten, so he'd have expected her back from dropping off the kids at school by now.

As it was, the drive-in theater sat empty and desolate, as it had for years, the only bright spot being the bright red chairs Kelly had placed outside of the silver trailer. He studied the overgrown lot, filled with knee-high grass and weeds, and the empty projection stands and concessions building. He'd heard the Blue Moon Haven Drive-In had been a real attraction back in its day, but he had never regretted its current neglected state. His goal had always been to raze it and plant another orchard. But that sense of peace he'd experienced last night watching the silent films with Kelly and the kids still lingered within him this morning . . . and he found himself curious as to what state the interiors of the buildings were in.

Before he could think better of it, Seth shoved his notepad and pen in his back pocket, walked across the property line and whistled for Patch to follow.

He walked to the concessions building, a large white structure positioned at the back center of the lot between two projection booths. Inside, it was in surprisingly good shape. The floors were clean, no mildew or mold clung to the tiled ceiling and the long counter lining the front of the building was still intact. Even the metal coverings over the windows still rolled up and down without squeaking or snagging. And an old-fashioned heavy-duty popcorn maker, which stood in one corner, seemed to be in good working order when Seth plugged it in and watched it light up.

The projection booths were next. Both buildings were piled high with boxes and boxes of old promotional materials, posters and frames, but buried behind the wall of paper goods in each projection booth were two five-foot-tall old-school projectors with five-foot-diameter reels. A note from Mae Bell was attached to each, reading: *Original 1952 projectors. Sword System. Original reels (1950–1960 films) we own are in canisters in the storage cabinet. When using, splice reels together in order listed inside the canister, load on the left side, weave up, over, then down through the lamphouse and onto the guide reel. Voilá!*

Seth grunted. *Voilá, huh?*

"What're you doing?"

He jumped and spun around to find Kelly standing in the doorway of the projector booth, her arms crossed over her chest and a confused look on her face.

Seth held up a hand. "Now, I know how this must look, but don't jump to conclusions, okay? I'm not here to spy or sabotage your renovation efforts."

Patch padded up to her side, sat down and whimpered for attention.

She bent, rubbing his head absently, as she narrowed her eyes and drawled, "Okay . . ."

"Watching the movie last night piqued my curiosity, and I thought I'd check the place out." He gestured toward the door of the projection booth. "The buildings were unlocked, so I figured I'd take a quick tour and see if Mae Bell had hung on to any of the original equipment that was here when the place first opened in the fifties."

"And?" she prompted. "What did you discover?"

He tapped the projector in front of him. "I discovered that Mae Bell left you quite a few classics, with directions attached. But somehow, I don't think manually loading twenty-thousand or more feet of film through an old-school Sword System will be that simple for the average, untrained individual."

She tilted her head, her confused frown deepening.

"Here." Seth held out the note Mae Bell had left taped to the projector. "Don't know if you've completed your tour yet, but Mae Bell left notes taped to everything. Only thing is, I'm not sure they'll be a whole lot of help to someone new to the equipment."

Kelly patted Patch's head once more, then straightened. "I've seen it, and I agree with you." She took the note from him, walked over to the projector and returned it to its original position. "I have no idea how to work that thing, but I can learn. And there's a digital projector in the other booth. Did you notice that one?"

Seth nodded. "I was surprised at that. I didn't think Mae Bell had purchased anything new for the property in years, but it looks as though she still worked out here up until she had her stroke and moved into the nursing home."

"She left the place in really great shape, all things considered." Kelly picked up a box that had fallen off a stack of other boxes, replaced it, then brushed the dust off her hands. "All the other booth needs is a good cleanup. This one, too, but it needs a digital projector as well."

"So you plan to keep the old projectors?"

"Of course. Mae Bell left a quality collection of film reels from the fifties and sixties, and I think people might enjoy a trip back to yesterday once in a while. They'd make for great retro nights in the summer."

"I can see that being a possibility," he said, grinning. "After the deep sleep that silent film put me in last night, I'd be willing to pay a few bucks to enjoy another night of classic films and good snoring outside on a warm, starry night."

She laughed. "I don't think I'll plaster your quote on any promotional flyers I distribute, but I'll take that as a compliment to great cinema."

"It was meant as a compliment." He admired her pretty features for a moment, taking in the kindness in her brown eyes and the slight dimple in her chin. "Thank you for dinner and the movie. I haven't had as good a night's sleep in a long time, and it was a welcome change. Though I'm sorry I was bad company."

She returned his stare, her eyes lingering on his smile. "You were great company. And I really appreciated your helping Todd see at least a little bit of beauty in silent film." Hesitating, she tossed her long hair back over her shoulders and rubbed her neck, avoiding his eyes. "I know we agreed to be good neighbors, but I think we've gotten along pretty well lately and we might have more to offer each other."

His trepidation at her words must have shown on his face, because she quickly held up a hand, palm out, and raised her brows.

"What I mean is, I could offer you warm meals after a long day of work in exchange for using your VCR player and letting Todd mooch off your internet service occasionally to do homework. And I was hoping that since it's worked out well so far . . . maybe we could try being friends, too?" She met his eyes, shrugging as her cheeks flushed. "I mean, seeing as how I just moved here and all, and you're the only person I've gotten to know a little bit, besides Mae Bell." A laugh burst from her lips. "And your sister, of course."

Seth's grin grew. "Oh, yeah. I forgot you shared your opinion of me with Tully."

Her eyes widened. "She told you what I said?"

That she thought he was easy on the eyes? Yeah, that much he remembered. He spread his hands. "It doesn't matter now, does it? I just regret the way I behaved when we first met."

"Well, I appreciated your help improving Todd's mood last night," she said quietly. "I've always been close to Daisy, but Todd and I are still getting to know each other better, and your smoothing things over between us last night, even for just a couple hours, was a welcome relief." She tilted her head. "So . . . can we try being friends then?"

"Yeah." He held out his hand. "Friends."

She took his hand and squeezed, and he stood there for a moment, between the dusty boxes and old projector, absorbing the soft warmth of her touch and shy smile. An unexpected urge to dip his head and brush his lips against hers washed over him. Instead, Seth released her hand and stepped back.

He withdrew his notepad from his back pocket, clicked his pen and smiled. "And as your friend, I have a few suggestions."

Kelly drummed her fingers on the steering wheel of her car as she waited in the student pickup line in the parking lot of Blue Moon Central, her mind racing through the priority list Seth had handed her several hours earlier.

Cut grass, weed-whack and plant a moon garden. Clean out projection booths. Unpack and keep usable equipment and discard old equipment. Paint exterior of concessions stand, projection booths and ticket stands. Repair projection screens. Hang colorful movie posters on exterior and interior walls of buildings for aesthetic appeal. Clean and test cooking equipment in concessions. Purchase and install a digital projector for the second projector booth.

Oh, gosh. Kelly dropped her head back against her seat's headrest and closed her eyes. Each item sounded like such a simple task, but they were only simple if one had unlimited time, money and opportunity.

As it stood, she'd be hard-pressed to complete a fraction of the tasks on the list by the time Mae Bell hoped to open in late spring.

Cut the grass. Weed-whack. Plant a moon garden. Clean. Paint. Test—

Someone banged on the window of the passenger door.

"Unlock the door," Todd shouted, pressing his nose against the glass. "We can't get in."

Daisy, standing beside Todd and holding his hand, jumped as the cars lined up behind Kelly honked impatiently.

"Okay, okay." Kelly unlocked the doors, hopped out and rounded the car to help Daisy into her booster seat. "My bad, okay? I was a little distracted."

"A little?" Todd snapped, hopping in the passenger seat and fastening his seat belt. "I'd been banging on the window for at least five seconds before you noticed."

"I said I was sorry." Kelly raced back to the driver's side, jumped in and pulled out, waving in apology to those behind her. "How was school today?"

"Horrible."

"You wanna elaborate?"

"Nope." Todd poked his earbuds in his ears, turned away and stared out of the window at the passing cars.

Kelly sighed and glanced in the rearview mirror. "Okay, guess you and I will enjoy a stimulating conversation without him. How was your day today, Daisy?"

Daisy smiled and started sucking her thumb.

"Okay," Kelly said. "Well, at least Mae Bell will be interested in holding a conversation."

She drove on through to the center of town, turned left into the nursing home lot and parked.

"Here again?" Todd asked, yanking his earbuds out.

"She is my boss, you know." Kelly opened her door. "Now, get out."

After unloading Daisy and Todd, Kelly grabbed a bag from the backseat and led the way inside. As usual, Mr. Haggart sat in his wheelchair by the door, but this time Kelly was prepared.

"Good afternoon, Mr. Haggart," Kelly said. "I brought you something special." She dug into the bag she'd carried in, withdrew a cold root beer and held it out to him. "Seth told me this is the kind you like."

Mr. Haggart looked momentarily surprised, but he accepted the root beer anyway and smiled. "This is exactly the kind I like, and it's a good thing you brought it," he said, "because the service here stinks."

Kadence Powell, standing at the nurses' station, frowned in Mr. Haggart's direction. "Now, I brought you seven glasses of water, two bowls of macaroni and cheese and three servings of chocolate pudding in the past three hours. I'd say I've waited on you enough today."

Kelly smiled in apology and said, "Oh, I didn't mean to imply Mr. Haggart wasn't being taken care of. We just thought we'd bring him something special for our visit today."

"You're meeting with Mrs. Larkin again today, I presume," Kadence said.

Kelly nodded.

"Go ahead," Kadence said, gesturing toward the hallway.

"Thank you," Kelly said.

She took Daisy's hand in hers and led the way down the hall to Mae Bell's room. The door was open, and Mae Bell was sitting on the edge of her bed, eagerly awaiting their arrival. Her hair was loose today, hanging around her shoulders in long white curls, and her eyelashes were extra thick.

"So," Mae Bell said, "do you have good news for me today?"

Wincing, Kelly forced a smile. "Well, we have a little bit of good news and then some not-so-good news."

"Please share." Mae Bell gestured toward two chairs positioned by the window. "And feel free to have a seat."

Kelly led Daisy over to the chairs and helped her sit down on one, then sat beside her in the other. Todd immediately went to the record player and began thumbing through Mae Bell's records again.

"I heard the two of you have begun attending school," Mae Bell said. "How do you like your classes, Todd?"

Todd rolled his eyes. "They're horrible."

Kelly waved a hand in the air. "That's all I've been able to get out of him so far."

"Well, it takes time for young ones to adjust to new environments," Mae Bell said. "Perhaps he just needs a chance to get to know everyone, then he'll settle in a little better."

"Whatever," Todd said, continuing to thumb through the records.

Kelly released a strained laugh. "As for the good news, I brought a revised list of priorities."

"Oh?" Mae Bell asked. "What was wrong with the first list?"

"Nothing. Nothing at all." Kelly withdrew a piece of paper from the bag she'd carried in and unfolded it. "It's just that Seth took a tour of the property and we discussed a few changes to the priority list."

Mae Bell stilled, her expression brightening. "You and Seth?"

"Yes."

"Your neighbor?" Mae Bell raised an eyebrow. "You

mean, the neighbor that's been trying to buy my land and raze the drive-in? The one you took an extreme disliking to upon first acquaintance?"

Kelly hesitated, the mischievous gleam in Mae Bell's eyes a bit too bright for her liking. "We have an understanding now. He has a VCR and he's been kind enough to let me use it to view the films you gave me, and I've brought him a couple meals in return."

"Ah, I see." Mae Bell grinned. "So the two of you are getting along better?"

"Yes." A wave of warmth rolled through Kelly and she pressed her lips together to hide her smile. "We're friends."

Mae Bell ran a hand over her hair, her eyes closing as she grinned wistfully. "That's how it all begins, my dear."

"Friends, Mae Bell," Kelly repeated quietly, sneaking a glance at the kids. Thankfully, Todd, earbuds stuffed back in his ears, was oblivious, and Daisy was busy staring out of the window at a cat who slinked along the hedges at a house across the street, hunting a bird. "Seth and I are friends. And, as I've said, he was kind enough to help me out with some changes that I would like to share with you."

Her grin vanished. "What kind of changes?"

"Well. . . ." Hands shaking, Kelly smoothed the paper across her thigh and sat up straighter. "I've watched several of the movies you left for me. I enjoyed all of them and"—she motioned to the kids—"even Todd and Daisy enjoyed them. So I've almost made it through the first item on your original priority list, and the changes I've made to the other priorities aren't big—they're just enhancements that I think will—"

"You don't have to explain yourself, my dear," Mae Bell said. "Please continue with the new priorities."

Kelly proceeded to share the new ideas, pausing every so often to gauge Mae Bell's expression. To her credit, she seemed to take it all in stride . . . until they reached the part about buying a new digital projector.

"I fear that won't fit within our budget," she said quietly. "I looked into purchasing one of those prior to moving here and I couldn't afford it. As things haven't improved since I've moved in, I can tell you with certainty that I can't afford it now, either."

"I was afraid of that," Kelly whispered. "How much does a digital projector usually run?"

"The cheapest usually cost around forty thousand dollars, and the fanciest come in at upward of two hundred thousand dollars." Mae Bell rubbed her forehead. "Although you might be able to get a discount on one of the cheaper models if you contact the gentleman I purchased the first one from."

Kelly blinked hard. "What kind of discount are we talking about? Say, thirty or maybe forty thousand bucks off?"

Mae Bell stood, crossed the room and retrieved a small business card from her dresser. She walked over to Kelly and handed it to her. "Give him a call and see what he says. And don't forget to mention I referred you."

"Mae Bell?" Kelly hesitated, turning the business card over in her hand. She hated to bring this up, but there was no way around the reality that very few people might show an interest in their new business endeavor. "The people I've spoken to in Blue Moon haven't been very enthusiastic about our reopening the drive-in."

Mae Bell sat on the edge of her bed and straightened the long scarf she wore around her neck. "They never are at first. Sometimes people need to see a finished product before they're able to see the beauty in it. That's what we're doing. We're reintroducing the beauty of cinema to Blue Moon."

"But . . ." Kelly forced herself to meet Mae Bell's eyes. "What if we can't pull it off? What will happen then?"

Mae Bell waved a hand in the air, but the fear that flashed briefly in her eyes was enough to break Kelly's heart. "There's no chance of that," she said, smiling. "Because I have you."

CHAPTER 8

Seth stood in the middle of Mae Bell's overgrown drive-in lot and wondered why he'd agreed to let Kelly get behind the wheel of his tractor.

"Wasps?" A look of horror filled her eyes as she looked down at him from her seat on the tractor. "What do you mean I'll need it for wasps?"

He lifted the spray bottle in his hand closer to her, shaking the bottle slightly. "It's a mixture of orange oil and soap. You'll need this if you run over a wasp's nest. If they start swarming you, just spritz 'em with this and it'll send 'em flying in the other direction."

She frowned. "You never mentioned anything about wasps."

"They like to build their nests in bushes and"—he gestured to the open field surrounding them—"there's nothing but bushes, weeds and grass out here, so there's bound to be a few in the area you're about to mow." He grinned. "But seeing as how you're afraid of a few little ol' wasps, you wanna hop down from there and let me take over?"

Frowning, she shook her head. "No way. I'm not bumming your TV, VCR, internet, tractor, bush hog *and* making you mow this lot, too. I'm perfectly capable of driving a tractor and clearing this field."

Man, he hoped so. Seth adjusted his cap on his head and glanced up at the sky. It was clear blue with several big puffy clouds drifting around to serve as cooling shade every now and then. And it was a good thing, too, seeing as how spring was beginning to settle in early this year, and the sun, though mild at nine-thirty in the morning, would grow hotter as the day progressed. Not to mention, although there was no better feeling than a hard day's work, the hot, sticky cling of clothes to sweaty skin after spending hours working under the afternoon sun was definitely an acquired taste.

But Seth was actually looking forward to the long hours he and Kelly planned to spend working on Mae Bell's property today.

"All I ask," Kelly said, "is that you show me what to do and how to do it once. I won't have to bother you again until I finish."

He leaned on the tractor and smiled up at her. "You're not a bother. I'm the one who offered, remember?"

And he'd been happy to do it, too. Yesterday afternoon, Kelly had shown up at his house with Todd, Daisy and a mouthwatering spread of home-cooked chili and peach cobbler, ready for their—er, *her*—routine afternoon of watching one of Mae Bell's films. He realized he'd begun to make a habit of filling his plate with whatever culinary delights she brought, plopping down on the sectional and viewing the movies, too.

But what he looked forward to the most, it seemed, was the soft scratch of Kelly's pen across paper as she took notes during the movie, Todd's sarcastic but humorous quips and Daisy's soft giggles during comedic moments in the film. All of that combined with a full stomach never failed to ease the day of hard work from Seth's muscles, send him to a state of pleasant relaxation and tug him into the deep sleep he'd enjoyed every night since Kelly had begun the late-afternoon movie ritual at his house.

As a result, he'd had more energy each morning and bounded through his daily chores in less time than usual, which meant he was already ahead of deadline for several tasks. With extra time to spare and curious to see what the drive-in would look like with a bit of sprucing up, he'd offered, between bites of chili last night, to help Kelly start work on her new priority list.

Kelly had readily agreed, and after dropping Todd and Daisy at school, she'd returned to the drive-in, spotted the tractor he'd driven over and had hopped right on it, eager to mow.

"Thank you for lending me your tractor and bush hog," Kelly said. "It would've taken me weeks to cut through the weeds on this lot if I'd used a lawn mower."

Seth laughed. "A regular lawn mower wouldn't have lasted more than five minutes cutting through this mess." He handed her the spray bottle and patted the edge of her seat. "We're burning daylight, so let's get started. Do you remember all of the prep steps, and have we finished them all?"

Her gaze lifted as she ticked each step off on her fingers. "First I lubricated the knuckles and shaft and checked to make sure all areas that needed to be greased were. Then I checked for leaks and loose plugs, as well as the oil and fuel—we're good on both counts. I made sure the bush hog was straight and level on both sides and that the wheel was turned in the right direction. And"—she glanced at the front end of the tractor, then the back end—"I've got it lined up just right."

"Watch what's in front of you at all times and keep

your eye out for anything that might pose a problem. All it takes is a knotty root or cut stump for that load bucket to snag, cause some major damage and put your safety at risk."

She waved his concern away. "I know, I know."

"And what are two ways you can stop if you run into problems?"

"Either push in the brake and clutch or turn it off with the key." She smiled and bounced twice with excitement. "So, what's next? Can I start?"

"Yes, but it's gonna be very lou—"

"Woo!" Kelly turned the key and jumped as the engine cranked, shattering the peaceful stillness of the lot. "Is it supposed to be this loud?" she yelled.

"Yes," he shouted back. "That's what I was trying to tell you. That's normal. Start when you're ready, but go at the slowest speed and I'll walk beside you until you get the hang of it."

She cupped her hand around her ear. "What?"

"Go slow! Very slow," he shouted louder. "I'll"—he made a walking motion with his fingers—"walk beside you."

"Oh, okay!" Grinning, she gripped the steering wheel, then eased forward, jostling in her seat as she ran over a small bump.

Things went well for the first few minutes. Kelly slowly drove the tractor in a straight line across the field, knocking down tall weeds and crushing thick bushes with the bush hog, leaving close-cut green grass in its wake.

"Nice job," Seth called out over the growl of the engine.

"What?" she yelled back.

He lifted both his thumbs in the air. "Nice job!"

She smiled down at him. "This is fun!"

"When you make this turn," he shouted, "keep the right tire inside the edge of what you just cleared. That'll leave nice clean lines." Something pinched his arm and he scratched it; then he continued walking beside the tractor. "And when you get to—"

Something dug into the back of his neck, then buzzed in his ear. He yanked his hat off and swatted at it just as another round of buzzing descended upon him.

"Seems we hit a wasps' nest already," he shouted, reaching up and tapping Kelly's thigh for the spray bottle. "Hand me the spray bottle."

"What?" Still smiling a mile wide, she spared him a cursory glance before pinning her attention back to the path in front of the tractor.

Another sting, another bite of pain. Flinching, Seth swatted his hat furiously in the air, batting away as many of the insects whirling about his face and chest as he could.

"Kelly, give me the spray bottle!" The wasps swarmed around him now, attacking his ears and neck. "Kelly! The spr—"

Seth took off running, swatting in every direction, yelping as another stinger dug into his neck. Weeds, grass and briars slowed his progress. He yanked his legs free of the tangled overgrowth and swatted as he went.

"Stop!" Kelly shouted at his back.

Focused on the increased buzzing, he ran faster.

"You have to stop for me to help you," she yelled again. "Stop, drop and roll!"

He'd wonder later why he did it, but in the heat of the moment, obeying her command seemed like the right thing to do, so he stopped in midstride, flung himself down into a somewhat-less-dense patch of weeds and rolled twice before he landed on his back.

He blinked as the air left his lungs and Kelly appeared above him, clutching the spray bottle in her hands and spraying it directly in his face. The onslaught of orange oil and soap continued for several seconds before he managed to pull his cap over his face, wave his hands in the air and catch her attention.

"That's enough," he shouted. The buzzing had stopped. "They're gone."

A fresh spray of orange oil hit his chest and neck. "There might be more."

"No, they're gone!" he gasped for breath through the hot cover of his cap. As the wet spray ceased hitting his neck, he removed it from his face and held his hands up in surrender. "They're gone, okay?"

Eyes wide, she dropped to her knees beside him and leaned close, inspecting his face and neck. "Are you okay? Are you allergic? Do you need to go to the hospital?"

"No." Her hands were soft and gentle and her cheek almost brushed his as she lifted his head and studied the back of his neck.

"Are you sure? I see one, two . . ."

Each brush of her warm fingertips and whisper of her breath caused his skin to tingle, making the throb of the stings disappear. A slow smile curved his lips. "I'm okay."

Her hands stilled on his neck and she sat back on her heels, her eyes narrowing on his grin. "I'll say."

She released his head, allowing it to fall backward to the ground.

He winced and rubbed the back of his head. "Hey, I'm injured here."

"You've got all of two stings, and you ran around like a toddler chasing bubbles." Despite her stern tone, her lips twitched and humor lit her eyes. "Mr. Beekeeper, huh? And you were worried about my lack of courage." She tossed the spray bottle on his chest, brushed her hands on her shorts to knock the dirt off her palms, then stood. "I'll have you know, I stopped the tractor just right, too. All on my own, I might add, so I think I qualify for solo duty." She smiled. "Think you'll still be able to weed-whack around the buildings while I mow? I mean"—she cocked her head to the side, her smile growing—"considering your wounds and all."

Seth folded his arms behind his head and sighed. "I suppose I might be able to work around my injuries."

Making a face, she kicked his foot good-naturedly, then marched back to the tractor, hopped on and cranked the engine. He sat up and watched her take the next turn seamlessly. She flashed him a proud smile as she passed.

Seth laughed, her optimistic nature and giddy delight at her new skill lightening his spirits . . . as she so often did lately, which made him remember exactly why he'd offered his tractor in the first place.

Four hours later, Seth met Kelly outside Mae Bell's trailer and accepted the cold soda she pressed into his hand with a sigh of gratitude.

"Thanks." He popped the top open, tilted his head back and glugged several generous swallows. The cool liquid coursed down to his gut, spreading a chill across his overheated suntanned skin. "Oh, man, I needed that."

After his unfortunate encounter with the wasps, Seth had grabbed his weed eater from his truck and attacked the knee-high weeds that had sprouted up around the two projection stands and concessions building, while Kelly continued mowing the field. By the time he'd finished that task, she had made it halfway across the field, so he tackled the next item on Kelly's new priority list and started hauling out old equipment, obsolete posters and trash, then loading it all in the bed of his pickup truck to haul away to the dump later that afternoon.

"It does hit the spot," Kelly said, taking a big gulp of her own soda. She turned to the freshly mowed field before them, inhaling the smell of grass on the warm spring air and stretching her arms out as though to frame it like a picture. "But so does this view! I can't believe what a difference knocking those weeds down made. The lot looks almost twice as big, and all that smooth green grass . . ." She set her soda on one of the chairs outside of the trailer and jogged toward the center of the field, calling back over her shoulder, "Makes me want to roll in it."

And roll, she did, skipping to the center of the field, dropping gracefully to the ground and rolling onto her back.

Smiling, Seth finished off his soda and walked across the field to her side. The sheer bliss on her face as she closed her eyes made him laugh. "Does it feel like a luxury memory foam mattress?"

"Nope." She cracked one eye open and looked up at him. "But it's sure nice to rest my bones under a beautiful spring sky. Come on," she drawled, "take a load off and appreciate our hard work."

He glanced at the trees bordering his property. "I should probably get the tractor back to my house and wash up the tools—"

"Oh, come on. Take a skip day."

He raised an eyebrow. "A 'skip day'?"

"Figure of speech." She opened her other eye. "Everyone deserves to take a break from the grind and skip work every now and then. Otherwise, what's the point of making a living, if you don't actually live? What are you, thirty-six, thirty-seven?"

"Thirty-eight."

She grinned. "Then it's way past time for your skip day."

Sighing, he eased himself down beside her on the grass and folded his arms behind his head.

She sniffed. "You smell like orange-scented dish soap."

"That's because someone hosed me down—unnecessarily, I might add—with wasp spray."

"I saved your life," she teased. "Now, relax and enjoy the beauty of nature when it's not stinging you."

Chuckling, he focused on the sky. "Yes, ma'am."

The sun shined brighter than it had this morning and the clouds had increased, creating big puffs of white that drifted together, then broke apart on the gentle breeze. They lay silent for a few minutes, appreciating the whisper of cool air against their sweat-slickened skin.

Seth shifted his back, settling more comfortably against the soft grass, and released a sigh of pleasure. "Got to admit, this is nice."

"Mmm-hmm."

He rolled his head to the side. Kelly had closed her eyes again and her cheeks had turned a pretty shade of pink beneath the warmth of the sun. Freckles were scattered across the bridge of her cute nose, more than likely a result of the hours spent working under the sun. And the most surprising thing was that she had seemed to enjoy every second of the hard work. Unlike some people who undertook outdoor chores and disliked it, she seemed to thrive on manual labor.

"Where'd you work before you came here?" he asked quietly, hesitant to disrupt the peaceful silence, but too curious not to ask.

Her lips twisted. "How much time do you have?"

He smiled. "A lot, apparently, since I'm taking a *skip day* and all."

She grew quiet, then took a deep breath and said, "A bakery, two grocery stores, a laundromat, the front desk at a motel. The place I hated the most was an all-night diner."

"Why'd you hate it?"

"Every afternoon, we had two regulars that came in. A man and woman who were homeless. They always had enough change for one cup of coffee and nothing more, but I think having a roof over their heads, a warm booth and a bit of company were what kept drawing them in. We always had extra food at the end of each shift, and I always slipped them some, but my boss found out and wouldn't allow me to give it to them. He'd rather throw it out than give away something for free. He said it was against company policy and that they were pests. I couldn't work for someone like that anymore. Or a company that was run with so little heart. So I quit and started looking for something else."

Seth frowned. "How many jobs did you hold down at a time?"

"No more than two at one time, and I had to cut back my hours when Laice . . ." Her voice caught and she bit her lip. "When Laice, Todd and Daisy's mom, passed away from breast cancer, and I took custody of them, I had to scale back my hours in order to take care of them properly. It's ironic, you know? When you're raising kids on your own, you have to work extra to provide for them. But then, you need to be there to take care of them, too, so you end up missing the most important things. I was constantly choosing what to sacrifice, like missing Daisy's performance in the Christmas play in order to work extra hours so I could pay that month's electric bill. Or the time I had to tell Todd he couldn't go on a field trip with the school to tour NASA, because I couldn't afford to pay the rent and buy him an airline ticket."

He searched her face, but she kept her eyes closed and her voice was emotionless. "What happened to

Todd and Daisy's father?" Her arm, lying in the grass, stiffened against his and he added, "If you don't mind my asking? I don't mean to pry."

"It's okay." She blew out a heavy breath. "He's around somewhere, doing something to serve his own purposes, I'm sure. Zane never was the dependable type." Her brow creased. "Though I can't say he didn't at least try. He'd never taken care of Todd and Daisy on his own before and he did try to take care of them for a couple months—well, he put more effort into it than he had anything else in his life. But in the end, he decided it was too much for him and dropped them off at my apartment and left. I haven't heard from him since."

Seth bit back a curse. "You mean he doesn't even call to check on them? To talk to them? Or let them know where he is if they need him?"

A humorless laugh burst from her lips. "Good luck with that. I've tried contacting his cousin, the only relative I know of, but even he has no idea where Zane is. There's a lawyer I touch base with every month, though. He's the one that drafted the will for Laice, naming me secondary guardian. I let him know where we are and how the kids are doing, just in case Zane has an attack of conscience one day and decides to look them up." Her eyes squeezed shut tighter. "That's the main reason Todd had such a strong reaction to you when he first met you. He has a hard time trusting anyone now—especially men. It was hard enough losing his mom, but having his dad choose to leave hurt Todd even deeper."

Seth released a sound of disgust as he thought of all of the grief Daisy and Todd must've endured after losing their mother, and all of the additional times they must've cried, worried and wondered where their father was . . . or if he was ever coming back.

"I know things like that happen," he said, "but I can't understand how a man could be so selfish."

"I can," she said softly. She faced him, rolling her head to the side and meeting his eyes. Her brown eyes were open now and filled with admiration. "But you'd never do something like that."

A sharp pain knifed through his chest as his last memory of Rachel, lying in his arms, her eyes closed and clothing bloodied, surfaced in his mind.

"What about you?" Kelly's words tugged him back to awareness. "Have you worked anywhere other than your orchard?"

He nodded, swallowing past the tight knot in his throat. "I had an odd job or two when I worked my way through college years ago, but having my own orchard was always my goal."

A look of admiration filled her eyes. "You went to college?"

"Yeah. Auburn University, for ag and plant pathology."

"Wow." Her expression fell, but the admiring look remained. "I always wanted to go to college, but could never afford it." She turned away and stared at the sky again, a muscle in her jaw clenching. "I'm going to make sure Todd has the opportunity, though. Even if I have to work twenty hours out of the day, he's going to be able to go. That's one of the reasons I took this job. I want Todd and Daisy to have a better life than I did. Whatever their dreams are, I want to help them come true."

Seth resisted the urge to skim the back of his hand along her smooth cheek and, instead, asked softly, "What were your dreams?"

Surprisingly, a wide smile broke out across her face as she faced him again. "You wouldn't believe me if I told you."

He smiled back. "Try me."

"I was going to live in a two-story country house with a red roof."

He laughed. "Like mine?"

"Yep." The tip of her tongue stuck out of the corner of her smile. "Although, I hadn't imagined as nice a kitchen as yours. And I was going to become rich off my cotton candy business, which I would operate out of my backyard, naturally."

Seth dipped his head. "Naturally."

"And," she went on with a giggle, "I was going to fly fighter jets in air shows on the weekends. See, easy peasy. I have *no* idea why I didn't follow through."

He laughed with her. "Given the nature of your aspirations, it's understandable that you chose a more predictable route."

"Until now." Her laughter trailed off. "I'm going to make this one work. Not just for Mae Bell, but for Todd and Daisy, too."

Seth studied her mouth, already missing her laugh and wishing her smile would return. He could help mow the grass, clean out projection booths and restore the drive-in, but he couldn't fix everything in Kelly's life. Though . . . he could try.

"And you? You did this for you, too, right?" He met her eyes again. "Because you deserve to be happy, Kelly. You truly do."

Her mouth parted as she searched his eyes and the pink in her cheeks deepened.

"There's something else you deserve, too," he said.

"What?" she whispered.

"A moon garden." He pointed to a stretch of green grass at the back edge of the lot. "Right over there. Some white daffodils and tulips. A few silver rhododendron and a few azaleas. Angel's trumpet and moon flower, and you'll have a new attraction to add to Blue

Moon Haven Drive-In." He did reach out then, brushing a damp strand of her brown hair off her pink cheek and tucking it behind her ear. "It'll bring an extra touch of magic under the stars."

Her eyes drifted closed at his touch, then fluttered back open as she smiled. "That'd be amazing."

"Good. We'll get started." He forced himself to withdraw his touch and stood, then grabbed her hands and tugged her to her feet. "How much time is left before you have to pick up Todd and Daisy?"

She held on to his hands as she gained her balance, looking a bit dazed. "Um . . . about a half hour or so."

"Perfect," he said, tugging her across the field toward his pickup. "Let's hop in my truck, take the trash to the dump and pick up the kids. Then we'll swing by the hardware shop in town—they have a greenhouse out back with a great selection—pick up a few plants to stick in the ground and take the kids out for a bite to eat at Tully's."

"Wait a minute." She dug her heels in until he paused and glanced over his shoulder. "There's one catch."

"And that is?"

"I used your tractor and took your time today, so dinner's on me."

He smiled. "Deal."

Kelly unbuckled Daisy from her booster seat and helped her down from the back of Seth's truck cab. "Ready for some honey taffy, sweet pea?"

Daisy smiled up at her, took her hand and tugged until Kelly was at ear level. "Can I have a triple burger, too?" she whispered.

Kelly hugged her close. "After all the hard work you did helping Seth and me pick out flowers, you betcha!"

After the hard work of mowing Mae Bell's field and clearing out old equipment and trash, Kelly and Seth did indeed hop in his truck and drive to the dump. Next they'd parked in the pickup line at Blue Moon Central and waited patiently for Todd and Daisy to stroll out of school. He'd made various suggestions as to which flowers to purchase for the garden and had stressed that white and silver-colored plants should be the dominant colors, maybe some pale pinks . . . and something else about how far apart to plant them and irrigation.

It had been hard to concentrate on his words. All Kelly could focus on was his mouth. His perfectly curved and welcoming lips. The first time he'd flashed his grin, she'd been taken aback by how it changed his expression, how it brightened his green eyes and added charisma to his already-substantial appeal. And his touch . . .

It had been such a small gesture, really: the fleeting, gentle brush of his knuckles against her cheek while they had lain on the soft grass under the spring sun. But something about that tender touch had tugged at her heart and warmed her chest.

"You did this for you, too, right?" he had whispered softly beside her as they'd rested on the freshly mowed field. "Because you deserve to be happy, Kelly."

As they had sat in his truck in the school's parking lot waiting for the kids to arrive, her hand had drifted up to her cheek more than once; while Seth talked about flowers, her fingertips lingered over the spot where he'd touched her, recalling the deep rumble of his quiet voice, his gentle words.

For the first time in a long time, she began to wonder what it'd be like to have someone by her side to face the challenges of life. Someone to care for and who would care for her in return. Someone to laugh with,

dream with and build a new life with. And not just anyone . . . but someone like Seth. A good, honest man so
unlike the grouch she'd thought he was when they'd
first met.

"Good. I'm starving!"

Kelly shook herself slightly and glanced up to find
Todd rounding the front of the truck.

"Can I get what I got last time?" Todd asked, rubbing
his stomach and eyeing the interior of Tully's Treats
through the window.

"I suppose," Kelly said. "So long as you promise to
eat all of the vegetables I put in front of you for dinner
tomorrow night."

He groaned, but nodded. "Whatever."

Seth locked his truck and joined them on the sidewalk in front of Tully's. "He's earned a hefty dinner
after all the work he put in hauling plants from the
greenhouse to the truck. I wouldn't have managed to
load all of them so fast without the extra muscle on
hand."

Todd turned away, remaining silent, but his mouth
moved in a small grin.

No sarcastic comment. No dry response. And he
hadn't complained a single time during the two hours
Kelly had roved around the greenhouse, debating over
which plants to invest in. He'd simply followed quietly,
his gaze moving from her to Seth and back as they discussed which plants would work best. He'd grabbed the
pots he was asked to transport and toted them to Seth's
truck without comment. Though his silent compliance
with their requests wasn't ideal, it was definitely an im-
provement over his recent moods.

Kelly smiled and ruffled Todd's hair. "Then let's get
this hardworking man inside and feed him."

They were able to get the same seats as the first time

Kelly and the kids had visited: an oversized booth with room for all of them. Kelly had just settled on one side with Daisy, while Seth and Todd sat on the other, when Tully walked up with menus in her hand.

Her step faltered as she reached the booth, her welcoming smile slipping and her eyes widening as she noticed Seth seated beside Todd. "Well," she said, blinking hard and recovering her full smile. "This is a surprise."

Seth smiled and held out his hand for the menus. "A man's gotta eat." He took the menus she gave him, giving one back to her, then passing the rest out to Kelly, Todd and Daisy. "I know what I want, but we may need a few minutes before we're ready."

"We . . . ?" Tully must've realized she was staring at all of them, because she closed her mouth and turned her attention to Kelly. "What have y'all been, uh, doing today?" She leaned close to Kelly and lowered her voice. "Has my brother been a better neighbor lately?"

"I can still hear you, Tully." Seth raised one eyebrow.

Tully narrowed her eyes. "Well, it's not exactly a secret that you weren't on your best behavior when y'all first met, dear brother."

"It's fine," Kelly hastened to say, waving a hand in the air. "We, um, we've actually been getting along great. Seth was kind enough to invite us over during the storm last week, and he then agreed to let me use his TV and VCR for a project I'm doing. He even brought his tractor around to the drive-in this morning, taught me how to use the brush hog and cleared out the projection booths and concessions stands, too."

Tully glanced from one of them to the other, studying their expressions. "Oh."

"And," Kelly added, smiling at Seth, "he even hauled off the trash and helped me pick out plants for a moon garden to add to the drive-in. I hadn't thought of it be-

fore, but I think it'd be a great way to showcase Mae
Bell's land, you know? It'll give guests an added attraction, and I thought that maybe down the road, if all
goes well, we could offer the drive-in lot as a location
for birthday parties, anniversaries, you name it. That
way, we'd have more than one revenue stream."

"Let's not jump too far ahead yet," Seth said, reaching into his back pocket and withdrawing a piece of
paper. "Those are great plans, but before we can start
adding more attractions, we need to get the main one
in place, and that means buying a new digital projector
for the second projection booth."

"I know." Kelly's shoulders slumped. "I'm worried
about that. Mae Bell said they're awful expensive."

"I made a few calls," Seth said, sliding the paper
across the table, "and Mae Bell was right. The guy she
referred you to was willing to give a pretty steep discount, but it's still a bit pricey."

Kelly picked up the paper, her eyes widening at the
number. "Oh, gosh. There's not enough money in the
budget to even come close to covering this. I mean, I
still have to buy paint, new frames for the posters we're
gonna hang, and snacks for the concessions building.
Plus, the guys that are repairing the holes in the projection screens for me next week are going to charge me
an arm and a leg." She looked up, the disappointed
look in Todd's eyes making her bite her lip. Well, at
least he'd refrained from commenting on her lack of
foresight this time. "I know I can pull this off," she said,
her voice shaking. "I just don't know how."

"I have an idea," Seth said, gesturing toward the
paper in Kelly's hand. "Turn it over."

She did, finding a new list of items. "Candy, baked
goods, crafts, quilts, model airplane contest . . ." She
frowned. "What is this?"

Seth smiled. "A fundraiser extravaganza hosted at Blue Moon Haven Drive-In. With enough sales, you'll be able to at least offset the cost of the new projector and, hopefully, drum up some interest in Blue Moon Haven Drive-In's grand reopening." He glanced at Tully and winked. "That's where you come in, dear sister," he drawled. "Would you be willing to donate some of your famous candy to the cause?"

Tully nodded eagerly and smiled. "Of course. How much of what and when?"

"I'll get back to you on the 'how much of what.'" He looked at Todd and Daisy. "I'm hoping these two will be willing to lend me their sugar expertise and help me make a list of the treats they think will sell best."

Daisy grinned and patted her menu.

Seth turned to Todd. "What do you say, buddy? You mind helping me out with this? And maybe the model airplane contest, too? I could use someone with your smarts to help organize it."

Todd thought this over for a moment, twiddling with a straw on the table. "Can I make a model airplane of my own and enter it in the contest, too?"

Seth grinned. "Of course."

"All right." Todd picked up his menu and started scanning it, his lips twitching on a proud smile. "I can do that."

Kelly stilled, taking a moment to appreciate the small spark of excitement she saw lighting Todd's eyes. "And for the 'when'?" she asked Seth, excitement stirring within her as well.

"Spring break's coming up soon for the kids, right?" he asked.

"The end of next week," Kelly affirmed.

Seth rubbed his chin, then said, "So you and I will work on rounding up sponsors for the fundraiser, finishing repairs over the next week, making sure the projection screens are spruced up and practicing with the projectors we have. Then, when the kids get out of school, they can help us paint and plant the Moon Garden and we'll hold the fundraiser at the end of spring break." He smiled. "How's that sound?"

Too good to be true.

"Perfect," Kelly said, brushing aside her hesitation and focusing on the promise of success in Seth's eyes. "Just perfect."

"It's settled, then." He turned to the kids. "Tully's got a pinball machine in the corner back there. After y'all order, you wanna play a round or two with me while we wait for the food?"

Todd's eyes lit up at the prospect; but not one to betray his feelings, he managed to hide his excitement and shrug as though it didn't matter either way. "Sure. If you want to, I guess."

"Great." Seth grinned. "Cuz I got enough quarters in my pocket to make champions out of us both."

Seth cajoled a grin out of Todd with that, and after placing their orders with Tully, the two left the booth and walked over to the pinball machine. Not to be left out of the fun, Daisy rose to her knees and whispered in Kelly's ear, asking if she could go, too.

"Of course." Kelly slid out of the booth so Daisy could hop down, then watched her sprint over to the pinball machine and join Seth and Todd.

Seth noticed her first and squatted down to her level to say something. Daisy hesitated, glancing back at Kelly, then nodded and put out her arms. Seth lifted her up, propping her on the edge of the pinball machine and supporting her with his arms so she could watch as Todd played.

Kelly's breath caught at the gesture . . . and Daisy's

hesitant trust of Seth. Yet another wonderful trait to add to his list of impressive qualities. "He's good with them," she whispered.

Tully, standing beside her, made a sound of agreement, then said with a heavy note of sorrow in her tone, "Yeah. He was the best dad in the world."

CHAPTER 9

Standing on the Blue Moon Haven Drive-In lot, Kelly dipped a roller in a tray of white paint. "I thought about going for a funky color, like hot pink or jewel purple, but decided it might be better to go with something less 'in your face.'"

She lifted the roller and painted a stripe along the side of the concessions building, then glanced over her shoulder at Seth.

"Whatcha think?" she asked.

He paused in the midst of cleaning the other half of the wall and eyed the paint stripe. "I think white was a sensible choice." He grinned. "We wouldn't want anyone to mistake this place for a nightclub."

Laughing, Kelly pretended to be offended. "What do you mean? You don't think hot pink would add a bit of pizazz?"

"Let's hold off on the pizazz until the first month of ticket sales comes in," he said.

Todd, who stood beside Seth, helping Daisy wipe a cleaning cloth over the wall, stopped what he was doing and made a face. "Don't you think white's kinda boring, though? We're trying to draw attention to the place, so bright colors might be a better choice."

Kelly froze. Todd kind of, sort of, taking her side for once? Actually agreeing with her initial idea of bright paint? It was a moment for the record books, and if she had her calendar, she might actually write it down.

Fact was, she'd been surprised more often than not over the past few days. Seth, true to his word, had pitched in overtime, working his orchard first thing in the morning, then crossing the property line to help Kelly tackle the remaining jobs on their priority list.

First they'd finished cleaning out the projection booths and picking up the last bits of trash around the buildings and grounds and hauling everything off to the dump. Next Seth had helped Kelly review the notes Mae Bell had attached to the projectors and they'd located the canisters of old film she'd managed to hang on to over the years. They'd dusted off each case, checked that the film was intact, then repackaged it and placed it in the canisters' storage shelving they'd discovered in a back corner of the projection booth, hidden by boxes. Seth had replaced several screws and banged out a few dents in the metal shelving so that the doors opened and closed smoothly again.

Throughout the week of repairs, Todd had been curious every day she'd picked him up from school prior to spring break. He'd clamored to see what new treasures Kelly and Seth had uncovered and was especially excited by the discovery of an old record player Kelly had unearthed in one of the back storage rooms of the concessions building. He'd even asked to borrow a few of Mae Bell's records during their most recent visit. She'd readily agreed, sending him off with an armload of vintage vinyl.

Todd had played each record at least a dozen times,

usually at full blast right before bed, but Kelly hadn't minded. There was something nostalgic and relaxing about the peppy jazz, soulful blues and soft ballads filling the trailer. And one night, she and Daisy had danced around the small living room, laughing, and had even managed to wring a laugh out of Todd.

It had felt like getting a glimpse into the past. A look at how the trailer, drive-in lot and life itself might've been at Mae Bell's drive-in. A place full of hope, dreams and entertainment. Each day, Kelly felt herself growing more and more attached to Blue Moon Haven Drive-In, and Todd had begun to feel a connection as well . . . This made the possibility of their project failing even more terrifying.

". . . could paint it a mixture of colors," Todd was saying.

Kelly jerked back into action and glanced at Todd as she resumed rolling paint along the concessions wall. "What'd you say?"

"I said, we could paint the ticket booth at the entrance different colors," Todd repeated. "That'd make it easier to see from the road—especially when it's lit up—and maybe it'll attract more guests on movie nights."

Kelly met his eyes and smiled, warmth coursing through her at his excited expression and friendly tone. Today had been the last day of school for Todd and Daisy and spring break had officially begun so they were both ready to start the festivities. "I think that's a great idea. How about we pick up some extra paint tomorrow and take care of that before the fundraiser?"

Todd smiled back. A genuine, honest-to-goodness smile. "Yeah. We can do that."

As he resumed wiping down the wall, Kelly looked at Seth over Todd's head. Seth raised his brows, a look of surprised pleasure crossing his face, though he shouldn't be all that surprised. Kelly had a hunch most of the change in Todd had been brought on by Seth.

After their visit to Tully's restaurant a week ago, Seth had driven them back to the drive-in and asked Todd to help unload the plants for the Moon Garden. Todd had done so, all of the time discussing the model airplane contest Seth had suggested as a fundraiser. The idea had apparently caught Todd's interest enough to lead him into starting a conversation with Seth. Over the past few days, they'd discussed the contest several more times and Todd had begun to devise his own plan for a model airplane.

"That'll work out well," Seth said, "since I planned on us all taking a trip to Glenville tomorrow. It's a bigger town, about twenty-five miles away, and there's a small, private airport there. One of the pilots who gives flying lessons is a buddy of mine from college, and when I called him up, he said he'd be happy to give us a tour."

The paint roller slipped out of Kelly's hands. "Seriously?"

Seth laughed at the look of ecstasy on her face. "Seriously. He said he'd give Todd an inside look so he'd have a better idea of how to improve the design for his model airplane." He dragged his forearm over his sweaty brow. "Oh, and I thought we could distribute some more flyers in Glenville to promote the fundraiser."

Kelly sighed. "Have I told you how wonderful you are?"

He chuckled and looked away, his lean cheeks flushing. "Once or twice."

"No, I mean it. You've thought of everything, every step of the way."

He shrugged. "It's no big deal."

To him, maybe, Kelly thought. But to her . . . his actions were pure gold.

Daisy, who'd been eyeing Kelly's paint roller with envy for the past five minutes, dropped her wiping cloth on the ground, walked over to the pile of paintbrushes on the ground and grabbed a small one of her own.

Kelly put down her paint roller and tried to reach her before she dunked the paintbrush in the bucket of paint. "Oh, Daisy, wai—"

Too late. She'd already gotten a big glob on the brush and spun around toward the wall.

"Hold on just a second, Daisy." Immediately Seth was by her side. He held his hands out. "Do you mind if I show you?"

Daisy stared at his hands for a few moments, searched his face, then nodded.

Seth guided her gently back to the paint bucket and showed her how to wipe the excess paint off the brush. Then he steered her back to the wall and helped guide her movements up and down to paint in a straight line.

Kelly smiled. Daisy was a bit too short to paint very high, but what she did paint was in a fairly straight line. "Nice job, Daisy."

"Very nice job," Seth echoed, smiling at Daisy's progress.

Daisy stopped painting, grabbed Seth's hand and tugged him down to eye level. She cupped her hand around his face and smiled up at him. "Thank you," she whispered.

Kelly stilled, her attention shooting to Todd, who met her eyes with an equally surprised expression. For the first time in months, Daisy had spoken to a stranger of her own volition, and the fact that she had chosen to speak to Seth didn't surprise Kelly. His gentle demeanor and patient disposition made him a natural father figure.

Kelly's breath caught, her belly flipping over at the thought. What was it Tully had said that night at her restaurant? Seth had been "the best dad in the world." Lying on the sofa in the trailer every night since then, staring up at the ceiling, Kelly had wondered what had happened to Seth's child. Had he had a son or a daughter? Maybe more than one child? And if he'd had children . . . what about a wife? He didn't wear a ring, had never mentioned a wife, and from what Kelly had been told by Mae Bell, he'd been living on his own for at least seven years.

So, what had happened to change it all?

"You're welcome," Seth whispered back to Daisy. There was a soft sheen in his eyes, as though he . . .

"You okay, Seth?" Kelly asked gently.

He nodded, his throat moving on a hard swallow as he straightened and resumed wiping down the wall. "Yeah. Everything's fine. Better than fine, in fact." He continued avoiding her eyes, wiping harder at the wall. "Way things are going so far, we oughta be finished with this building by noon and finished painting the projection booths by three or four, which means—"

"We'll have plenty of time to watch TV," Todd finished for him. He glanced up at Seth. "We still get to come watch a movie at your place tonight, right?" He shot a look at Kelly. "Not one of those silent things, but one me and Daisy choose, right? You promised."

That prompted a smile from Seth. "Of course. I always keep my promises."

Which made the mystery of his child's absence even more odd. Kelly bit her lip and resumed painting, figuring it was time to take Mae Bell's advice again and go right to the source for the answer.

* * *

Seth backed away from the projection booth, propped his fists on his hips and admired Todd's handiwork. "Looks good, Todd. Real good."

"No dirt, uneven spots or anything, right?" Todd asked expectantly.

Seth looked down at Todd, who eyed him with nervous apprehension, and smiled. "Looks like a professional job, kid. If we paid professional painters, I doubt they'd be able to do any better."

That made Todd smile . . . and Kelly as well. She stood several feet away by the concessions building with Daisy, rinsing off with a hose the paintbrushes and rollers they'd used, watching Todd's face. An equally pleased look of joy entered her expression, too.

Seth gestured toward Kelly and Daisy, who still scrubbed paintbrushes by the concessions building. "Why don't we round these paint trays up and take them over to Kelly and help scrub them down? It'll make things go faster."

Thirty minutes later, the paintbrushes and rollers were thoroughly rinsed, the paint trays were scrubbed clean, the paint buckets resealed and all of it had been loaded into the bed of Seth's truck.

"Your place?" Kelly asked, shoving her hair back off her forehead as Seth closed the tailgate.

"My place," Seth affirmed. "And there's no need to worry about picking anything up to eat. I got a couple pizzas in the freezer that'll be perfect for this occasion."

Kelly grinned. "'This occasion'? You mean a day spent painting buildings on your new neighbor's drive-in lot, which also happens to be the property you want to buy?" she teased.

"Yes," he said. "This very one."

Laughing, he nudged her toward the passenger seat, then climbed into the driver's seat. Once Daisy was settled in her booster seat and Todd comfortably in the back of the cab, Seth drove to his house. Patch was waiting for them when they arrived. He was stretched out on the front porch, his head resting on his front paws, but sprang upright when he spotted Seth's truck and bounded down the porch steps to greet them.

"Hold up there, boy," Seth said, hopping out of the truck. "Did you miss me?"

Squatting, he rubbed Patch's ears and patted his back, smiling as Patch yipped with excitement. During their day of painting, Patch had moseyed over to Mae Bell's property several times, butting his head against everyone's legs until he received a pet, then bounding off into the orchard to chase a bird or squirrel. Apparently, he'd run himself out and returned to the porch to take a nap, but now, having caught sight of Kelly, Todd and Daisy exiting the truck, it was back to playtime.

"Oooof." Kelly stumbled back against the truck door as Patch lunged against her middle, stuck his paws on her chest and started licking her neck. "Oh, I missed you, too, Patch," she said, laughing, and turning her face in an attempt to avoid Patch's onslaught of attention. "Maybe not quite as much as you seemed to miss me, though."

"Patch, down." Seth patted his leg and Patch obeyed, releasing Kelly and lowering himself to the ground. "Y'all come on in and get comfortable. It won't take me long to get the pizza—"

A small hand gripped Seth's from behind, halting his words. He glanced down to find Daisy snuggled against his leg, her hand holding his.

Seth smiled softly, assailed by a rush of emotion— adoration, pain, grief and happiness—all mixed in one. He blinked back the sting of tears and smiled. "Does pizza sound good to you, Daisy?"

"Yes." No whisper in his ear. No hiding her response behind her hand. Just the sweet sound of her voice, clear as a bell.

Seth glanced at Kelly, and she looked away, tears glistening in her eyes.

"She likes you," Todd said. "If she talks to you, you're okay in her book." Shrugging, he spun around and headed for the front porch, waving them on as he went. "Come on, Seth. I'm starving and want to watch a movie. You promised."

A man of his word, Seth set two hot pepperoni pizzas with extra cheese on the kitchen island forty-five minutes later. In twenty minutes it was all gone, along with three 2-liter bottles of soda. Seemed a day of painting made a person hungry . . . especially, Seth learned, Todd.

The boy sat back on the sectional now, groaning and rubbing his belly.

"How many slices did you eat, kid?" Seth asked, smiling.

"Six." He burped. "It was good, too."

"Todd." Kelly shot him a stern look, but her lips twitched and humor lit her eyes. "Excuse yourself, please. Or better yet, don't do it in public at all."

Shrugging, Todd apologized, then grabbed the remote, turned on the TV and looked at Daisy. "What d'you want to watch, Daisy?"

She shrugged and continued petting Patch, who sat by her side, a look of sheer doggy bliss on his face. Moments later, Daisy yawned and Patch followed suit.

"Looks like someone needs to hit the sack early tonight," Kelly said softly.

Daisy's eyes widened. She shook her head vigorously and hugged Patch closer.

"Okay. You and Todd can stay and watch one movie, but once it's over, it's time to go back to the trailer and turn in."

"But it's the first night of spring break." Todd frowned. "Can't we stay for at least two?"

"I'm sorry, but not tonight," Kelly said, standing. She placed her palm in the center of her lower back and stretched, moaning low. "My back is killing me from all that painting, and we all need a good night's sleep. Including Seth."

Seth drained the last swig of soda from his cup, then stood up. "Why don't I grab us another soda and we can sit outside while they watch the movie? There's a great view of the stars from the front steps."

Kelly smiled. "Sounds good to me."

"I'll meet you out there."

Seth helped Todd and Daisy choose a movie on an internet site and stream it through the HDTV, grabbed two cans of soda from the refrigerator and joined Kelly on the porch.

She was seated on the bottom porch step, leaning back on her hands, her face tipped up and her gaze fixed on the stars in the night sky above.

He walked down the steps and sat beside her, passing one of the cans of soda to her.

"Thanks." She popped the top and took a sip, then pointed at the sky. "Is that the Little Dipper?"

Seth followed her line of sight and nodded. "Yeah. And the moon is"—he pointed to her left—"right over there. It's barely a sliver tonight, which is good for us. Means we should have a big beautiful full moon for the grand opening."

"You were right. It's a beautiful view." She grew quiet for a moment, then asked, "Did you choose this land because you knew it had an incredible view?"

Her words were innocent, even nonchalant. But for some reason, they made him hesitate. "Yeah. There were only a few lots on the market like this one when I began looking for a place to build years ago, and Mae Bell wasn't selling, as you know." He bumped his shoulder against hers, smiling when she laughed. "I had it narrowed down to this spot and one other, and I swung by both places one night on a full moon, saw the view from here and just knew this was it." He gestured toward a white stone sitting on the edge of the flower bed by the front steps. "See that rock? It was resting in the driveway a few feet away from me that night. I grabbed it and set it right where it is now, to mark where I wanted to build the front porch."

"Sounds like you should've been an architect."

He shook his head. "Nah. It interests me, but the orchard has my heart."

"Why do you love it so much?"

He mulled the question over for a few moments, taking another sip of soda and studying the shadowy figures of his trees under the stars. "It's always peaceful there. There's nothing but roots, soil, air and sun, and they all work together for one purpose. They're all distinct parts of a bigger whole. There's no fighting or fussing. No pushing or pulling." His jaw tightened. "No accidents. Things happen for a reason out there, and they happen quietly and peacefully." He looked up, raising his eyes above the watery blur along his lower lashes. "There's time. So much time. Anything bad that's on the horizon, like disease or infestation, anything that would harm the trees, you can see it coming and stop it."

He continued staring at the sky, the stars melding together.

She stirred beside him, her soft palm closing over the back of his hand, her fingers weaving between his. "Tully told me you were a great father."

Seth's breath caught and he swallowed hard against the lump rising in his throat.

"You don't have to tell me if you don't want to," Kelly said softly.

"Her name was Rachel." For some strange reason, it felt good saying her name out loud. It brought some of the pain inside his chest out into the open, where it had more room to breathe. "She used to watch me work in the orchard every morning on the weekends. Her favorite tree was the one you were trying to cut down that first day." He grew silent, but then continued. "I got her a bike when she turned seven. It was her first big-girl bike, with no training wheels, and it had a pink frame and lots of yellow strings on the handlebars. My ex-wife, Madeline, didn't want her to have one. She thought it'd be better to wait one more year, but Rachel wanted that bike so much, I gave in." A ghost of a grin moved his lips as he recalled how happy his little girl had been when she set eyes on that bike. "She loved it. Hopped right on it and rode circles in front of the house all morning. Eventually she got bored of that. Wanted a bigger challenge. So she asked if she could ride out farther."

He stopped, his body trembling, and Kelly's hand curled tighter around his, urging him on.

"I walked beside her, the whole way, watched her every move. When we got to the road, there was no one. Not a single car in either direction. So I let her keep riding and kept my eye on her. The next day, she wanted to do the same thing, but I had work to do, so I told her to wait for me and stay in the driveway." He closed his eyes and inhaled, the words leaving him on a rush. "I didn't know she'd left the driveway until I heard the horn. It was one of those big blasts from a transfer truck that make your heart stop. Except it went on and on, like the guy just lay on the horn and didn't let up. I noticed she was gone, and I ran as fast as I could. I could see her. I put my eyes on her and she put hers on me, but it was too late. She couldn't get off the road fast enough, and the truck didn't have time to stop. Rachel and I were still in the road when Madeline came home from work that day."

A tremor ran through Kelly's hand into his own, and her head lowered, her cheek resting on his shoulder. She wove her other arm around his and held him close.

"I just couldn't get there in time."

Kelly squeezed him closer. "It wasn't your fault."

He nodded. "It was an accident. That's what everyone said. That's what I told myself, but it doesn't change how I feel. It doesn't change how that moment plays over and over in my mind. It doesn't change how bad I want to go back. Not then and not now."

They fell silent, staring at the stars, Kelly holding on to him, her breathing timed with his own.

"What was she like?" she asked softly.

Wet heat trickled down his cheeks and he wiped his face. "She loved mornings. She jumped out of bed like there was no better moment in her life than sunrise. Pancakes were her favorite and she loved dogs." He managed a smile. "She would've hugged Patch until he passed out if she'd ever met him. She was smart as a whip, ahead of just about everyone in her class. She loved to talk about space, climb trees and look at the sky." His smile grew as tears coursed more heavily down his cheeks. "And she loved me. She told me so every day."

Kelly hugged him closer, pressing her warm palm against his chest, right over his heart. Her quiet tears joined his own, easing the pain more than his angry silence ever had, and her next words brought him more peace than he'd felt in years. "Rachel was happy you were her father."

CHAPTER 10

K elly had never expected a ride in a truck with two kids, a dog and a handsome man could be such crazy fun.

"Woooo! Woo! Woo!" Daisy howled from the back-seat in tandem with Patch, howling to the music Seth played on the truck's radio as he drove.

"Make her stop!" Todd begged, cupping his hands over his ears. "Make them both stop."

Kelly glanced in the rearview mirror and smiled. Though he pouted, a smile tugged at Todd's mouth and his eyes lit up with laughter. The goober was having a ball, but didn't want to admit it. It was a special Saturday—the first full day of spring break—and the big fundraiser day was exactly one week away.

At the high-pitched sound of Daisy and Patch's next round of howls, Seth joined in, tipping his chin up, meeting Daisy's eyes in the rearview mirror and howling right along with her.

Kelly glanced between the two of them, the bright

smiles on both of their faces making her heart turn over in her chest.

Last night, she had sat with Seth on his front porch under the stars for hours after he'd shared the details about Rachel's death. She'd hugged him close and cried for his loss, grief and pain, and though he hadn't made a sound, she'd felt hot tears roll down his cheek and onto her temple as she'd rested her head against his chest. She hadn't looked up at him—it had seemed too private a moment—but she'd held on for as long as he allowed her. And, by eleven o'clock that night, he'd been the one to gently nudge her awake, offer a small smile and suggest she and the kids stay in one of his guest rooms for the night.

She'd been tempted to accept, but thought better of it. Something in his eyes, a lingering shadow, she supposed, had led her to believe he might be better off having his home to himself for the rest of the night. To have time to process what he'd shared and recover from the renewed grief he'd experienced, and that it might be better for him to do that without Todd and Daisy's presence . . . and perhaps, even her own.

So she'd gone inside, found Todd, Daisy and Patch sprawled on the sectional, sound asleep, and had reluctantly woken them. Seth had driven them back to their trailer and she'd carried Daisy, who still slept, inside; then Kelly lingered outside of the door of the trailer as he left, watching the taillights of his truck fade into the dark night.

Kelly had stayed awake most of last night, staring at the ceiling, unable to think of much else than the distress in Seth's eyes when he'd spoken of losing his daughter. Her heart had ached so much for him that hot tears had continued rolling down her cheeks most of the night.

Seth had shown up earlier than expected the next morning, preparing the part of the field they had marked off for the Moon Garden and unpacking the flowers from their plant holders, preparing to plant them. Patch had followed him and had come running toward the trailer the moment Kelly had opened the door.

Soon enough, Kelly, Todd and Daisy had all joined Seth in planting the flowers. Within a couple hours, the garden was finished—and gorgeous—just as Seth had said it would be. Though the blooms on the nocturnal flowers wouldn't open until that night, the flower bed already added a lush and elegant air to the grounds.

"Thank you for planting the Moon Garden this morning," Kelly told Seth now. "I couldn't quite picture it in my mind when you mentioned it, and it's more beautiful than I could have imagined."

"You're welcome." He removed one hand from the steering wheel, reached over and squeezed her hand. "I had fun spending time with you, Todd and Daisy. Laughing with y'all took the work out of it."

That was true. Kelly placed her hand over his and smiled down at their joined hands, recalling the jokes Seth and Todd had shared and the mini dirt fight they'd all gotten into at one point, forcing everyone to wash up before loading up in the truck for their day trip.

"So, what's the plan?" Todd asked from the backseat. "How long will it take to get to the airport for the tour?"

Seth squeezed her hand once more, then returned his hand to the steering wheel and smiled at Todd in the rearview mirror. "It only takes about half an hour to get to Glenville, but Kelly and I thought it'd be a good idea to stop by the nursing home on the way."

Surprisingly, Todd didn't complain. He simply nodded and rubbed Patch's ears. As a matter of fact, Todd hadn't even brought his earbuds or music with him. That alone was enough to make Kelly take a second look.

"What?" Todd frowned as Kelly swiveled in her seat for the third time to glance at him.

"Nothing. I'm just . . . glad the plan works for everyone today." She pulled in a deep breath and held up her hands. "So here's the thing. I want Mae Bell and Mr. Haggart to come to the fundraiser Saturday, but I have to get permission from the nurse in order to transport them off the grounds," she drawled. "So I'm gonna have to do a lot of begging. And pleading. And possibly bribing when we get there."

"No problem," Todd said. "Me and Seth packed a cooler full of root beer before we left."

"It's mostly Kadence, the nurse, that I'm concerned about." Kelly swiveled around once more in her seat and sent a pleading look to Todd. "Would you please be extra-special sweet to the nurse today? No critical observations or judgment calls, okay? Just kind, polite, how's-the-weather conversation."

She stiffened as Todd pursed his lips and narrowed his eyes, studying her as though he might protest. Instead, he just shrugged.

"I suppose I can handle that," he said before looking out of the window at the passing scenery.

Kelly turned back around in her seat and smiled at Seth, whispering softly, "Well, hallelujah."

The Silver Stay nursing home was business as usual when they arrived. Mr. Haggart sat by the door, pounding the arm of his wheelchair with his fist, demanding root beer, and Nurse Powell was behind the reception desk answering the phone.

"Psst," Todd whispered, slipping inside the lobby with Patch on a leash. "We brought you something, Mr. Haggart."

Mr. Haggart's face lit up at the sight of Patch and he stretched his arm out. "Oh, you got a right fine mutt there, kid. That's a beaut! What's his name?"

"Patch," Todd said. "He belongs to Seth."

Mr. Haggart chuckled as Patch padded up to his wheelchair, laid his chin on Mr. Haggart's lap and groaned with contentment as the old man scratched Patch's head. "Don't get to see too many dogs anymore, being cooped up in this crazy place."

"Seth." Kadence hung up the phone and rounded the desk, eyeing Patch. "You know we don't usually allow pets in."

"I know." Seth dipped his head in apology. "But I thought a visit from Patch might cheer Mr. Haggart up, and the kids were looking forward to bringing him to visit." He glanced at Daisy, who stood by his side, holding his hand. "We enjoy spending time with Patch, don't we, Daisy?"

Daisy nodded, then walked over to Patch, kissed his head and smiled at Kadence.

Kadence's icy frown melted just a bit as she looked back at Daisy, then broke into a full smile. "Oh, all right. But just this once, and only because she's such a cutie."

"Thank you, Nurse Powell," Todd said, even going so far as to crack a polite smile.

Kadence looked surprised, then confused, but seemed genuinely pleased at Todd's pleasant behavior. "You're welcome. But like I said, just this once."

Biting her lip, Kelly eased around Seth and stepped forward hesitantly. "There's one other thing I'm hoping you'll allow just this once, Kadence."

Her frown returned as she faced Kelly. "And what's that?"

Not wanting to disappoint Mr. Haggart in case the answer was no, Kelly walked over to Kadence, leaned close and whispered, "I was hoping you might consider letting Mae Bell and Mr. Haggart take a field trip of sorts next Saturday."

Kadence's eyes widened as she shook her head, but Kelly held up a hand.

"It won't be far. Just up the road to Mae Bell's drive-in. We've put a lot of work into renovating the place and we're holding a fundraiser next Saturday afternoon to raise money for a new digital projector. I think Mr. Haggart would enjoy spending the afternoon outside, and I know Mae Bell will be anxious to see what we've done." She quickly added, "You won't have to lift a finger. I'd pick them both up in Seth's truck, stay with them all afternoon and drive them back here as soon as the fundraiser ends."

Kadence frowned again, but looked contemplative as she glanced at Mr. Haggart. She smiled slightly when he laughed as Patch kissed his face.

"Please, Kadence. I know you care deeply for them, and I'd love to help do something special for them both."

She sighed. "Okay. But I expect you to stick by their side all afternoon and return them safe and sound at the end of the fundraiser."

Kelly smiled with relief. "I promise." She turned around to face Seth and the kids and gave them a thumbs-up.

Seth strode over. "We really appreciate this, Kadence."

Kadence grinned. "You're welcome." Her voice lowered. "And anytime you feel up to having company yourself, I'm just a call away."

Seth ducked his head and rubbed the back of his neck, glancing at Kelly underneath his lashes.

"I, uh . . . I'd like to speak to Mae Bell before we go," Kelly said, heading toward the hallway leading to Mae

Bell's room. "Do you mind looking after Todd and Daisy for a few minutes?"

Seth nodded. "Take as long as you need."

Kelly murmured a thank-you and headed down the hall, eager to escape the awkward moment.

Mae Bell was standing in the open doorway of her room when Kelly arrived. "I'm so glad to see you. I've been anxious for another update all week. Do you have any pictures of the renovations so far?"

"Better than that," Kelly said, taking Mae Bell's hands in hers and smiling. "I'm going to pick you and Mr. Haggart up next Saturday and take you to Blue Moon Haven Drive-In for our first—and hopefully only—fundraiser."

"A fundraiser?" Mae Bell asked.

Kelly nodded. "Seth suggested we host a fundraiser to raise the money we need for the new digital projector. He even pitched in on the renovations. Worked as hard if not harder than I did most days, and we've managed to clean out the projection booths, mow the field, paint all the buildings and plant a moon garden."

Mae Bell clapped her hands together and closed her eyes. "That sounds heavenly." Her smile slipped as she looked at Kelly. "Do you think the fundraiser will be a success?"

"I hope so," Kelly said. "So far, we have Seth's sister, Tully, donating enough sweets from her restaurant for a candy stand, two churches in town offered to set up a baked-goods stand and a craft stand for local artists, and Seth and Todd have organized a model airplane contest." She grinned. "That's what I've been most excited to see. Seth is taking us to Glenville when we leave here to meet a pilot he went to college with. His friend has agreed to take us all on a tour of the airport where he works and help Todd with his model airplane design for the contest."

Mae Bell grew quiet, but her smile widened. "You and the kids are spending a lot of time with Seth lately, aren't you?"

Kelly sighed. "We are."

"And how is that going?"

Kelly eased past Mae Bell and walked over to the window, glancing at Seth's truck parked in the lot. "Did you see us arrive?"

"Oh, dear," she said, laughing. "The view from my window is the highlight of most of my mornings. And, yes, I watched you arrive."

Kelly touched the curtain beside her, running her fingers over the lacy material. "So you noticed how well he's getting along with Daisy and Todd?" She glanced over her shoulder at Mae Bell and tried to smile. "Daisy even talks to him now, without whispering or hiding. And Todd's temper has calmed down. He is more motivated to take part in the renovation projects. He even agreed with me this morning—that's never happened before."

Mae Bell smiled gently. "But this scares you."

Kelly frowned. "I didn't say that."

"You didn't have to. You don't make a habit of hiding your emotions, and it's right there in your eyes." Mae Bell crossed the room and stood by Kelly at the window. "What are you afraid of?"

Kelly wound the hem of the lace curtain around her fingers, rubbing the fabric. "He told me about Rachel last night," she said quietly. "About how he lost her and how hard it's been for him."

Mae Bell sighed. "That was a difficult time for quite a few people. So many loved Rachel and her family. Madeline was inconsolable."

"Does he . . . does he keep in touch with her?" Kelly asked.

"Madeline?"

Kelly nodded.

"I don't know. I know she moved away nine years ago when they divorced, and I haven't heard very much about her since. I think she was eager to move on from the loss and start over."

Kelly bit her lip. "That's what I'm afraid of." At Mae Bell's frown, she said, "I've always believed in happy endings, and yet Seth had his, every bit of it." She managed a small smile. "A beautiful country house with a red roof, a wife and daughter. A life he worked hard for and loved, and it only took a moment for it all to fall apart." Her chin trembled and she blinked hard, willing away the tears pricking the backs of her eyes. "What would make this time different? How would a potential new life with me, Todd and Daisy work out better for him . . . or for me and the kids?"

"Kelly—"

"I'm a secondary guardian, not a mom," she blurted. Despite her best efforts, a tear escaped and rolled down her cheek. "I have no idea what I'm doing ninety percent of the time, whereas Seth was a perfect dad from all accounts and from what I've seen of him and his interactions with Todd and Daisy. When I heard about what happened to Rachel, I couldn't help wondering what kind of awful things could happen to Todd and Daisy under my watch? I make mistakes all the time. I'm used to living on my own and following my whims"— she spread her arms, gesturing around her—"like this one. Coming out here. I quit my job and came out here on a whim, expecting this to be magically better."

"No, you didn't." Mae Bell touched her shoulders gently and turned Kelly to face her. Her eyes, kind and patient, searched Kelly's expression, her voice firm. "You left a life that was less than what it should have been for something better. You did something a lot of people never do, not once, in their lifetimes. You took a chance, a real chance, for something better. And you didn't do it just for you—you did it to provide a better life for the kids. That's the kind of sacrifice good mothers make."

Kelly blinked back a fresh wave of tears. "Todd hates me."

"No, he doesn't—"

"He thinks I'm not capable of taking care of him and Daisy . . . and most days, I think he's right. I want so much for them. I love them so much. I don't want to fail them."

"Is that why you won't say they're yours?" Mae Bell asked quietly.

Kelly stiffened. "What do you mean?"

"When you first arrived, I asked if Todd and Daisy were your children, and you said no. That you were just taking care of them. From the way Todd reacted, I assumed that was something you did often."

It was. Kelly cringed, thinking about all of the times she'd corrected strangers, emphasizing she wasn't Todd and Daisy's mother.

"I'm not the kind of mom Laice was," she whispered. "I'm not mom material at all."

Mae Bell tapped her finger under Kelly's chin and lifted her face until their eyes met. "You are a wonderful mother, and this gamble you took has had a touch of luck on it from day one. Look at what happened with Seth. The two of you started off on the wrong foot, and now, things between you have taken a completely different turn. I wish I could offer you a guarantee, but I can't. Life is scary and there's no way to predict what's coming. Committing and following through to the best of your ability is the best any of us can do." She sighed, hugging Kelly close. "You just have to have faith. We both just have to have faith."

* * *

Seth eased away from Mae Bell's room and retraced his steps down the hall of the nursing home, his chest aching over what he'd unintentionally overheard: *"I've always believed in happy endings, and yet Seth had his . . . and it only took a moment for it all to fall apart."*

He winced and kneaded the back of his neck with his hand. The fear in her voice had made him long to wrap his arms around her and hold her close. To tell her that there was still good in the world, and that she had been the one to show it to him.

For eight years after Rachel's death, he had hidden himself behind a wall of pain, grief and anger, refusing to come out or let anyone else in. He'd gone through the motions each day with little care as to what the next held and no interest in the future. At heart, he'd believed that there were no happy endings after losing Rachel. That any happiness he managed to steal from life was only a tease that would either be snatched away or fade with time, leaving him with nothing more than emptiness and regret.

But then, Kelly had arrived with Todd and Daisy, upending his predictable existence and introducing a whole lot of chaos.

He smiled as he walked back into the lobby of the nursing home and watched Daisy and Todd sit on a sofa near Mr. Haggart, laughing as they listened to one of his jokes. At first, Daisy and Todd's presence had unnerved him—Daisy especially. She made him recall his unanswered prayers that Rachel would somehow return to him, safe and well. That things could return to the way they had been when he, Rachel and Madeline had lived happy, relatively uneventful lives, secure in the knowledge that tomorrow would be more of the same.

But . . .

His smile fell. As Mae Bell had said, there were no guarantees, and Kelly's fears that whatever was beginning to bloom between them might end before it even had a chance to begin were well-founded, given what he'd experienced in the past.

Yet he found himself still wanting to try. He still wanted to explore a relationship with Kelly—and not a friendship, either. The emotions Kelly had begun to stir within him went far deeper than friendship, the intensity of his feelings for her surprising him. He hadn't felt anything like it in his life so far . . . and he had no desire to give up on it anytime soon. Or at all, for that matter.

"Is Kelly coming? I'm hungry and y'all said we could go out to eat before we went to the tour."

He stopped in the center of the lobby, glancing at the sofa where Todd was looking at him expectantly, awaiting an answer. "She's still talking to Mae Bell. We'll give her a few minutes, and if she doesn't come out soon, I'll go back and get her."

Seth glanced over his shoulder at the empty hallway behind him, his jaw clenching. No way would he go back to the way things were—empty, alone and predictable. He was ready to take a chance as Kelly had, coming to Blue Moon, and he wanted to take that chance with Kelly, Todd and Daisy.

Two hours later, after a stop along the road for lunch, Seth pulled into the Glenville Airport parking lot and parked his truck.

"The planes are smaller than I thought they'd be," Todd said from the backseat of the cab. He craned his neck, leaning forward between Seth and Kelly to get a better look at the runway. "How many do they have here again?"

"It depends," Seth said, cutting the engine. "Some days, a private jet or two will fly in and stay put a week or so. Other days, only small local planes are here." He glanced at Kelly, who had scooted forward in the passenger seat, her face all but plastered against the windshield as she scanned the layout before them. "How 'bout we hop out and see if we can find my buddy, Clark. He'll show us the ins and outs of the place."

She tore her gaze off the runway and faced him, her excited expression and bright smile relieving some of the worries he'd carried as they'd driven away from the nursing home earlier. Her expression had looked drawn and her eyes had been slightly puffy as though she'd been crying when she left Mae Bell's room, but after a leisurely lunch with the kids and a peaceful drive to Glenville, she seemed her ordinary self and almost giddy with anticipation as he mentioned the tour of the airport. Perhaps she was just eager for a distraction.

"Yes!" She unsnapped her seat belt, thrust open her door and hopped out, pausing briefly to stick her head back in the truck's cab and say in a rush, "Now, get out, y'all. I'm ready to see some planes."

Clark, Seth's friend, was waiting for them inside the small terminal building. "Good to see you, Seth."

"And you." Smiling, Seth shook his hand. "You haven't changed much since I last saw you."

Clark patted his belly and laughed. "Well, now, that's not exactly true. I've put on a few reserves for the winter. But you're still as fit as you used to be. How's the pecan business going?"

They reminisced for a few minutes, while Todd wandered around the small terminal, getting a good look at things, and Daisy stuck close to Kelly's side. Toward the end of their conversation, Todd returned and nudged Kelly, pointing to various areas of interest around the terminal.

"I got some guests with me, eager to see the inner workings of your establishment." Seth gestured toward Kelly. "This is Kelly, my . . ." He hesitated, wanting to put a name to their relationship, but not quite able to find the right one.

Kelly beat him to it. "Neighbor." She shook Clark's hand. "I'm Seth's neighbor."

Seth frowned. It was worse than he'd expected. *Friends* would've been an unwelcome word for the intense emotions he had for Kelly, but it seemed Kelly had booted them to less than that. Now, they were just . . . *neighbors*.

His mouth twisted, but inwardly he gave himself a pep talk. The confusion wouldn't last long because he planned to be open and honest with Kelly about what he was feeling. And the sooner, the better.

"Kelly has partnered with Mae Bell," Seth said. "They're throwing a fundraiser to earn money for the grand reopening of Blue Moon Haven Drive-In."

"Oh, yeah?" Clark asked. "I'll let my dad know. He used to go there back in the day. He'd visit his aunt out in Blue Moon for the summer, spend some time on the farm. He loved it there. Said some of the best memories he had were of that drive-in." He grinned at Kelly. "When he was a teenager, he had a big ol' dented-up Cadillac that drove like a beauty and had a trunk the size of a bedroom. He said his friends used to pile in there on the nights they'd go to the drive-in and he'd sneak them in for free."

Kelly laughed. "That's pretty brave to trust someone enough to let them stuff you in a locked trunk. I'll have to do some trunk inspections if we manage to get to opening night."

"'If'?" he asked. "I was hoping to finagle a date from you to share with my dad."

Kelly grimaced. "We're still in the renovation phase, and our budget is stretched pretty thin. All our hopes are pinned on raising enough funds this weekend to buy a new digital projector."

Clark made a sound of disappointment. "Well, if there's something I can do to help, please let me know. I know my dad would love a chance to spend another night at the drive-in."

"Appreciate that." Seth smiled. "It'd be great if you could make it out there this Saturday for the fundraiser. We could catch up on old times and"—he glanced at Kelly—"I don't think you have anyone formally lined up to judge the model airplane contest, do you?"

She shook her head, looking at Clark hopefully. "Oh, it'd be wonderful to have a true pilot judge the contest . . . That is, if you could spare the time?"

"You kidding me?" Clark grinned. "I'll make the time. And I'll bring my dad with me. Give him a chance to look around and reminisce." He rubbed his hands together. "Y'all ready to take a look around and get up close and personal with some planes?" He glanced at Todd and Daisy, then smiled. "I see you brought your son and daughter with you today." He waved at Daisy. "What're your names, guys?"

"They're not my . . ." Kelly looked at Todd, hesitated, then said, "They're excited to see everything." She reached out and squeezed Todd's shoulder. "Especially Todd. He's been working on a model airplane with Seth for our fundraiser contest and he was hoping to get some construction tips from you while he's here."

Todd stared up at her, a wary look of surprise in his eyes.

Seth held his breath, waiting for a reaction from Todd, but if he'd softened any toward Kelly, he didn't let it show.

Instead, he nodded and held out his hand to Clark. "I'm Todd. Thank you for letting us come and look around."

Seth glanced at Kelly, who appeared as shocked as he was at Todd's polite response, but she looked away and hid her smile, probably thinking the same as Seth: It was better not to mention it and just appreciate the moment.

Over the next hour, they toured the whole airport, starting with the terminal. Clark showed them around the check-in and checkout stations, baggage claim and the small café that served coffee and pastries. Outside of the terminal, he pointed out the control tower and runway, then led them inside the hangar to take a closer look at the planes.

"Wow," Kelly said.

"Double wow," Todd echoed.

Looking at each other, Kelly and Todd burst out laughing. Seth, standing nearby with Daisy, crossed his arms over his chest and smiled. He'd hoped the airport tour would entertain Kelly and hopefully fulfill at least part of the dream she had of being around airplanes (even if they weren't fighter jets).

Seth's smile widened as Kelly and Todd approached a silver-and-blue light aircraft with triple black lines down the middle.

Kelly touched the side of the plane and drifted her hand lightly along its body, asking softly, "What kind is this?"

"That's a Cirrus SR22," Clark said, walking over and opening the doors. "This one belongs to me. I use it a lot for training. Want to take a look inside?"

Kelly's eyes widened and she walked over to the open door with an air of stupefied amazement. "I'd love to."

Stifling a laugh, Seth watched as Clark helped Kelly into the plane, then joined her inside and walked her through the equipment, highlighting the instrument panel and special interior features.

Daisy tugged on the hem of Seth's shirt. "Can I get in with Kelly?"

Seth smiled. "Sure thing."

He walked Daisy over and helped her inside, watching as she settled onto Kelly's lap and stared with rapt interest at the controls as Clark continued pointing out different features. Seth leaned on the side of the airplane, listening for a few minutes as well, then joined Todd at the back of the plane.

Todd had one of Kelly's notebooks in his hand. He'd been carrying it around in his back pocket for most of the day. He drew slowly on the paper, while studying the plane, a look of fierce concentration on his face.

Seth peered over his shoulder. "Sketching this for your model?"

Todd nodded. "It's a nice one. Looks sharper than I expected for a small plane. I want to get the details just right for mine."

"May I take a look?"

Todd nodded and handed it over.

The drawing was remarkably intricate. "You've got a lot of talent, Todd." Seth drew his finger over the drawing. "You captured the details just right."

"Thanks." Todd took the notepad and resumed drawing. "I think with a few tweaks, the model I've already started will look just like it. I just hope it flies as well as Clark says this one does."

"Just keep in mind that the idea of the contest is to have fun and not solely to win."

Todd continued drawing, his brow furrowing as he focused intently. "I know."

Seth shoved his hands in his pockets and rocked back on his heels. "Kelly loves planes, too."

"I know."

Seth grinned. "Said she dreamed of flying fighter jets when she was a girl."

"I know."

"You know what else she dreamed of?" Seth asked.

"A cotton candy factory and a big house with a red roof like yours. She's told us about it a thousand times and talked about it during the entire drive from Birmingham to Blue Moon when we moved here."

"What else do you know about her?"

Todd's movements slowed, the pencil he held growing still over the paper. "She was my mom's best friend," he said softly. "And I know she misses her. A lot."

"And you?"

His mouth tightened. "I miss my mom, too." He looked up, meeting Seth's eyes, a hard look in them. "My dad left us. That's why we're with Kelly."

"I know," Seth said softly.

"He's in Florida."

Seth glanced at Todd in surprise. "Are you sure about that?"

"Yeah. He gave me his number before he left. Said I could call him anytime. I called him right before we left Birmingham to come here, told him Kelly was moving us here, so he'd know where we were."

Seth hesitated, glancing at Kelly and Daisy, who still sat in the plane, talking with Clark. "Does Kelly know you have his number?"

Todd lowered his head, staring at the drawing in his hand. "No. My dad told me to give it to her, but . . ."

Seth gripped Todd's shoulder and squeezed, waiting until the boy looked up and met his eyes. "Why didn't you give it to her?"

"Because I didn't want her to call him."

"Why?" Seth prompted.

Todd's mouth trembled. "Because I was hoping that she'd . . . that she'd . . ." He ducked his head again. "I bet Dad will come back for us." He looked up again, a determined look in his eyes. "Sometimes I think he will. And Kelly probably wants him to come back for us, you know? She doesn't really want us. The only reason she took us at all is because she promised my mom she would."

Seth shook his head. "That's not true, Todd. I've known her a lot shorter time than you, but I know that everything she does is because it's what she thinks is best for you and Daisy. She enjoys having you both with her."

Todd searched Seth's eyes for a moment, then glanced at Kelly. "Maybe. Maybe not. But it doesn't matter anyway. Dad can take us back whenever he wants. We're not hers, you know."

Seth sighed and squeezed Todd's shoulder. "She cares for you and Daisy very much," he said quietly. "More than you know. And she's doing her best. I hope you'll think about giving her a fair chance."

CHAPTER 11

Kelly opened the side door of the Silver Stay nursing home, stepped back and waited as Mr. Haggart wheeled himself out of the door and onto the ramp leading to the parking lot. It had been one week since she'd last visited the nursing home and gotten permission to take Mae Bell and Mr. Haggart on the fundraiser field trip and the big day had finally arrived.

"Ain't it a gorgeous day," Mr. Haggart said, inhaling deeply and glancing around.

Kelly tipped her head back, soaking up the warm spring sunshine, then smiled at the deep green grass that had grown in the lawns of neighboring homes, overtaking the dormant winter ground. Honeysuckle had sprouted along the hedges lining the front porch of the nursing home and the trees danced gently in the warm breeze.

"Yeah," she agreed. It was a perfect day for Blue Moon Haven Drive-In's first fundraiser. "It's absolutely gorgeous."

"You know what'd make it even better?" Mr. Haggart slowed his wheelchair and raised an eyebrow, flashing a pleading look in Kelly's direction. "A cigarette. Ain't no better way to break in a bright, beautiful spring day such as this than a fat pack of ciggies and a cold six-pack of root beer."

"Forget it, Jimmy." High heels clacked slowly down the hallway of the nursing home to the open doorway, accompanied by the rhythmic click of a cane. "There will be no cigarettes on this trip, and you're not suckering sweet Kelly into buying you any." Mae Bell, dressed to the nines in a long white spring dress, walked slowly out onto the ramp and squinted against the bright sunlight.

Kelly moved to Mae Bell's side and cupped her elbow. "How're you doing? Are you feeling weak at all?"

Eyes closed, Mae Bell leaned more heavily on her cane and pulled in a strong breath. "I'm fine. Just allow me a moment to get my bearings and all will be well." After a couple more breaths, she slowly opened her eyes, took in her surroundings and smiled. "Oh, beautiful world, what fun we shall have today."

Kelly bit back a laugh and stuck close to Mae Bell's side as they followed Mr. Haggart along the ramp to the parking lot. She led them to Seth's truck and opened the doors of the cab.

Mae Bell poked her head inside the cab, then glanced at Kelly. "Where are the little ones?"

"Todd and Daisy are at the drive-in helping Seth guide everyone in and set up the booths so things will be ready to go on time. The fundraiser officially starts in"—Kelly glanced at her wristwatch—"one hour. And the two of you are our guests of honor."

Mr. Haggart scoffed. "If you want to honor me, give me a cigarette and a root beer."

Mae Bell propped one hand on her hip. "Look here, Jimmy. We have not vacated the premises of Silver Stay as of yet, and I'd be more than happy to tell Kadence you'd rather stay put and have her take your less-than-cheerful backside right back to that lobby window, where it came from."

Mr. Haggart pursed his lips, considering this, then smacked the arm of his wheelchair. "What're we waiting around here, holding everyone up for, woman? We're guests of honor. Get in the truck."

Fifteen minutes later, after a ride to the outskirts of Blue Moon filled with anecdotes from Mr. Haggart, Kelly pulled into the entrance of Blue Moon Haven Drive-In. She smiled at the grand impression the newly renovated sign and ticket booths lent to the driveway and sneaked a peek at Mae Bell to gauge her reaction.

"Oh, my . . ." Eyes wide and lashes fluttering, Mae Bell, seated in the backseat of the cab, grabbed the headrests of both seats in front of her and leaned forward, craning her neck for a better view of the entrance. "You've restored its beauty. Made it even better than the original, I think."

The massive sign, fourteen feet high and forty-eight feet wide, had been stripped, sanded and repainted a crisp, clean white. Large letters, which had barely clung to the sign before, had all been replaced with bright blue neon lights that spelled out BLUE MOON HAVEN DRIVE-IN and glowed at night. Each of the two ticket booths had been painted blue and silver, the interiors cleaned from top to bottom, and as Kelly drove through the left ticket entrance, Todd and Daisy stuck their heads out of the ticket booth window and waved.

"There's Todd and Daisy," Kelly said, glancing at Mae Bell. "They came out to welcome you. They were both excited to hear you were able to come today."

"And they look right at home," Mae Bell said, smiling as she waved back at the siblings. "That's just how a drive-in should feel for children and their parents alike. A home away from home."

Kelly rolled down her window and smiled at the pair. "You guys on ticket duty?"

"Yep," Todd said. "Seth asked us to direct people to their booths as they arrive."

"How many have made it here so far?" Kelly asked.

He pressed his lips together, thinking, then said, "There's nine different booths and eight people have shown up so far."

"Oh." Kelly forced a smile and tried to sound upbeat. "There's still over an hour until the fundraiser kicks off. The rest will probably trickle in soon."

Or at least she sure hoped so. Most of Mae Bell's budget had been spent renovating and salvaging what was already at Blue Moon Haven Drive-In, buying rights to screen current films and restocking concessions. There'd been very little left over to set aside for a new digital projector. They'd need every penny they could raise from today's festivities.

"It's still early yet," Todd said. "And Mr. Clark's already here. Seth is showing him and his dad around the place." He whispered something to Daisy, who nodded, withdrew something from under the counter and passed it to Todd, who then held it out to Kelly, smiling. "This is for you, Mr. Haggart," Todd said. "There's plenty more inside for you when you want another." He smiled and gestured wide with one arm. "Welcome to Blue Moon Haven Drive-In. I hope you enjoy your visit."

Kelly laughed. "Perfect delivery of both the welcome line and"—she took the bottle he held out and passed it to Mr. Haggart—"the root beer."

Mr. Haggart took the soda, popped off the cap, took

a big swig, then made a sound of satisfaction. "Yes sirree, Todd. This right here's the best welcome I've had in years."

"Seth has a place set up special for y'all," Todd said, pointing toward the Moon Garden. "There's a table over there by the garden."

"Thank you for holding things down here," Kelly told Todd and Daisy. "You're doing a great job leading, Todd, and I really appreciate it."

He smiled and a faint blush bloomed across his cheeks. "I wanted to help. It's no big deal."

"It's a big deal to me," Kelly said softly.

A horn honked and she glanced in the rearview mirror to see that four more cars and trucks had arrived, lining up behind her to enter the Blue Moon Haven Drive-In grounds.

"Best get to moving," Mr. Haggart said, taking another gulp of root beer. "Looks like your moneymakers are starting to arrive."

"Thank goodness." Saying a silent prayer of thanks, Kelly shifted back into drive and pulled off, slowly driving across the open field and past a table and several chairs set up by the Moon Garden.

"It's unrecognizable." Mr. Haggart scooted forward an inch more on his seat. His eyes lit up with excitement as he glanced out of the windows of the truck in each direction. "Who cleared the field?"

"Seth was good enough to loan me his tractor and show me how to run it." Kelly waved one hand toward the sprawling field, where the cars and trucks behind her were spreading out along the outskirts of the wide property. "All this was covered with so many weeds you could barely walk through it, and the briars were so dense, they'd tangle in your shorts and almost yank you down. I wanted to clear plenty of space and preserve the original areas of the lot that guests used for picnics and small group gatherings on the lawn. That way guests who want to enjoy more of the outdoor viewing experience outside of their cars will have the option of viewing the movie with friends directly under the stars with no car roof impeding the view. We're keeping everything as close to its original family-oriented design as possible with plenty of viewing options. Blue Moon Haven used to be more than just a space for cars—it was a space for gathering and celebrating the outdoors as well."

Chuckling, Mr. Haggart glanced back at Mae Bell. "You remember the last screening you held out here, Mae Bell?"

Smile softening, she slowly nodded. "*Midnight Wind.* It was late September, if I recall correctly, and our last showing prior to shutting down."

"You'd already set up for fall," Mr. Haggart said, grinning. "You had pumpkins, scarecrows and fall banners all over the place. And *Midnight Wind* was the perfect choice—a bittersweet romance between the undead." He laughed and nudged Kelly's elbow. "Oddities were always in great supply in movies back then. The stranger or more ridiculous the plot line, the more fun it was to watch." He sighed. "I, for one, loved those films. I miss those days."

Kelly patted his hand. "If all goes well today, you'll have the opportunity to enjoy plenty of them again. If Mae Bell and I get this business off the ground, I'll pick you and Mae Bell up for a showing every week on a night of your choice."

"*When,*" Mae Bell stressed. "*When* we get this business off the ground, you mean."

Kelly parked the truck behind the Moon Garden, between two trees bordering Seth's orchard, and echoed Mae Bell's sentiment with a confident smile despite the small, nervous tremor running through her. "When our business takes off, you'll both be able to enjoy Blue Moon Haven Drive-In whenever you'd like."

"Would you look at that?" Mr. Haggart boomed from the passenger seat. "They got a big ol' bucket of iced root beer on that table over there." He tapped the windshield, drained the last of the root beer bottle he held and laughed wholeheartedly. "My day's already made, folks!"

After helping Mr. Haggart and Mae Bell out of the truck, Kelly led them over to the large table Mr. Haggart had pointed out. Sure enough, there was a huge bucket filled with ice and root beer sitting in the center of the table, which had been draped with an elegant lace tablecloth. Two trays, one laden with strawberries, grapes and blueberries, and the other with cheese cubes and slices of ham, were positioned on either end of the table. A pitcher of cold lemonade, two glasses and two ceramic plates completed the place settings.

"Oh, you found my tablecloth," Mae Bell squealed with delight. She reached out, lifted the hem of the tablecloth and ran her fingers gently along the lace. "In the past, Blue Moon Haven Drive-In always had a special viewing table, and this is what I always used to make it a bit more elegant for guests."

Kelly was at a loss. "I have no idea where—"

"I found it." Seth sauntered up with Clark and an older man at his side. "It was packed inside a box in one of the projection booths, along with the trays and place settings. Had a note on it, like everything else, detailing what it was and how it was to be used." He walked over to Mae Bell and took her hands in his. "I thought it'd be a welcome sight and that you might enjoy using it for yourself for a change."

Kelly's chest warmed as Mae Bell brushed Seth's hands aside and wrapped her arms around him.

"By that touch alone, you've made this day wonderful already," Mae Bell said, hugging him close. "Thank you, Seth."

"You're welcome." Seth squeezed her back gently, then released her and helped her sit in one of the chairs at the table. "Now, sit back and just enjoy the day. Everything's taken care of and the fundraiser will start soon, so there'll be plenty of sights and festivities to enjoy."

He helped slide her chair closer to the table, then patted Mr. Haggart's shoulder as he rolled his wheelchair up to the table and settled at Mae Bell's side. "How's that bucket of root beer look to you, Mr. Haggart? Think it'll get you through the afternoon?"

He guffawed, grabbed a root beer from the bucket and popped off the cap. "You done fixed me up, Seth. I'm good to go for the rest of the day."

Seth laughed. "Glad to hear it." He gestured toward Clark and the older man. "This is Clark, a friend of mine from college, and his father—"

"Brighton Wellings," Mae Bell said, running a hand over her long silver hair. "He and I go way back." She raised an eyebrow. "You didn't smuggle anyone inside for free today, did you?"

Clark's father, chuckling, shook his head. "Not today, Mae Bell."

"You best not try it," she teased, smiling. "Because I've got your number." She glanced at Kelly and wagged a finger at Brighton. "When we were teenagers, this man tried to pull a fast one every time I worked the ticket booth. My father put me in charge of ticket sales and we'd come up short every night Brighton graced us with his—and at least four of his friends'—presence. He thought he could get away with anything, so long as he flashed that charismatic smile of his."

Brighton smiled wide. "I only used it on you, Mae Bell. After all, you were a sight for any man to behold.

And may I say, you look even more gorgeous today than you did all those years ago?"

Mae Bell arched her eyebrows. "Oh, you certainly may." She held out her hand. "Come have a seat by me and keep me company."

Kelly grinned as Seth slipped away from the others to stand by her side. "It's so good to see Mae Bell and Mr. Haggart enjoying themselves. Thank you for doing this, Seth."

He smiled down at her. "No problem. I've been looking forward to this as much as they have, I think. It's nice to see some life in this place again."

"Hmm." Kelly eyed his expression, but only pleased excitement showed on his face as he glanced around. "Even though you had other plans for the property?"

His eyes returned to her, the warmth in the green depths making her still. He dipped his head, his lips brushing the shell of her ear softly as he spoke his next words. "Plans change, Kelly." The light scent of his cologne, masculine and inviting, combined with the heat of his broad chest as it pressed against her shoulder. "And lately I'm discovering that any plans that involve you attract me the most."

Breath catching, Kelly started to speak, but Seth's warm, muscular presence disappeared as he walked away, retrieved a stack of papers off the edge of Mae Bell and Mr. Haggart's table and rejoined Clark. Her attention lingered on his strong hands as he thumbed through the papers, then pulled out one sheet and handed it to Clark, his tempting mouth moving as he spoke to his friend.

Something had shifted between them the night she'd consoled him on his porch under the stars, holding him close as he'd grieved the loss of his daughter. The friendship they'd begun to build had been so fresh and new; she hadn't expected so many other emotions to get tangled in as well. So much so, she'd found herself admiring him a bit too long on occasion. Wondering what it might be like to be closer to him. To share her fears as well as her dreams. To have that same sense of close comfort and compassion she'd felt from him as they lay on the freshly cut grass of the field beneath the sun when she had shared her worries about Todd and Daisy and her anger regarding Zane.

Seth had been so understanding, so kind and reassuring, that she couldn't help but want to be near him. To be close enough to feel his comforting strength and patient support, as before.

A rumble of engines and boisterous chatter echoed across the field as a new string of cars and trucks, many more than before, drove onto the grounds.

Kelly rubbed her shaky palms across her shorts and squared her shoulders. Now was not the time to daydream about Seth. It was time to work and, hopefully, raise enough funds to revive Mae Bell's dream.

Hours later, Seth, standing on the edge of the field, squeezed Todd's shoulder, leaned down and said, "Hands steady, keep your eyes on it at all times and don't crash into the competition."

"Got it." Todd, holding the handle of the control line connected to his model airplane, nodded as Seth lifted the plane off the ground and held it up with one hand on each of the wings. "When Clark says start, I'm supposed to plug in the battery, spin the propeller, then guide it with the handle and control line after it hits the air."

"That's it." Seth flashed an encouraging smile. "You're ready, bud."

More than ready, Seth would say. Todd had been chomping at the bit to fly his model airplane in this competition ever since they'd visited the Glenville airport and toured with Clark. When they'd returned home, Todd went straight to the trailer and dove head-first into putting the finishing touches on his plane, and Kelly had mentioned he'd spent every spare moment of his spring break week painting his plane with the same design of the Cirrus SR22 Clark had shown them during the tour.

Two days ago, Todd had run across the property line at daybreak to seek out Seth as he worked in the orchard. He'd offered to pitch in and help in exchange for Seth's coming to the drive-in to help him practice his first flight. Seth, almost as eager as Todd to see the model embark upon its debut flight, had readily agreed.

The model airplane competition had been specified as control line, and both he and Todd had had to conduct extensive research to build the correct equipment for the plane to fly. But, with trial and error, they'd succeeded in getting the plane off the ground several times, and Todd had practiced flying it with fierce concentration, often refusing to stop for lunch, while Seth, Kelly and Daisy sat on the edge of the field, eating sandwiches and cheering him on.

"Go, Todd!"

Seth glanced to the left of the field where Kelly sat, with Daisy on her lap, in a chair beside Mae Bell. All smiles, Kelly and Daisy waved, cheering Todd on.

A pleasant tug of affection stirred in Seth's chest at the sight, his smile widening as a feeling of comfort and happiness, which he hadn't felt in years, swept through him. Months ago, he wouldn't have been able to imagine ever looking at a little girl without his heart breaking with memories of Rachel. When he'd first met Daisy, he was sure he'd never be able to accept her presence without hurting.

But lately . . . something had changed. Ever since the night he'd spoken to Kelly about Rachel, he'd found himself more and more able to let go of the pain that had consumed him for years. Not only the pain, but the guilt as well.

He stilled, his hands tightening around the wings of Todd's model airplane as his gaze settled on Rachel's tree just off to the right of his line of sight. The tree conjured up memories of Rachel climbing, settling onto one of the strongest limbs and smiling at her accomplishments. In his mind, he could even hear her voice, calling to him, just as he had when he'd worked in the orchard near her, exchanging jokes and anecdotes as she had watched him work.

But those memories, he was surprised to discover, no longer hurt as much as they had in the past. Now, he found himself able to focus more on the joy of her smile. On how happy she'd been.

"Rachel was happy you were her father."

Peace settled within his heart, relaxing his limbs and easing his guilt, at the memory of Kelly's gentle words that night he'd spent speaking of Rachel on his porch. Rachel had been happy, and he had, in some small way, been a part of that.

He glanced down at Todd, who studied the plane Seth held anxiously, then looked up at Seth and smiled.

Yeah, he'd helped make Rachel happy . . . just as he was helping Todd and Daisy find happiness now. He met Todd's eyes, his chest lifting at the admiration in the boy's eyes and feeling that strong rush of contentment he'd felt as a father. A feeling he wanted to experience again with Todd and Daisy.

"Everyone ready?"

Seth blinked as Todd turned away and bounced in place with excitement. The large circle the competitors had formed was made up of fathers, mothers and grandparents, standing with their sons, daughters or grandchildren, eagerly anticipating the release of the planes.

After helping Kelly get Mae Bell and Mr. Haggart settled at the head table, Seth had joined Clark and gone over the rules and procedures of the model airplane competition. As they'd spoken, several new lines of vehicles had poured into the Blue Moon Haven Drive-In lot.

The crowd had swelled throughout the afternoon as families had taken photos of the crafts they'd purchased and treats they'd enjoyed and posted them to social media, and soon the drive-in grounds were so full, people had begun to park their cars in a line down the side of the road leading to the drive-in's entrance.

From the looks of it, Blue Moon Haven Drive-In's fundraiser was poised to be a success.

"Plug in your batteries," Clark shouted, raising his arm in the air.

Todd, his hands shaking with nervous tension, reached past Seth's arms to the back of the model plane, plugged in the battery and smiled when it beeped, signaling the craft was ready for flight.

"At my command, you'll take flight," Clark directed. He smiled, glancing at the crowd gathered in a circle around the competitors, their good-natured groans and pleas for the competition to begin growing louder with each passing second. "Ready. Steady. Start!"

Todd spun the propeller and the small motor growled, then kicked into a steady buzz. When the propellers hit optimal speed, Seth released the model airplane, as did the other competitors who formed the circle around the field, and the crowd of onlookers cheered as the model planes hit the sky, darting in every direction.

Todd made faces as he struggled to control his plane in the spring breeze and dodge other planes, turning himself in circles as he lifted and lowered the handle, guiding the plane safely between other aircrafts and showing off its best assets.

"Looking sharp," Seth complimented him, moving alongside him and tipping his head back to take in the action.

Planes buzzed and swept low, causing onlookers to duck and laugh with excitement. Kelly and Daisy had left their chairs and stood, jumping and cheering from the sidelines, urging Todd on.

The flight continued for several more minutes until a few planes started dropping out of the sky as their batteries ran out of juice. Soon Clark signaled the end of the competition.

"All right," he shouted over the jubilant chatter of participants and onlookers. "Land your planes and I'll take a final look at each one."

After all of the planes landed, Clark began making his last round of inspections, pausing by each competitor to admire their plane and take notes. Kelly and Daisy wove their way through the crowd to join Seth and Todd.

Daisy threw her arms around Todd's waist and squeezed. "You were great! Bet you get first place."

Smiling, Todd lifted his chin and hugged her. "Thanks, Daisy."

"It flew perfectly," Kelly said, ruffling his hair. She lifted her arms toward him, but hesitated, then patted his shoulder and smiled instead. "I'm so proud of you."

Todd's grin grew. "I didn't do it on my own." He glanced up at Seth. "Seth helped me a lot."

Seth patted Todd's back, a sense of pride he hadn't felt in a long time rushing through him as he said softly, "We both worked hard."

Finished with his inspections, Clark moved to the center of the competitors' circle and waved his arms to get everyone's attention. "Okay, folks, we have a decision. It was difficult to make, considering all the talent we had today, and I want to assure all the competitors that they did an excellent job. Let's give them a round of applause for all their hard work."

The crowd clapped and whistles and cheers peppered the air before it quieted down.

"After a lot of deliberation, I'd like to introduce our three winners. Third place goes to Joey Dale. Congratulations, Joey."

Joey, a tall, gangly teenager, jogged to the center of the circle and accepted his ribbon from Clark with a big smile.

"Second place goes to . . ." Clark paused for dramatic effect, then said, "Todd Campbell."

Seth bit his tongue, holding back a sigh of disappointment on Todd's behalf, but he smiled and patted Todd's back. "Good job, Todd."

Surprisingly, Todd's smile was even bigger, without an ounce of disappointment at all. He ran to the center of the competitors' circle, accepted his second-place ribbon from Clark and smiled even wider as Clark hugged him for a brief second before moving on to announce the first-place winner.

"And coming in first place is Annie Wells," Clark announced. "Let's give Annie a round of applause."

Annie, a cute young girl around Todd's age, jogged across the field and joined the two boys. After accepting her ribbon and thanking Clark, she took her place beside Todd for pictures, exchanging several glances with him as they posed for different people taking their photo. Todd blushed a deep red by the fourth picture and turned to Annie to strike up a conversation.

Chuckling, Seth leaned over to Kelly and whispered, "From the looks of it, I think Todd might be happier about losing to Annie than he was about getting that second-place ribbon."

Kelly laughed and leaned closer, her soft arm pressing against his. "I think you're right."

It felt like the most natural thing in the world as Seth lifted his arm and looped it about Kelly's shoulders, pulling her closer to his side. And Daisy, standing in front of Kelly, glanced up at him and smiled, then wrapped her arms around his left knee and hugged his leg, snuggling close.

For a moment, as they watched Todd and Annie chat, Seth felt . . . at home. More than that, even. It felt like . . . family.

"Seth?"

Kelly's soft voice brought Seth's eyes back to her and he smiled as her brown hair shined in the sunlight. "Hmm?"

"Someone's trying to get your attention." She pointed at a spot across the field. "Over there. By Rachel's tree."

He looked across the field, his gaze settling on a woman who stood beside Rachel's tree, her arm raised in a hesitant wave, a mixture of pain and polite greeting on her face.

"Who is she?" Kelly asked.

Seth froze, his arm tightening around Kelly's shoulder as a renewed surge of guilt swept over him. "Madeline," he said, his voice hoarse. "My ex-wife."

CHAPTER 12

Seven years had not changed Madeline at all, it seemed. Her long blond hair still hung loose about her shoulders, her outfit of slacks and a blouse were perfectly color coordinated with her earrings and necklace, and she stood tall and confident, as she always had.

Except she twisted her hands together at her waist and eyed him nervously as he approached.

Reluctantly Seth continued weaving his way through couples, kids and model airplanes toward Madeline, who stood on the opposite side of Blue Moon Haven Drive-In's grounds. She stared at him as he approached, leaning against Rachel's tree and casting glances over his right shoulder toward the spot where he had left Kelly and Daisy.

He looked back, his chest tightening at the sight of Kelly, Daisy and Todd, who had rejoined them and was showing off his red second-place ribbon. He felt a pang of regret at having left Kelly the way he had.

He hadn't had time to explain Madeline's presence—he couldn't even manage to do that for himself—and he hadn't been able to offer any reassurances that there was very little left between him and Madeline, not with Daisy standing by Kelly's side, looking up at him with those big brown eyes and hanging on to his every word.

No. The best he'd been able to do was to squeeze Kelly's shoulder prior to releasing her, then meet her eyes and say, "I'll be back soon."

And now, Kelly stood in the same place he had left her with Daisy and Todd, whose smiles had both dimmed a bit as they watched him walk away from them and cross his property line to join Madeline.

"I didn't mean to intrude." Straightening, Madeline smoothed a hand over her pink silk blouse and tucked her long blond hair behind one ear. "I went to our— your— house first, but I saw your truck wasn't there, and when I heard all the noise . . ." She motioned toward the crowd still milling around the field behind him. "I thought I'd walk over and see what all the fuss was about." She smiled, but it was forced, and died quickly. "I guess you finally managed to talk Mae Bell into selling you the property?"

Seth shook his head. "No. The drive-in still belongs to Mae Bell. She's hired someone to restore it for her, get the business back up and running again."

"Oh. I see." Her eyes drifted away from him and returned to that spot over his right shoulder. "And are they friends of Mae Bell's?"

He glanced back again, stifling the urge to return to Kelly, who had thrown an arm around both Daisy and Todd and was leading them away toward the table where Mae Bell and Mr. Haggart still sat.

"Yeah, and mine." He faced Madeline. "Kelly and the two kids, Todd and Daisy, are friends of mine as well."

"Daisy," she said softly, her blue eyes moving slowly

over the field, tracing Daisy's steps. Her chin trembled. "She's about the same age as. . . "

As Rachel. Seth dipped his head. There was no need for her to finish the sentence. He knew what was on her mind . . . and heart.

"Yeah," he said quietly. "I'm surprised to see you."

The sad look in her eyes receded slightly and a smile reappeared. "Don't you mean, what am I doing here?" Her gaze moved over his face, taking in what he was sure were new lines and a wrinkle or two. Changes the passage of seven years had brought to both their faces, he noticed now that he was able to view her expression up close. "I miss how blunt you always were about everything," she continued. "I've never met anyone as brutally honest as you."

He managed a smile. "Not even since you left?"

"No. Not even since I left." Her smile fell and she looked down at her manicured hands, twisting a diamond ring around the fourth finger on her left hand.

"Are you married?" Sincere surprise shook him, but as the emotion subsided, he was pleased—and somewhat relieved—to discover he felt genuinely happy for her.

She looked up, a hesitant and somewhat-guilty look in her eyes. "Engaged. Or maybe I will be." She blushed. "I accepted the ring, but said I wasn't sure and that I'd have to think about it." Her lips trembled. "That's selfish of me, isn't it? And so unfair to him."

Seth bit his lip, unable to read the look in her eyes and unsure how to respond. Instead, he touched her elbow, then gestured toward the orchard. "Want to take a walk? It'll be quieter at the house."

She ducked her head, but nodded, and fell in step beside him as they walked past Rachel's tree and into his orchard, making their way through the maze of trees and ducking beneath low-hanging branches. It was getting late, the afternoon sun slipping lower on the horizon, and they both had to lift their hands to shade their eyes from the sharp sunlight as they continued through the orchard and walked onto the driveway leading to Seth's house.

"It hasn't changed much," Madeline said, looking at the house and lawn. "You've kept things very similar to the way they were."

"Outside, the place is exactly the same," Seth said softly. "But inside, it's a different story."

She didn't look at him. Just kept staring straight ahead at the house they used to live in together. "It's the same for me. Except . . ." She looked away, her gaze settling on a spot in the distance, on the other side of the orchard. "I don't know if I want to invite anyone in again."

Seth dragged his boot across the dirt of the driveway. "What's his name?"

"Allen Wright. He teaches at an elementary school. Loves kids." Her voice shook. "He wants to have at least two of his own." She turned her head, meeting his eyes again, and managed a weak smile. "What is Daisy like?"

Seth smiled. A real smile, full of admiration, with no trace of the grief and guilt he had carried for so long. "She's wonderful. Very shy and doesn't speak much, but I expect that's because she lost her mother to cancer." His mouth twisted. "Her father didn't stick around. That's how she and her brother ended up with Kelly."

"And Kelly? What's she like?"

His skin tingled at the mention of her name, a ripple of excitement and tenderness moving through him. "She's great." He ducked his head, hiding his smile. *Great* was the understatement of the year. Kelly filled his heart and mind, her presence restoring a sense of peace and hope within his heart. Even her flaws and imperfections were endearing.

"Do you love her?" Madeline asked quietly.

Seth thought for a moment, that feeling of tenderness welling up in his chest until he thought his heart might burst. "Yeah." He glanced up, facing Madeline. "Yes, I do. Very much."

She smiled. "I'm happy for you."

The sincerity in her eyes brought him relief. "Thank you." He hesitated, searching her expression, then said, "Are you wondering how it feels? Starting over?"

Her smile fell and she bit her lip, fear in her eyes as she nodded.

"It's scary at first," he said softly. "And it hurts—it hurts so much." He turned away and stared at the house, recalling the first night Kelly and the kids had invaded his living room. "It feels like a betrayal, having someone new in your life—especially children. I felt like I was letting Rachel down. Letting her go."

He faced Madeline again, noting the tears welling along her lower lashes, and thought of the peace that had moved through him sitting on his porch that night with Kelly. When her gentle touch and tender words had reminded him of the good times he'd had with Rachel.

"Rachel was happy," he said, his voice catching. "What happened that day . . ." He swallowed hard. "I'll never be able to completely let it go. I'll probably always wonder 'what if' or 'if only.' But I've learned to accept that sometimes things that happen aren't my choice or in my control. And I choose—every day—to focus on the good memories. That way, I'll never really let her go."

A sob escaped her. "I can't help but think I should've stayed. I think about all the things I could've tried that might have helped us work things out. That . . . that I was selfish for leaving you when you were hurting so much. And now, here I am, thinking about getting married again. H-having another child."

He reached out, wiping away a tear that slipped from her lashes and rolled down her cheek. "You deserve to be happy, Madeline. To get married and have children. You deserve to love and live again. We both do. We lost our baby girl and we tried our hardest to make things work, but it wasn't meant to be. You were right to move on. You don't owe me anything, and you shouldn't feel guilty about wanting to start over." He nudged her chin up with his knuckle. "We both have more to give in life. And it's what Rachel would've wanted."

A smile broke through her tears. She closed her eyes, quieting a sob, then opened them and stepped forward, easing her arms around him and hugging him close. "Thank you, Seth."

He smoothed his hand over her hair and hugged her back gently, a sense of closure he hadn't known he was missing easing over him. Seth grinned. "Now, get back home and give Allen his answer."

Releasing him, she stepped away and wiped her eyes, then started jogging toward her car. "I'm on my way."

And Madeline?

She paused and looked back, her hand on the driver's-side door of her car.

"Be happy, okay?"

She smiled. "I will."

From the tidy stacks of bills spread out over Mae Bell's fancy lace tablecloth, Blue Moon Haven Drive-In's first fundraiser had been a success. But Kelly worried it hadn't been quite successful enough.

"One thousand eight hundred, one thousand nine

hundred, two thousand," Mae Bell said, counting the last bill in her hand and placing it on the stack in front of her on the table. She glanced up at Kelly, a hopeful expression on her face. "Do we have enough?"

Kelly sighed. "Mr. Haggart? How much do you have in your stack?"

Mr. Haggart, seated in his wheelchair beside Mae Bell, held up one hand, which still clutched a few bills, while he continued counting with his other hand. His mouth moved with each placement of a new bill on the stack until he finally reached the end.

"Nine hundred, seventy-six dollars and thirty-five cents." Mr. Haggart slumped back in his wheelchair, blinking heavily. "Where's that put ya?"

Kelly leaned over the table, pulled out the paper she'd used to track funds and added up the total. Straightening, she shook her head. "Not close enough. Even adding this to what's left in Mae Bell's expense budget, it's not enough to cover the new digital projector. We'd need at least four thousand more dollars to cover the purchase."

Mae Bell's hopeful expression fell, and she looked around the field, slowly taking in the leftover remnants of the fundraiser, which had ended an hour ago.

Kelly rubbed the knot that had formed in the back of her neck and glanced around, too, estimating how long it would take to clean up. Soda cans, candy wrappers and paper cones that had once held cotton candy littered the freshly cut field, streamers and pieces of model airplanes that had either crashed or fallen apart were strewn along the property line between the drive-in and Seth's orchard. And there was no telling how much elbow grease the restroom in the concessions building would need after dozens of people had trekked in and out of it from the field. Everything was peaceful and quiet again now, with Todd and Daisy picking up trash, along with a few guests who'd stayed behind to help. Mae Bell and Mr. Haggart remained at the table Seth had set up for them, helping Kelly count the money the event had made.

An hour earlier, after the model airplane contest, Blue Moon Haven Drive-In's grounds had been bustling with activity. The crowd had parted, some families grouping around the winners of the contest to congratulate them, while others revisited the stands that formed a circle around the field to browse arts and crafts, bargain over homemade quilts and afghans, and buy one last treat from Tully's candy stand. Then the visitors had eventually all walked to their cars and left the drive-in, taking flyers, which announced the grand opening next Saturday, which Todd handed to them through the open windows of their vehicles as they left the lot.

Only the prospect of holding a grand opening next weekend without the benefit of an additional digital projector was an outcome Kelly had been hoping to avoid.

"We could do just fine without the second projector, though," Mae Bell said, patting the table nervously. "Couldn't we?"

"We could," Kelly said. "But having only one screening at a time would cut our profits in half, and we need all the profit we can get to purchase rights to new films."

"But there's still an original projector in the other projection booth," Mae Bell said. "Why can't we use that? Show an older film?"

"It's a great idea, but I don't think it'd draw the crowd we need right now." Kelly shook her head. "The best use of the vintage films we have is to arrange a theme night and attract targeted audiences from a greater distance. Screening newer movies will have the best immediate impact financially."

Mae Bell grew quiet for a few minutes, the only sounds the chatter of a couple guests across the field and Todd and Daisy's laughter as they played around, tossing trash into a garbage bag as though they were shooting hoops of basketball.

"How long would we be able to stay open with only one digital projector in use?" Mae Bell asked.

Kelly looked down and picked at the hem of her T-shirt. "I don't know. It's hard to tell. A month. Maybe two?" She glanced at Mae Bell, the sad look in the older woman's eyes making her wince. "I promise I'll do everything I can to keep Blue Moon Haven open, Mae Bell."

Footsteps fell across the grass at their backs and soon Clark and his father, Brighton, walked up, smiling.

"We're headed out," Clark said. "But I wanted to thank you and Seth for inviting me to judge the model airplane contest today. I haven't had that much fun in a while. Seeing those kids discover a love for aviation made it that much more enjoyable."

"And spending time with you," Brighton said, gently lifting Mae Bell's hand and kissing the back of it, "is always a joy."

Mae Bell's smile returned. "You always were a flirt, Brighton." She tossed her long hair over her shoulder and winked. "But a welcome flirt."

"I'll see you at the grand opening." Brighton patted Clark's shoulder. "My son here has promised to come out with me and enjoy his first movie at a drive-in."

"We'd be thrilled for you to join us." The pep faded from Mae Bell's tone. "It's a good thing you're coming early, though, because we're not sure how many showings we'll be able to manage before we'll have to close Blue Moon Haven Drive-In for good."

Brighton frowned. "I thought the fundraiser went

well. A lot of people showed, and it seemed as though items were selling right and left from the stands."

Kelly nodded. "Yes, and we're grateful for every person and every penny. Thing is, it just wasn't quite enough. We need a second digital projector to make enough profit to keep the drive-in running on a regular basis, and we didn't make enough."

"How much are you lacking?" Brighton asked.

Kelly picked up the paper she'd used to add figures and showed it to Brighton and Clark.

"Mmm." Brighton pursed his lips. "That's a hefty chunk. Who're you buying the projector from?"

"A friend of Mae Bell's." Kelly returned the paper to the table as she relayed the man's name. "He's giving us a great discount, but we're still short."

Brighton glanced at Mae Bell, then nodded. "Well, we'll be hoping for the best for you." He cast one last smile at Mae Bell. "And we'll definitely be here opening night."

With one more goodbye, Clark and Brighton walked across the field to their truck.

Kelly watched them leave, then glanced up at the sky, noting the sunlight had begun to fade. "Well," she said, glancing at Mae Bell and Mr. Haggart, "it's time we pack this money up and get you two back. I promised Nurse Powell I'd have you inside your room by sunset."

Mae Bell sighed. "I hate to go back, but this has been a lovely day. The best I've had in years." She smiled, her eyes glistening. "Thank you, Kelly."

Kelly smiled, her voice catching at the gratitude in Mae Bell's eyes. "You're welcome."

"Yep," Mr. Haggart said, grinning. "You can't beat a sunny day of cold root beer, friends and freedom."

They packed up the money, and Kelly called Todd and Daisy over, instructing them to help her get Mae

Bell and Mr. Haggart back in the truck. Once everyone was loaded up, and Mr. Haggart had the last root beer out of the bucket in his hand, Kelly cranked the engine and pulled out. She glanced in the rearview mirror at the trees in the distance, hoping for a glimpse of Seth.

After he'd left with his ex-wife over an hour ago, she hadn't seen or heard from him. Several times, Todd and Daisy had asked when he was returning, but she hadn't had an answer for them. And, with each passing minute, she'd begun to grow more impatient at his absence as well.

Not that she was worried, she assured herself as she drove toward the Blue Moon city limits. Seth was a good man. An honest man. And though he hadn't spoken of his ex-wife but once, she hadn't picked up on any lingering tension or unrequited feelings on his part.

Her stomach sank at the thought, and she gripped the steering wheel tighter as she turned into the parking lot of Silver Stay nursing home. What if she'd misread Seth? What if, that night on the porch, he hadn't been just grieving over the loss of his daughter? What if he'd been grieving over the loss of his wife, too?

"You're picking us up again next Saturday for the grand opening, right?"

Kelly blinked and faced Mr. Haggart, who sat in the passenger seat. An excited look gleamed in his eye. "Of course, Mr. Haggart." She motioned toward the windshield where, outside, the sun was just beginning to dip below the horizon. "I got you and Mae Bell back safely before sundown, so I'm fairly certain I can talk Nurse Powell into letting you attend the grand opening. And maybe she'd even like to attend, too."

"I hope so," Mae Bell said from the backseat of the truck's cab. "We'll need every ticket sale we can get." She reached up and squeezed Kelly's shoulder. "You've done a great job, Kelly."

Kelly met her eyes in the rearview mirror, saying quietly, "Maybe not great enough, though."

Mae Bell patted her shoulder once, then let go. "You've done your best to help me make my dream a reality. Nothing will ever change that."

Kelly hoped so. She really did. But without the new projector or a healthy infusion of cash, neither of which the grand opening would produce, Mae Bell's dream would fall apart even quicker than it had the first time around.

After helping Mr. Haggart and Mae Bell to their rooms, Kelly drove back to the drive-in and Todd regaled her and Daisy with details of the model airplane contest. His excitement was infectious and Daisy was all smiles, giggling at the sound effects Todd made as he described the movement of the planes and the sounds of their battery-powered motors.

"You think we can have another contest?" Todd asked from the passenger seat as they drew closer to the drive-in.

Kelly couldn't quite meet his eyes. Instead, she kept her gaze pinned firmly on the road ahead, watching the headlights of Seth's truck illuminate the grassy ditches and sprawling fields on both sides of the road. Night had fallen and she was grateful for the dim interior of the truck's cab that helped hide her expression.

"I don't know, Todd." More than likely not, she thought. Without utilizing both screens, the profits from each screening wouldn't be enough to float the drive-in for long, but she couldn't tell him that now. Not when she'd promised both him and Daisy so much. "We need to focus on opening night right now. We only have one week to prepare, and you and Daisy go back to school Monday, so we'll be very busy between now and then trying to drum up attendance and give the best show we possibly can."

Even in the dark cab, she could feel his gaze on her, picking apart her words and tone.

"You're afraid we won't make enough to stay open, aren't you?" he asked.

She bit her lip, slowing the truck as they reached the entrance to the drive-in. "I didn't say that, Todd."

"You didn't have to." He sat back in his seat and fell silent, his tone heavy with skepticism and disappointment.

"Seth!"

Kelly smiled at Daisy's shout and glanced in the rearview mirror. Daisy, seated in the backseat of the truck's cab, pointed between the front seats toward the windshield and bounced in her seat with excitement.

Sure enough, Seth was back. He'd turned on all of the outdoor lights on the projection booths and concessions building and had put the headlights of her car on, pointing them toward the table he'd set up on the back edge of the field by the Moon Garden. A large plastic box was on the table and he was packing away the plates, cups and what was left of the snacks Mae Bell and Mr. Haggart had left behind. Hearing the rumble of the engine approach, he turned and waved, smiling as Kelly parked the truck nearby.

Todd hopped out of the truck and jogged over to Seth, talking a mile a minute. Kelly helped Daisy out of her booster seat and joined him.

". . . you see how it beat everyone?" Todd was asking Seth. "She was awesome!"

"Who're we talking about?" Kelly asked, smiling as Daisy skipped past her and hugged Seth's leg.

"Annie," Seth said, returning Daisy's hug and smiling. "The girl who won first place. According to Todd, she has mad skills when it comes to building model planes."

"She's amazing." Todd's hands moved as he talked, gesturing through the air. "It was unbelievable what her plane could do. It spun, it dipped, it surged." He smiled wide. "It was perfect."

Seth grinned. "Sounds like you're a pretty big fan of Annie's."

Todd blushed.

"Nothing wrong with that," Seth said, ruffling Todd's hair. "It's great meeting new people and making friends."

Todd's cheeks darkened to a deeper red. He stuck his hands in his pockets and grinned. "I got her number. She got mine, too. Said she'd call me tonight and tell me how she made her plane. Give me a few tips for how to make mine better." He glanced at Kelly. "You think it'd be okay if I invited her over one day after school?"

Kelly smiled, catching Seth's eye as she murmured under her breath, "And so it begins." She nodded at Todd. "I think we can arrange that. But let's wait until after the grand opening, okay? We need to put all our energy into setting things up for a successful night."

"Okay." Todd looked up at Seth. "Want us to help pack this stuff up?"

"Nah, I think you and Daisy have earned a rest." Seth gestured toward the grassy field, now clear of trash and debris. "You two did a great job cleaning up after the fundraiser."

"I second that." Kelly held out her hand for Daisy, and when she walked over, she gave Daisy a hug. "Why don't you two go inside the trailer, take turns having a shower and settle in? I'll get something ready for you to eat by the time you're done."

Daisy blinked her big brown eyes up at Kelly and smiled. "Can we have hot dogs?"

Kelly pursed her lips, then said, "I think that can be arranged."

Satisfied, Daisy skipped off toward the trailer, and when Todd ran past her, she joined him, racing inside.

"Wish I had their energy," Seth said, smiling.

"Don't we all?" Catching herself staring at his smile, Kelly walked over to the table, picked up a plastic freezer bag and started transferring leftover fruit from a dish into it.

"Todd's pretty proud of himself, as he should be." Seth joined her, picked up the large metal bucket that had held Mr. Haggart's root beers and dumped out water and what was left of the ice. "He worked hard on his plane, took missing first place in stride and was more than cordial to the first-place winner."

Kelly kept her eyes focused on her task, lifted the plate she'd emptied of the fruit and shook excess water off it before placing it in the large box on top of the table. "He did a wonderful job, but I think the change in his attitude and perception of others is due to your influence on him. His temperament has improved dramatically since the two of you began spending more time together."

"He's still a bit standoffish and doesn't talk about his feelings very easily, if at all." His strong hands stilled in the act of picking up a glass, but his thumb tapped the edge of a plate he held. "He has a sharp mind and compassionate nature, but keeps most people at arm's length."

Kelly grabbed a napkin and wiped a few crumbs off Mae Bell's lace tablecloth.

"He behaves very similarly to someone else I know," he continued. "There's a million and one questions going on inside that beautiful mind of his, but he just won't open up."

Kelly stopped wiping, leaned heavily on the table and faced him across it. "What do you want to know, Seth?"

He eyed her silently for a moment, then leaned onto the table, too, lining his body up to hers and bringing his face closer. "I want to know what you're thinking. What you're feeling."

"About what?"

He frowned. "About why I was gone as long as I was. About what Madeline and I talked about. Or whatever else you think might be going on between me and my ex-wife. I think any one of those places is a good starting point."

Her arms shook and her palms grew hot against the table, but she licked her lips and forced herself to speak. "Okay. So, why were you gone so long?"

"Madeline had some worries and wanted to talk," he said softly. "She and I were best friends before we were ever married, and I imagine she thought of me when she wanted honest advice from an old friend."

"A *friend*?" She flexed her hands, rubbing her fingertips against the intricate lace of the tablecloth. "Is that all?"

"That's all. Madeline may have been the one to file for divorce, but we both knew our marriage had ended."

Kelly sagged, surprised at the depth of relief settling over her. "And . . . what did she want to talk about? If you don't mind my asking?"

He came around the table to stand beside her. "I keep no secrets from you, Kelly. You can always ask anything of me." His head dipped, his green eyes seeking hers, the warmth in them making her breath catch. "She's been proposed to, but wasn't sure she was ready to start over yet. Or rather, she felt too guilty to start over."

"Guilty about what?"

"About losing Rachel. And about leaving me."

Kelly closed her eyes briefly, then forced herself to face him head-on. "Does she want to come back?"

"No." He leaned closer, and she could smell the spicy scent of his cologne, feel his soft breath against her cheek. "She wanted to let go and move on."

"And . . . did she?"

"Yes." His hand moved, lifting to cup her cheek. His palm was warm and firm against her skin. "Just like I want to move on with you."

Her mouth parted and she found herself leaning forward another inch, wanting to feel him close again. Wanting his arms around her, his broad chest beneath her temple. Wanting to find safety and support in his arms.

"With me?" she managed to ask.

"Yes." His other hand lifted, cupping her face, tipping up her chin and bringing her eyes back to his. "I love you, Kelly."

Her breath caught, a rush of emotion surging to her chest, filling her heart to the point of overflowing. "Y-you love me?"

He brought his mouth to hers, his warm lips brushing hers, parting them as he whispered again, "I love you, Kelly."

Her eyes fluttered shut as he kissed her, his callused thumbs gliding gently along her cheekbones, his long eyelashes tickling her cheek, the taste of him—comforting, tender and passionate, all in one—overwhelming her senses.

She wove her fingers through his thick hair and cupped the back of his head, drawing him closer, kissing him deeper. Her blood rushed and her limbs grew heavy, urging her to press more heavily against him, seeking the heat of his strong chest. He lifted his mouth, pulling in a strong breath, and she tilted her head, inviting his mouth to move along her neck, his warm lips sending delicious shivers over every inch of her skin.

Her mouth moved as well, forming words she barely caught before they escaped her lips. "I . . . I love—"

Kelly's eyes sprang open, her chest lifting on a ragged inhale as his mouth trailed kisses along her collarbone and lower, into the vee of her T-shirt.

"I . . . Seth, wait."

He stopped immediately, allowing her hands to cradle his head and tug him away from her chest. Breathing heavily, he stepped back and straightened, taking her hands gently in his. "What's wrong?"

"I . . ." She licked her lips, the taste of him hitting her tongue, sending a fresh wave of heat through her. "I can't do this now. We can't start something with each other that I . . . that we might not be able to end well."

He dragged his teeth over his bottom lip and drew in a few more ragged breaths before focusing on her eyes. "What do you mean?" He blinked, confusion clouding his gaze. "I'm talking about beginning. A new beginning. For us, for the kids."

"It's the kids I'm thinking about." Squeezing his hands once more, she tugged hers from his hold, straightened her shirt and picked up a glass from the table. "I'm already risking too much as it is. The way things are headed, Mae Bell and I will have to close the drivein within a month or two if we're unable to pull in the profit we need to keep it afloat, and I just don't see us staying open, with the limited resources we have right now."

Seth watched her closely, his eyes studying her face, then following her hands as they placed the glass in the box and reached for another. "That's a financial concern. I'm talking about your heart."

"Everything I do has to be in Todd and Daisy's best interest."

"I love Todd and Daisy, too, and I know how much

they mean to you. I would never have approached you if I didn't plan on—"

"It's not a matter of planning."

"Then what is this abo—"

"It's a matter of what you don't see coming."

He stiffened. "What do you mean?"

She closed her eyes, willing back hot tears. "I mean, what makes this time different? How do we know this will work out between us? That we'll manage to make things work and that it won't fall apart down the road? What will happen to Todd and Daisy? They've already lost two parents once before. I don't want to risk them losing out again."

Seth sighed, the sound harsh and ragged in the night air. "You won't lose me." He reached out, slid one hand beneath her long hair and kneaded her nape gently. "That's what I'm trying to tell you. I'm here to stay. I want to be here for you and the kids forever. I love y—"

"But that's what you told her, too, isn't it?" A sob burst from Kelly's lips, and she threw her arms around him and pulled him close, burying her face against his neck to avoid the pained look in his eyes. "I'm sorry, Seth. I'm so sorry to say any of this, but you asked how I felt and what I was thinking and this is it." His big hands settled on her back, his fingers splaying against her, and she closed her eyes and held him closer. "I used to think happy endings were always there—just within reach. That you just had to believe, want them and work hard enough for them, but that's not the case. Things can fall apart at any time, no matter how well you think they're going. We—Todd and Daisy—could lose everything in just a moment. They've already lost everything."

"Kelly . . ." His hands smoothed her hair back and his lips brushed her temple. "I wish I could assure you that we'd never run into trouble. That things will always be perfect between us, but I know that's not a reality. We'll argue, have disagreements, different needs at different times. And other times, we'll be happier than we ever imagined possible. All that and more is unavoidable—expected even." He nuzzled his cheek against her hair. "I can't give you an answer that will ease your fears or your worries, but I can tell you—without a shred of hesitation or doubt—that a life with you, Todd and Daisy is what I want." A low sound of frustration left him. "No . . . it's what I need."

He raised his head, gripped her shoulders and eased her back, then nudged her chin up, waiting until her eyes met his. "I love you. I will always love you, no matter what we face. I know that deep in my soul—unfortunately, there's no way for me to prove it to you in the way you're asking. I can't give you a perfect future. I can only swear to you that I'll do everything I can to make each day the best either of us—or the kids—ever had."

She swallowed past the tight knot in her throat and wiped her eyes. "I . . . I wish things were different, but they're not. I can't take this risk with you right now. I can't risk losing you and hurting Todd and Daisy." Heart breaking, she squeezed his shoulders, her fingers moving over the curves of his biceps, forearms and hands, memorizing every detail of his solid strength beneath her hands. "I'd rather have you forever as a friend than risk losing you as something more."

Seth's jaw hardened. "What I feel for you is so much more than that." He searched her eyes, looked down at their entwined hands, then withdrew his touch and stepped back. "I don't want to just be your friend, Kelly." His mouth twisted, a rueful smile appearing as he met her eyes again. "I want to be your everything. And I'm not giving up on you. Or us."

CHAPTER 13

Seth steadied himself on the top rung of his nine-foot ladder and strung a strand of outdoor solar lights along the limb of a tree on the property line between his orchard and the Blue Moon Haven Drive-In lot.

"There." He studied his handiwork, then glanced down where Patch sat on the ground beside the ladder, panting up at him. "How's it look? Festive?"

Patch barked and wagged his tail.

He smiled. "I'll take that as a yes." And he hoped Kelly and the kids would be just as excited when they arrived home from school and saw it, too.

Inhaling, he savored the fresh spring air as he glanced about the grounds. Last weekend, after confessing his feelings for Kelly, he'd returned to his house, surprised and disappointed. He'd been caught off guard by Kelly's feelings, though he did take comfort in what he guessed might have almost been an admission of love as well. Or at least he hoped so. He was sure he'd seen it in her eyes, and even more sure that he'd felt it in her kiss.

His blood rushed at the memory of her lips against

his, her arms around him and her fingers moving through his hair. Even his skull had tingled at her touch, his whole body buzzing and throbbing as though it had suddenly been brought to life by her attention. He'd never felt emotions so strongly before—not even with Madeline. But unfortunately, while the intensity of what he and Kelly shared revived and energized him, it seemed to have the opposite effect on her. Where he saw passion, happiness and a thrilling future, she saw only the potential for mistakes, regrets and endings.

Frowning, he climbed back down the ladder, knelt beside Patch and rubbed his ears. He could understand her hesitation, especially considering the financial instability of the drive-in and the recent turmoil Todd and Daisy had endured, losing both parents. But what he couldn't resolve was how to find a way to prove to Kelly that there could be a happy ending for all of them. He'd been prepared for a lot of different scenarios when he had decided to tell her he loved her, the worst being that she might not reciprocate his feelings. But instead, he'd been faced with a different and more intimidating problem: how to entice her into taking a chance.

"Come on, bud." He stood and clucked his tongue for Patch to follow him. "We need to haul that load of wood over here so it'll be ready for the kids when they get home."

Another surprise he hoped Todd and Daisy would enjoy . . . and that Kelly would appreciate. Given that he'd spent the past several days trying and failing to get Kelly to see his side of things and take a chance on a relationship with him, he'd decided to up the ante, show her how all in he actually was. He could only hope it'd be enough to prove to her, in some small way, that he was intent upon moving forward and starting fresh with her and the kids.

One hour later, Seth was unloading the last of several four-by-four posts from the bed of his truck when Kelly's car drove through the entrance of the drive-in and parked near the trailer. The doors opened and Todd and Daisy sprang out of the car and ran over, dropping their book bags on the ground along the way.

"Hey!" Kelly waved her arms and shouted after them, stopping to pick up their bags as she followed in their wake. "This isn't where your book bags go, guys."

"What you got all that for?" Todd, out of breath, drew to a stop beside one stack of lumber and nudged it with his foot. "You building something?"

Seth smiled as he hefted a concrete block from the bed of his truck. "Yep."

"Whatcha building?" asked Daisy, her cheeks pink.

"A surprise." Seth set the concrete block on the ground and grabbed another, placing it near the first. "Take a look at the blueprints." He jerked his chin toward his truck. "See if you can figure out what it is."

Eyes bright with excitement, Todd and Daisy shot over to the truck, searching the empty bed, rummaging around in the toolbox, then climbing into the cab to finally find the blueprints he'd left on the front seat.

"What's all this?" Kelly, arms holding the kids' bags, stopped by one of the concrete blocks and frowned. "You starting a new beehive or something?"

He grinned. "Nope."

"It's a house!" Todd shouted, jogging over with Daisy, blueprints in hand. "You're building another house?"

Seth narrowed his eyes, "You're close . . . but not quite correct."

Daisy stared at the lumber on the ground, then studied Seth, her gaze moving over his shoulder to the tall tree behind him. A bright smile appeared. "For the tree!" She bounced up and down, glancing at Todd. "He's making a house for the tree."

Laughing, Seth walked over, lifted her up and kissed her forehead, then set her back down on her feet. "You got it, sweetheart." He stepped back and swept his arm toward the tree behind him. "Right here. We're gonna build the fanciest-schmanciest tree house your beautiful eyes have ever seen."

Daisy clasped her hands in front of her and twisted from side to side, her cheeks blushing. "I never seen one before."

"Well, you will today." Seth held his hand out toward Todd. "Why don't we let Kelly take a look and see what she thinks." When he had the blueprints in hand, he turned to Kelly and offered them to her. "Your approval is required before we proceed. Nothing's set in stone, and everything I've unloaded can be reloaded and taken back to the hardware store today if you're not happy with the plan."

Todd groaned. "Aw, come o—"

Seth held a finger to his lips and raised one eyebrow, whispering, "She hasn't given an answer yet. Give her a chance to look at the blueprints."

Kelly studied the blueprints in her hand, then glanced at the lumber and tools spread out on the ground by his side. She frowned and walked closer. "Which tree are you planning to build this on?"

He pointed to the tree at his back. "This one."

Her eyes followed the direction he indicated, her frown deepening. "But that's Rachel's tree," she whispered.

"I know." Meeting her eyes, Seth lifted his hand, hesitating briefly, then tucked an errant strand of hair behind her ear. "But now it belongs to Daisy and Todd. It can serve as their own private viewing balcony on opening night." He grinned and gestured toward the lights he'd strung between the trees along the property line between his orchard and Mae Bell's field. "They all do. They belong to all of us."

Her eyes widened and her lips trembled as she examined the strands of lights draped elegantly along the property line. "Solar lights?" She glanced around. "You strung them up?"

"I surrounded the place with them. Even tacked them along the edges of the projection booths and concessions building, and I plan on adding more to the entrance if you like them." He held up a hand. "I did check first. They won't interfere with the film screenings or the projection booths. The lights provide a glow more than anything. I thought it'd complement the Moon Garden, and the flowers should be in bloom by opening night. I'm hoping it'll add just the right ambience to create a bit of magic in the atmosphere."

Kelly swiveled in a circle slowly, taking it all in, then watched Todd and Daisy as they explored the lumber and tools, chatting to each other, their tones full of happy anticipation. She faced him again. "Yeah," she said softly, her gaze roving over his face. "I think it will."

Seth touched her cheek, his fingers lingering on her smooth skin. "Are you sure?"

A hesitant smile moved her lips as she said, "We'll give it a try."

Three hours later, Seth, along with help from Kelly and the kids, had built the foundation using four-by-four posts and concrete blocks to ensure safety. Next they worked on building the platform, attaching the floor joists to the tree. Then Seth and Kelly used his miter saw to cut four-by-four posts into angle braces for stability. Daisy and Todd covered their ears as Seth and Kelly worked, jumping and skipping around nearby trees in excitement as the initial steps of the vision drawn in the blueprints began to materialize in front of their eyes.

"How much longer?" Todd asked when Seth finished cutting the last four-by-four post. "Will it be ready by opening night on Saturday?"

Seth wiped his sweaty brow with the back of his hand and smiled. "With luck, it will be." He glanced at the sun, noting how low it had slipped as he and Kelly had worked. "Today's Thursday, and we should be able to squeeze in attaching the deck boards to the platform today. We'll knock off when it gets dark, and Kelly and I will start again in the morning while you're at school. If all goes well, by the time you get home, it should be ready to go. Only thing left would be to stain or paint it—if you and Daisy decide to. But you should be able to sit in it on opening night to watch the movie if you'd like."

"Can I bring Cassie, too?" Daisy asked.

Seth glanced at Kelly in question.

"Her doll," Kelly clarified, smiling. "Cassie has lost her pants, two toes and one eyebrow, but she's still a great playmate."

Seth laughed. "Ah, I see. I've noticed her lugging it around a lot but had never been formally introduced."

Kelly laughed, too.

He smiled wider, grateful to see Kelly happy again, and unable to stop glancing at her as he worked. She'd worked as hard as, if not harder, than he had building the foundation and deck of the tree house, but hadn't complained a single time. Over the duration of the afternoon, the sun had tanned her bare arms and neck, cast a pink hue along her cheekbones and sprinkled freckles over the bridge of her nose. Her hair was damp, clinging to her jaw and neck, but in Seth's opinion, she looked more beautiful than she ever had before.

"This is the best exercise I've had in a long time," she

said, helping him attach a two-foot angle brace to the foundation with a three-inch nail.

"I agree with you there." Seth hammered the nail home, checked that it was secure, then grabbed another angle brace. "Do you feel like tackling the deck boards today? If you're getting tired, we can knock off early. I think we'll still have time to finish by the time Todd and Daisy get home from school tomorrow."

"No, I'm good." She held the angle brace in place as he hammered, and when he finished, she said softly, "I do have one question, though."

Seth grabbed a towel Kelly had brought out earlier and wiped the sweat from the back of his neck. "Shoot."

"How much did these materials cost you?" A worried expression crossed her face. "I know it wasn't cheap and I'd like to pitch in at least—"

"Uh-uh." Seth held up a hand. "This was my idea and my treat. No need to pitch in anything but your time." He grinned. "And time with you is worth more to me than any amount of money."

Kelly rolled her eyes and hit his shoulder playfully. "What a charmer you are. That's the smoothest line I've heard in months."

He winked. "You know it, baby."

Laughing, she gave him another playful shove, then grabbed another angle brace.

They continued to work for the next hour, attaching the last angle brace, then connecting the deck boards to the platform and attaching it around the tree. Soon the foundation and deck were complete, sturdy and ready for occupants.

Todd was the first one to hop onto the platform. He climbed the ladder, jumped onto the deck with both feet, tipped his head back and spread his arms wide. "Woo-hoo! It's awesome, Seth."

"Well, wait until we get the walls and roof on," Seth said. "You'll really be impressed then."

"I want to try, too," Daisy said, reaching up her arms to Kelly.

"We'll all have a go." Kelly slid her hands under Daisy's arms and lifted her up onto the ladder, then helped her climb up to the platform. "Don't let her fall, Todd. There aren't any railings for her to hold on to yet." She placed her own foot on the bottom rung of the ladder and looked back at Seth. "Is it safe for all of us, do you think?"

"Of course." Smiling, Seth walked over, grabbed her waist and hoisted her up to the top rung of the ladder. "It'll hold us all easily."

Kelly squealed, flailing her arms until they settled on the platform. Then Todd, laughing, grabbed one of her hands while Daisy grabbed the other and they pulled her the rest of the way up. Soon she was standing beside Todd and Daisy, spreading her arms wide and shouting into the orchard as well, laughing as her voice echoed back along with Todd's and Daisy's.

"Get up here, Seth." Kelly bent over the ladder and held out her hand. "Take a moment to enjoy your hard work with us."

Now, that was an offer he couldn't refuse. Smiling, Seth took Kelly's hand and tugged gently, pulling himself to the top rung of the ladder and mounting the platform so that he could stand beside Kelly. He rocked on his heels for a few minutes in each direction, testing the stability of the structure, and found it sturdy and solid.

"We did a darn good job, if I do say so myself," he said, smiling at Kelly.

"Yeah." She stopped, her mouth parting as she studied his face, then said, "We did."

We. He never knew one word could feel so precious, but there it was. His heart turned right over in his chest, hearing it on Kelly's lips. To his surprise, she moved closer, slipped her arm around his waist and pressed her cheek to his chest. He lifted his arm and placed it around her shoulders, hugging her close.

"Cassie'll love it," Daisy said, edging her way in-between Kelly and Seth and hugging his leg.

"I bet this would be a great control tower for flying our planes," Todd said, standing beside Seth and nudging him with his elbow. "What d'ya think?"

A smile spread across Seth's face as he wrapped his arm around Todd's shoulders, hugged him, then ruffled his hair. "I think that'd be perfect." His throat was so constricted with emotion, he could hardly speak. It'd been years since he'd felt the sense of pride that came from being a father. From making a child happy. Tenderness washed over him in waves as he glanced down at Kelly and met her brown eyes. The sight of her, Todd and Daisy, happy and close, felt like . . . family. "Just perfect."

An engine rumbled at their backs and Seth released Todd to swivel around and glance behind him. A truck rumbled through the entrance of the drive-in, then drove slowly across the field, stopping in front of the trailer. The door opened and a man got out. He stood in front of the trailer, staring for a moment, then turned and, shielding his eyes, looked over at where they stood on the tree house platform.

Seth squeezed Kelly's shoulder. "You've got company."

She lifted her head from his chest and looked over his shoulder. Some of the color left her cheeks, a paleness taking its place.

"Who is it?" he asked.

Her mouth opened, then closed soundlessly before she managed to speak. "Zane," she whispered. "It's Todd and Daisy's dad."

Kelly watched, frozen in place, as Todd scrambled down the ladder of the tree house platform and hit the ground running toward the truck parked outside of the trailer.

"Dad!" Grass kicked up behind his tennis shoes as he raced across the field. "You came!"

Zane, standing beside his truck, waved, then knelt with his arms spread open as Todd approached. He rocked back on his heels as Todd thrust himself into his arms, hugging him tightly.

"Did you know he was coming?"

The deep rumble of Seth's quiet voice sounded close by Kelly's ear. She shook her head. "No," she said through stiff lips. "I've been unable to reach him for months. I didn't even know he knew where we were. Unless . . ." Her mind raced, her heart pounding faster as possible reasons for Zane's visit tangled her thoughts, each one more frightening—and potentially painful—than the one before. "He must have called the lawyer who dealt with our guardianship. What if he . . . ?"

"Kelly?" Daisy tugged at the hem of her T-shirt, her big brown eyes widening as she stared up, her chin trembling. "Why's Daddy here? Will he stay, too?"

Despite her disdain for the way Zane had abandoned Todd and Daisy, Kelly couldn't help but feel a wave of empathy, and a speck of hope she hadn't thought she harbored. Had Zane possibly been thinking of—and missing—his kids?

"I don't know why your daddy's here, baby." She smoothed her hand over Daisy's wind-tousled hair and forced a smile. "If I had to guess, I'd say he's missed you and Todd very much and wants to see you." She hesitated at the surprise in Daisy's eyes. "Would you like to go over and tell him hello?"

Daisy's brow creased as she thought it over, her gaze moving across the field to where Zane, now standing, smiled down at Todd, who spoke rapidly, his hands moving in big gestures in the air. "Will you go with me?"

Kelly held out her hand. "Of course."

"Okay," she said softly.

"Come here, sweet Daisy," Seth said.

Having climbed down the ladder, Seth stood on the ground and held up his arms to help Daisy down from the platform of the tree house. She walked across the platform into his arms and waited patiently for Kelly to join her.

Kelly paused at the top of the ladder, putting her hand in Seth's and meeting his eyes. "Why would he show up now?" she whispered. "After all this time?"

Expression blank, he shook his head and whispered back, "We won't know until we talk to him." He smiled, but it looked just as empty as the one she'd offered Daisy. "We'll find out soon enough."

Kelly accepted his help down from the platform and joined Daisy as they made their way slowly across the field. She held Daisy's hand tightly while they walked, smiling when Daisy glanced up, her eyes filled with a mixture of excitement and uncertainty. Kelly glanced back as they drew nearer to Todd and Zane, her eyes drawn to the tree house platform where, just minutes before, she, Seth, Todd and Daisy had stood, grouped tightly together, overlooking the orchard and drive-in. The comfort, hope and closeness she'd felt in that moment had driven her back into Seth's arms and she'd felt, for the first time in years, as though she'd finally found home.

She faced forward again, her steps faltering slightly as she refocused on Zane. Why, after all this time without a word, had he returned out of the blue? What was his motive? She clutched Daisy's hand tighter as Zane tore his attention away from Todd and smiled at Daisy.

"There's my Daisy." Zane, tall and fit, looking healthier than he had when Kelly had last seen him several months ago, smiled that lopsided grin of his and spread his arms. "I've missed you guys."

Biting her lip, Daisy looked up at Kelly and raised her eyebrows.

"It's okay," Kelly said, forcing another smile.

Confusion receding slightly, Daisy released Kelly's hand and ran over to Zane, hugging him tightly as he closed his arms around her.

Kelly bit her lip, stifling a fresh surge of anger. It was for the best, she reminded herself, that Todd and Daisy have some sort of relationship with Zane. So long as he meant to see that relationship through and not disappear into thin air again with no thought to their emotional or physical well-being. But she couldn't avoid the resentment that surfaced at his surprise reappearance . . . or the need to shake some sense into him, both of which made her hands tremble.

". . . thought about you both so much," Zane was saying. "I've wondered how you guys were doing."

"Then why didn't you call?" The words left Kelly's lips before she could think better of them. "Or write? Or even leave a number where we could reach you?"

Zane frowned, confusion clouding his expression. "You could've contacted me at any time. I left my number with you."

Kelly scoffed. "No, you didn't. I even called your cousin to try to track you down, but he didn't know how to reach you."

Zane's mouth twisted. "You know I don't keep in

touch with him. I may move around a lot, but I always keep the same cell number, and I gave that to Todd on the day I left them with you."

Kelly glanced at Todd, who shoved his hands in his pockets and looked down, twisting the toe of his shoe against the grass. "Todd? Did you have Zane's number all this time and not give it to me?"

Todd's cheeks flushed and he nodded, but continued to stare at the ground.

Kelly spread her hands. "Why didn't you give it to me? Why didn't you tell me?"

He remained silent for a moment, then said softly, "I didn't want you to have it."

A sound of frustration burst from Kelly's lips. "Why?"

Todd looked up, a wounded look in his eyes as he met her gaze. "Because I wanted to stay in one place for a while instead of being bounced around again. And I was hoping you'd decide you wanted us for real—not just because you promised Mom you'd keep us. I just . . . I just wanted you to want us. You only took us because you had to—not because you loved us."

"'To want you'?" Kelly's vision blurred and she looked away, struggling to sift through the implications of his words. "You thought I—that I didn't want you? Didn't love you?" She faced Todd, whose face blanched at her expression, as she asked softly, "Is that what you still think?"

His mouth opened and closed soundlessly; then he looked back down at his feet, his chin trembling. "Yeah, I guess. We aren't yours. You said so yourself. You told Mrs. Mae Bell that when we first met her at the nursing home." He rubbed his eyes. "And you told anyone else who asked the same thing. You never planned on keeping us."

Daisy left Zane's arms and walked over to Kelly, taking her hand and whispering, "Please don't cry, Kelly. I don't think that."

Kelly blinked rapidly, clearing the tears from her eyes, her throat constricting so tightly she couldn't speak.

Seth cleared his throat and stepped forward, offering his hand to Zane. "I'm Seth Morgan."

"Zane Campbell." He shook Seth's hand, smiling tightly. "I'm Todd and Daisy's dad." He motioned toward the tree house in the distance. "That your handiwork?"

Seth nodded. "Mine, Kelly's and the kids'. Everyone pitched in."

Zane made a sound of agreement. "Guess that kind of project would take everyone's help."

Everyone working together. Like a family. Kelly turned away, brushing the tears from her eyes surreptitiously and swallowed hard. All this time, Todd had thought she hadn't truly cared for him and Daisy . . . and it was her own fault. She had been hesitant to commit herself fully to being a mom but not because she didn't love them . . . because she was afraid she wouldn't measure up. And here she'd done just that. She'd failed Todd by leading him to believe she didn't love him or want him. And Zane had arrived at the perfect moment to swoop in like a perfect parent and take over.

How could she have forgotten so easily? She should've known this wouldn't work out the way she'd hoped. If she'd learned anything from her time here in Blue Moon, it was that happy endings were much more difficult to come by than she'd once thought. And here she was, being tempted to believe things would fall in line seamlessly, Todd would trust and admire her, Daisy would be happy, the drive-in would thrive and they'd settle in with a good man who loved them.

She looked at Seth, a pang moving through her at the thought of losing what might have been. The dream of finally finding a home, a family and their own, albeit imperfect, happy ending.

"Daisy, Todd," Kelly said quietly. "Would you please go inside the trailer with Seth for a few minutes? I'd like to talk to Zane in private."

Todd looked up, his frown deepening. "But—"

"Please, Todd." Kelly tensed in anticipation of his refusal, but after holding her gaze for a few moments, he nodded and held his hand out to Daisy. "Come on, Daisy."

Kelly glanced at Seth. "Do you mind watching th—"

Seth held up his hand. "Not at all," he said softly. "Take your time."

Kelly waited until they had walked to the trailer and gone inside before facing Zane again. He returned her stare, his features so like Todd's.

"I'm sorry I didn't greet you better," she said quietly. "You turning up here today just caught me by surprise."

He dipped his head. "It's all right. I understand how you feel. You didn't know I'd given Todd a way for you to contact me." A wry smile twisted his lips. "He was angry at me for leaving him and Daisy and resented me for that. And I imagine he transferred some of that anger on to you, too. I always knew Todd was stubborn, but I didn't think he'd take it quite that far. In his defense, he . . ." His tone softened. "He was—and still is—grieving. I had no doubts that you loved him and Daisy both. That you'd take great care of them."

"Is that why you never called? Never visited? Never bothered to check on them?" She tried. She really did. But it was impossible to keep the bitterness out of her tone.

Zane grimaced and looked away. His profile—strong

jaw, aquiline nose and muscular physique—was just as clean-cut as it had been months ago. He'd always put extra time and effort into his appearance. If only he'd bestowed half as much of that attention on his own children. Though when it came to Laice, Kelly had to give him credit. He had loved Laice—to a fault almost. He'd showered her with affection, spent every free moment he had with her and cared for her more deeply than Kelly had ever thought him capable of feeling.

But that intensity of emotion had morphed into a curse of sorts when Laice had died. After her passing, Zane had become consumed with grief and had been unable to care for Todd and Daisy, much less acknowledge or address the pain they were wrestling with at the loss of their mother.

"I was going through a hard time, Kell—"

"Todd and Daisy were going through a hard time," she said, balling her fists by her sides. "Did you think about them while you were cruising away from my place, leaving your kids behind to—"

"You think I wanted to leave them? I never . . ." Zane's voice cracked, and he dragged his hand through his hair, mussing the carefully combed strands. "I love my kids, Kelly. Always have."

The slight sheen of tears in his eyes and conviction in his voice rocked her back on her heels. "I don't doubt that," she admitted quietly. In his own selfish way, Zane did love Daisy and Todd. "I just wish you could have set aside your own interests and taken care of theirs."

He lifted his chin, meeting her gaze head-on. "That's why I'm here now. I'm taking them with me. And judging from what Todd said earlier, I think I came at the right time. Todd knows who he belongs with."

Kelly's stomach sank. "Zane, please don't. They've

been with me for months. We've just settled into a routine and started feeling like . . . like . . ." *A family.* She winced. "Like things are looking up. For all of us."

"I appreciate all you've done, but Todd and Daisy are my children and—"

"Please."

His jaw clenched and his mouth thinned into a tight line. "They're not yours, Kelly. I know you wish they were, but they're not. They never have been."

She froze, her fists slowly unfurling at her sides and her heart slowly breaking. The phrase sounded offensive now and she couldn't believe she'd ever uttered the words in Todd's presence before. Todd had every right to be angry with her for insisting he and Daisy didn't belong to her and not helping them feel secure with her. For not reassuring them every day that she loved and wanted them both.

For once, Zane was right . . . and there was nothing she could say.

CHAPTER 14

"How much longer are they gonna be out there?" Seth joined Todd by the front window of the trailer and peered out, watching as Zane spoke and Kelly's face turned pale. "I don't know," he murmured. "I expect they have a lot to talk about."

Todd frowned. "But they've been out there forever."

Daisy, seated on the sofa in the living area a few feet away, hugged her legs to her chest and rested her chin on her knees. "Is Daddy gonna stay here with us?"

Todd glanced back at her, a conflicting mixture of hope and fear in his expression. "Probably not. I bet he came here for us. He wants us back."

"Todd." Seth squeezed his shoulder. "Let's not jump to conclusions." Though thinking back to what Kelly had shared with him as they'd lain on the freshly cut field those weeks ago, he was certain that Kelly, as secondary guardian, had little say in whatever Zane decided to do about Todd and Daisy's custody. "I'm sure that soon enough your dad will explain his reasons for coming. He's already said he missed both of you very much. I'm sure that was his primary reason for coming."

Todd lifted his chin. "He wants us."

Seth smiled and cupped the back of his head in a comforting gesture. "I know."

"I don't want to go with him." Daisy curled her arms tighter around her legs. "I don't want to leave here."

"Well, you'll just have to," Todd snapped.

"No, I won't! I want to stay with Kelly." Daisy scowled. "I won't go."

"You will if Dad says so," Todd said, his voice shaking. "Kelly's not our mom. She doesn't have any say, and if Dad says we're gonna go, we'll go."

"Nah-ah. I don't have to go if I don't want t—"

"Yes, you will." Todd's tone turned hard. "You don't have a choi—"

"I won't!" Sobbing, Daisy sprang off the sofa, ran over to Seth and threw her arms around his leg. "Tell him I won't go, Seth. Tell him!"

Seth immediately drew her close and smoothed his hand over her soft hair, his heart aching. "Todd," he said quietly. "I think it's better that we not discuss this now, okay? There's no need to upset Daisy any more than she already is." He glanced down, waiting until Todd looked up and met his eyes. "You think you can grab a couple sodas out of the fridge and keep Daisy company on the sofa while I go check in with your dad and Kelly?"

Todd's mouth trembled, and if the moisture lining his lower lashes was any indication, he was dangerously close to tears himself. But after a moment, he blinked hard and squared his shoulders, then held his hand out to Daisy. "Come on, Daisy. Let's get something to drink."

Seth watched as Todd led Daisy to the refrigerator, grabbed two sodas, then led her over to the sofa. Once they sat, Todd placed his arm around her shoulders and hugged her close. Daisy, no longer sobbing, but still teary-eyed, snuggled deeper into Todd's side and sipped her soda.

Drawing in a deep breath, Seth opened the door and walked out, joining Kelly and Zane by Zane's truck.

". . . take 'em tonight, drive back out to Glenville," Zane was saying. "I'm staying at a room in one of the motels there and figure me and the kids will stay there tonight, then hit the road first thing in the morning."

"Not tonight." Seth shoved his hands in his pockets to keep from reaching for Kelly, her drawn expression and the pain in her eyes making his jaw clench. Zane might have the upper hand when it came to custody of Todd and Daisy, but he wasn't entitled to walk all over Kelly in the process. "We're not doing anything tonight."

Zane shot him a look of disapproval. "Excuse me?" He frowned, his eyes narrowing as they roved over Seth from head to toe. "This is between me, Kelly and my kids. It has nothing to do with you."

Seth narrowed his eyes. "Anything that has to do with Kelly involves me, and I'm telling you, we're not making any decisions tonight."

Zane stiffened. "Those are my kids in there and—"

"I'm not arguing with you on that," Seth said calmly. "That's not something any of us are debating, and I can tell you now that all Kelly has ever wanted is what's best for Todd and Daisy. And no matter what her personal feelings may be toward you, she's always wanted you to have a strong relationship with them."

Zane's shoulders lowered and he relaxed back on his heels, his guard dropping a bit. "Then I don't understand why it's such an issue for me to pick up my kids and take them with me."

Seth tipped his head back and gestured toward the sky. The sun had set over a half hour ago and the stars had emerged, twinkling brightly in the black velvet night sky. "It's late. Daisy's in there crying on the sofa, worried about what's going to happen next, and Todd's getting angrier by the second." He faced Zane again and offered an apologetic smile. "Don't get me wrong. I'm not putting that on you. This is a difficult situation for all of us. It's just, things like this tend to rock a kid's world, and it's best for Todd and Daisy if we slow this down a bit."

Zane opened his mouth and held up a hand, moving as though to protest, but Seth shook his head.

"I'm not trying to make this difficult," he continued. "And I think I know you want what's best for Todd and Daisy, too, right?"

Zane held his stare for a moment, then slowly nodded.

"All I'm proposing is that we sleep on this tonight. It's Thursday." Seth motioned toward the trailer. "Let Todd and Daisy stick to their routine and finish out the school week by attending school tomorrow. That'll give you and Kelly a chance to get a good night's rest and think things through. If you still feel the same way about taking them tomorrow, then Kelly and I will be better prepared to help ease them into the transition."

Zane glanced from Seth to Kelly, considering this, then reluctantly conceded. "All right. I see what you're saying, and all things considered, I think that might be best." He looked over his shoulder, a frown appearing. "But . . ."

"No one's asking you to walk away from 'em tonight." Seth gestured toward the orchard. "My place is just next door and I got plenty of room. You're welcome to spend the night there and I'll cover whatever amount you would've paid at the motel in Glenville. That way, you'll rest easy, still being near the kids tonight and tomorrow, and we won't have to upset them by seeing you leave again without them right off the bat."

Zane hesitated.

Seth spread his hands. "What do you have to lose?"

He sighed. "Okay. I'll take you up on the offer and I thank you for it."

Seth blew out a breath, relieved that he'd gained at least an inch of breathing room for Kelly. It wasn't much, but it was better than she'd had initially. "Go back out through the drive-in entrance, take a left onto the main road, then another left at the first dirt road you see. Follow that driveway till you reach a house and park wherever you'd like. I'll be right behind you."

Zane nodded and pulled his keys from his pocket, turning them over twice in his hand as he glanced at Kelly, then headed for his truck.

Seth stood still by Kelly's side, watching as Zane started his truck, flipped on the headlights and drove back toward the main road. Seth didn't move until the red taillights of his truck disappeared around the bend. Silence fell over the field, the only sound the whisper of the night breeze through the trees of his orchard and a spring chorus of crickets.

Seth held out his hand slowly and whispered, "I'm sorry, Kelly."

She was in his arms instantly, burying her face against his chest and sobbing. Heart breaking, he wrapped his arms around her and held her tightly, pressing his cheek against her hair and smoothing one palm across her back in comforting circles.

"I h-had no idea he'd show up like this." Her voice caught on a sob, and she shook against him. "I . . . I always knew he could, but never actually thought we'd see him again so soon. And for him to show up now. Just when—"

Her sobs deepened, her fingers twisting in his shirt.

Seth closed his eyes and willed his own tears back. "I'll talk to him. See what his intentions are. Try to find out if he's really serious or if this is just a spur-of-the-moment decision. If it is, I'll try to get him to see reason. I'll try to explain to him why Todd and Daisy are better off with you."

"It doesn't matter what you say." Her tears began to slow, but her entire body still shook against his. "He's their father. I have no right to Todd and Daisy without his approval. And Todd knows that as well as I do. He always has. And my insistence that he and Daisy aren't mine just kept confirming Todd's belief that I didn't want them." She lifted her face from his chest slowly and looked up at him, her chin wobbling. "I just can't help but worry what will happen down the road. When juggling work and two kids interferes with whatever else Zane normally does." A fresh surge of tears welled in her eyes. "He'll break their hearts again."

Seth cupped her jaw and brushed his thumbs over her cheekbones, wiping away her tears. "We can only control ourselves," he said softly, "not the people around us. The only thing we can do now is hope he sees reason."

A look of sad resignation entered her expression. "And if he doesn't?"

"Then we do the same thing you've been doing all this time." He tried to smile, but failed. Instead, he kissed her forehead, cradled her face in his hands and touched his forehead to hers. "We do what's best for Todd and Daisy."

Ten minutes later, after saying goodbye to Todd and Daisy, Seth walked through his orchard and back to his house. Zane stood outside in the driveway, leaning against his parked truck, waiting for him.

"Sorry for the wait," Seth said, striding across the front lawn.

Zane took a deep drag from a cigarette he held and blew out the smoke slowly. "Not a problem. It's nice out here." He glanced around, his expression hard to read in the low glow of the stars. "You've got a nice place."

"Thank you."

"How long you been living out here?"

Seth looked up at his house, a small smile lifting his mouth as he looked at the red roof Kelly had so admired. "About fifteen years." He returned his attention to Zane. "You?"

"I was living in Florida but just got a place back in Birmingham. One-story house. Nothing like this."

Seth watched him take another drag of his cigarette. "Been there long?"

One corner of Zane's mouth lifted. "Investigating my suitability, are you?"

Seth kept his expression blank. "I think it's a fair question. You haven't been around for a while. You show up with no notice. Not trying to offend you, just trying to find out what your plans are for Todd and Daisy."

Reaching the end of his cigarette, Zane flicked the butt to the driveway and ground the embers out with the heel of his shoe. "You've gotten pretty close to my kids, haven't you?"

"Yes."

Zane studied his face, his eyes narrowing. "You don't think I should have them, do you?"

Seth shook his head. "I didn't say that. I don't even know you." He sighed. "But I'd be lying if I said I didn't have reservations about you, or concerns about Todd and Daisy's well-being. From what I've seen, Kelly's taken great care of them for quite some time now. She's got them settled well here. They're finally getting into a routine at school and gaining ground on the drive-in renovations. The grand opening is this Saturday, and they were looking forward to it."

"I didn't come here to interrupt Kelly's plans with the kids," Zane said. "But I miss them, and I have a right to them. I'm grateful to her for taking care of them—especially for as long as she has. But they're my children, not Kelly's."

Seth strolled over to Zane's truck and propped his elbows on the hood of the vehicle, leaning into them and striving to inject a casual tone into his voice. "You've said that a lot—that they're your children and they belong to you. But what I haven't heard you mention is what you are to them . . . or, more specifically, what you plan to offer them."

Facing Seth, Zane rested one arm on the hood of his truck and frowned. "I'm their father and I'm going to take care of them. Give them a home, get them back in school in Birmingham."

Seth nodded. "That's a good start. But I guess what I'm really wondering is why you left them with Kelly in the first place."

Zane's expression fell, his gaze drifting down and his fingers splaying against the hood of his truck. "Laice—my wife—died, and I had a hard time getting over losing her. She was it for me, you know. I just couldn't let her go." He looked up, meeting Seth's eyes, his mouth set in a tight line. "I know a lot of people say you should just get over it and move on, but I couldn't. You ever felt like that before?"

Seth stilled, a familiar pain—not as sharp as before, but still present—moving through his chest as he returned Zane's stare. The pain in the other man's eyes mirrored his own, and though the last thing he wanted was to empathize with Zane, he understood his grief and appreciated how difficult it was to move on after losing someone so dear. "Yeah." But still . . .

"You left them, though. Not just for a few days or a week or two, but for months with no updates of any sort, from what Kelly has told me. She said you didn't even call to check on them, to see how they were faring through all this."

"I knew Kelly would take care of them," he said firmly. "Otherwise, I wouldn't have left them with her."

"But what about their emotional needs?" Seth shook his head. "You basically dropped them off on her doorstep and drove off with no assurances or promise that you'd ever return. Todd and Daisy had just lost their mother. Can you imagine how difficult it must have been for them to lose their father, too?"

Zane straightened and dragged his hand through his hair. "I know I messed up. I know I should've handled things better, but I can't take that back now. All I can do is move forward."

Seth's hands clenched together on the hood of the truck. How could he blame Zane for making a mistake amid a cloud of grief and pain, then having a change of heart and wanting to rectify that same mistake? Wasn't that what he was trying to do himself? Let go of the past, of his grief and anger, and start fresh with Kelly and the kids?

Something Kelly had said last weekend, the night of the fundraiser, resurfaced in his mind.

"What makes this time different?" he asked softly.

Zane's brow furrowed. "What do you mean?"

"I mean, you say you made a mistake leaving them. That you weren't able to handle things at the time. I assume you mean juggling the pain of losing your wife and taking care of two kids on your own—both of which anyone would agree are great challenges." Seth straightened as well and shoved his hands in his pockets. "What I'm asking is, how do you know you'll be able to take care of Todd and Daisy on your own now?"

Zane scoffed. "Same as Kelly, I expect."

"Yeah," Seth continued gently, "but this is a huge move for Todd and Daisy. Can you understand why Kelly and I are concerned that if you're not sure, that if down the road you change your mind again, your leaving a second time might devastate Todd and Daisy?"

Zane dragged a hand over his face and kneaded the back of his neck. "I can't see the future, man, and quite frankly, I don't owe you any explanation. I'm Todd and Daisy's father, and I have a right to take them with me."

"Yes," Seth echoed. "You have every right to take them. I'm just asking you to please think it through before you act. Kelly's made a good home for Todd and Daisy here. She's taken great care of them and would continue to do so, given the chance." He held out his hand in supplication. "All I'm asking, as someone who loves your son and daughter, is that you sleep on it. Give the decision a little more thought and just be sure you're committed before you disrupt their lives again."

Zane stared at him, the anger slowly receding from his expression and an uncertain resignation taking its place. "All right. I'll give it some thought tonight. But that's all I'm agreeing to."

Seth stepped back and nodded. "Thank you." He swept his arm toward the front porch of his house. "Please come on in. I'll show you your room and get you a drink. You're welcome to settle in, and let me know if you need anything."

A somewhat-friendly smile returned to Zane's face. "Thanks again, man. I appreciate you setting me up so I don't have to drive back to Glenville."

Seth led the way up the front porch steps, unlocked

the door and invited Zane to precede him inside. Patch was waiting patiently by the door, his tail wagging furiously as Seth walked in.

"Hey, buddy." Seth squatted beside Patch and rubbed his ears. "You ready for some supper?"

Patch barked, sniffed around Zane's legs, then shuffled to the kitchen, barking twice more along the way.

Zane smiled. A real one this time. "Nice dog you got there. I've been thinking about getting one for Todd. You think he'd like that?"

Seth paused in midstride toward the kitchen, glancing back at Zane over his shoulder. The question alone unsettled him. It was as though Zane knew nothing at all about his own son . . . and maybe even less about being a good parent. "Yeah," he said slowly. "I think he would. Look . . . if you're ever uncomfortable calling Kelly for help, I'd be happy to give you my number if you'd like. Anytime you have questions about what Todd and Daisy might like or need, I'd be happy to give my advice. No questions on my part, just help whenever you might need it."

That, at least, he could do to help make the transition easier for Todd and Daisy.

Zane nodded, his gaze drifting off as though in thought. Then he shoved his truck keys in his pockets and looked around the room. "I'd be fine on the couch if that'll save you some extra cleaning tomorrow and keep me out of your hair."

"No need for that," Seth said. "The guest room's upstairs. Second on the left. You can go take a look and let me know if you need anything. Bathroom's right across the hall. Sleep as late as you like in the morning. The kids leave for school early and won't be back until after three tomorrow afternoon."

Zane murmured another thank-you, then headed up the staircase, glancing around as he went.

Seth waited until he was out of sight, then walked to the kitchen, grabbed a can of dog food from one of the cabinets and fed Patch, patting the dog's back as he dug into his dinner.

"Let's hope he has a change of heart," Seth whispered to Patch.

Because the last thing he'd ever want was for Kelly to feel the pain of losing the two children she loved.

Kelly unrolled the tape measure in her hand and measured out a two-by-four stud from the lumber Seth had left behind in the drive-in lot yesterday. She marked the wood with a pencil and ran it through the miter saw, carefully making sure the cut was accurate. When she finished, she moved the stud over to the tree and propped it against the base of the trunk.

She looked at Seth's orchard, peering past the thick trunks and sprawling branches in anticipation of Zane's arrival. But the orchard remained undisturbed. Despite the strong warmth of the morning sun, a chill ran through her.

Kelly spun away from the orchard, returned to the stack of lumber on the ground and lifted another piece of wood onto the saw table. Her movements were abrupt and automatic, but the loud buzz of the saw filled her ears and drowned out her thoughts, allowing her a moment's peace from the turmoil that had warred within her over the past several hours.

Yesterday after Zane had left to drive to Seth's house, Seth had hugged her tightly one last time, promised to return in the morning, then walked past the halfway-built tree house into his orchard, disappearing into the night. As Kelly watched him leave, an unexpected urge hit her, tempting her to rush back into the trailer, pack up everything she and the kids had brought with them, then bundle Todd and Daisy into the car and take off. She'd drive without stopping until enough distance had been put between her and Zane that the fear pricking the back of her neck would ease so she could breathe again. Then she, Todd and Daisy would look for a new place they could call home. A new start. A new life.

The saw reached the end of the wood she'd loaded and the two-by-four was cut. Kelly turned off the saw, removed her safety glasses and pinched the bridge of her nose with her gloved hand.

None of what she'd dreamed about in that moment last night was a viable option and she'd never do it, of course. But last night, for the briefest of panic-filled moments, she'd wanted to try. And the worst thing about it was that she wasn't even dreaming of doing it for Todd and Daisy's sake, but for her own.

She stared at the empty driveway of the drive-in lot, recalling how quiet they'd both been this morning when she'd driven them to school and dropped them off. They hadn't asked any questions about Zane or what was to come. They'd simply sat silently in their seats and stared out of the window, then murmured quiet goodbyes as they'd exited the car and walked into school. The biggest difference being that instead of Todd's usual routine of walking five steps ahead of Daisy, and only casually checking behind him to make sure she made it inside, this time, they held each other's hands, walking side by side through the entrance and a few steps beyond. It was as though they sought comfort in each other.

The sight had almost broken Kelly's heart. She'd driven home with hot tears rolling down her cheeks the entire way.

She stilled, her eyes moving to the silver trailer at the back of the lot. The outdoor chairs she had bought still sat in front, colorful and inviting. Each window shined in the morning light and sparkled every now and then as the sun rose higher as though winking in approval of the beautiful day. And every square inch of the small interior had become as comfortable and welcoming as Mae Bell had promised.

A bittersweet emotion filled her chest. The little Royal Mansion of Mae Bell's dreams had indeed become her own. This place had become home—for Kelly and the kids . . . with Seth. Her breath caught, the idea of losing both Seth and the kids too much to bear. Now, when she, Todd and Daisy had finally found a place of their own . . . a family and dream of their own . . . Zane could rip it all away.

"You started without me."

Kelly jumped and glanced over her shoulder to find Seth weaving his way through the last two trees and striding up to her. Just the sight of his kind, peaceful expression was enough to ease some of the tension from her limbs.

"I couldn't sleep last night," she said. "And after I dropped the kids off, I knew it'd be fruitless to try again, so I figured I'd come on out and work on the tree house some more."

Seth frowned. "Kinda dangerous handling power tools alone when you're not well-rested. I hope you're being careful."

"I am." She bit her lip. "Has Zane changed his mind?"

Sadness filled his eyes. "No. He got up early this morning and started making calls to try to reenroll Daisy and Todd in their old school back in Birmingham. He's afraid he may have to try another school district after the trouble Todd caused there before. He asked me if I'd touch base with you and see if you could help get them packed and ready to leave this afternoon, as soon as possible after they return from school."

Her shoulders slumped. It was as she'd expected, but

the idea of losing Todd and Daisy hurt even more than losing Laice had.

"How were they doing this morning?" Seth asked.

She shrugged, then walked over to the stack of lumber and lifted another piece of wood from the pile. "Todd managed to help Daisy stop crying last night, but even he was teary-eyed when he went to bed, and neither of them touched their breakfast this morning. I think they're afraid, confused, excited and unsure. They don't really know how to feel, and at the same time, I think they're feeling so much they don't know how to respond."

Seth moved quickly, lifting the long post from her arms and placing it on the saw table. He placed his palms flat on the wood and leaned forward, catching her eye, and asked softly, "And how are you doing?"

Kelly tugged off her other glove and dragged a hand over her face. "I don't know how to feel, either. I mean . . ." Her mouth trembled and she pressed her lips together and looked away, trying to keep the tears at bay. "I want them to have a relationship with Zane—of course, I do. But I don't want that relationship to come at the expense of my losing them altogether." Her voice shook and she inhaled deeply before continuing. "Sometimes I wish he'd just leave again, but I hate myself even more for wishing that, because I know it would just break their hearts again." She looked up, blinking past the tears filling her eyes as she met Seth's eyes. "What kind of parent does that make me?"

Seth walked around the table and drew her close, his big palms moving in slow circles over her back. "A great one. One who loves those kids as much as herself and wants what's best for them. There's nothing selfish about loving someone and wanting them with you."

Kelly buried her face against his warm throat and breathed him in, finding comfort in his embrace. "Like you tried to tell me last week?" she asked quietly. "When you told me you loved me and asked me to take a chance on a future together?"

His hands stilled against her back for a moment, then resumed moving in slow circles again. "Yeah."

She lifted her head and looked up at him, studying the kindness in his eyes, his patient expression. He'd been through so much, losing Rachel and a marriage he thought would last forever, yet . . . here he was, standing before her just as he had been for weeks now, ready and willing to take a chance on life and love again. With her.

"You love Todd and Daisy just as much as I do, don't you?" she whispered.

He nodded, the same pain she felt clouding his eyes.

"I've never met a man as good as you," she said, lifting her hand and cupping his jaw in her hands. The stubble lining his jaw was rough against her fingertips. She smoothed her thumbs across his lean cheeks, managing a small smile despite the pain roiling inside. "I love you, Seth, and I wish I'd had the courage to tell you so last weekend. I wish I'd been able to see that a happy ending doesn't have to be perfect to be happy. I wish I had told you how much I admire your kindness, patience and concern for others. How gentle and compassionate you are with Todd and Daisy. And how it's just as hard for me to imagine losing you as it is for me to think of losing Todd and Daisy."

She lifted onto her toes and touched her mouth to his. Immediately he folded his arms tighter around her, dipped his head and deepened the kiss. His stubble-lined jaw brushed her cheek, his taste touched her tongue and his hand lifted, his palm cupping the back of her head gently.

A tear fell from Kelly's eyes and slipped between them. Seth lifted his head, his mouth and cheeks flushed from her kiss, and drifted his thumbs below her eyes, wiping away the rest of her tears.

"We'll be okay, Kelly," he whispered. "Whatever comes, we'll still have each other. I promise you that."

She closed her eyes and inhaled, breathing in his spicy scent and taking comfort in the strength of his tender touch. "Thank you for everything. For letting Zane stay with you and giving me one more day with Todd and Daisy. For sticking around through all this."

A crooked smile crossed his face as he said softly, "Where else would I want to be?"

An engine rumbled past the entrance of the drive-in. Kelly released Seth and turned, watching as a van drove over to one of the projection booths and parked. Doors opened and two men got out, one waving at Kelly and Seth from across the field.

Kelly lifted her hand, shielding her eyes from the sharp rays of the sun. "Who is that? I wasn't expecting any guests today."

A puzzled look crossed Seth's face as he peered across the field. "That's Clark." He waved back. "Not sure who the other guy is, but let's hope it's good news for a change."

They walked across the field and joined the two men by the projection booth.

Seth greeted Clark first, shaking his hand and smiling. "What brings you all the way out here this morning?"

Clark grinned. "My dad, believe it or not. He had an errand for me to run, and this time, I was more than happy to carry it out." He nodded at Kelly, then gestured toward the man beside him. "Kelly, I'd like you to meet Gerald Manning. He manages several online specialty businesses, one of which happens to sell digital projectors."

Gerald, a tall man in his midthirties, shook Kelly's

hand and smiled. "Sorry to show up out of the blue, but Clark's dad was adamant that we have the product out here and installed by noon. He said y'all had some kind of big opening tomorrow night?"

"Yeah." Kelly frowned. "Our grand opening. But what product are you talking about?"

"Come on back and take a look." Gerald led the way to the back of the van, opened the double doors and motioned toward a large piece of equipment sitting in the center of the van. "A Christie CP2315-RGB laser projector. You get 2K, 4K and 3-D on this bad girl. Top of its line, easy to install, and you won't have to purchase any additional parts to make it work. She's good to go as soon as I get her set up in your booth."

"But . . ." Kelly stepped back from the van and spread her hands. "There's no way we can afford this. I already priced a cheaper model weeks ago and we couldn't even afford that one with a steep discount."

Gerald held up his hand. "No problem. This one's already bought, paid for and in your name. Well"—he reached in his back pocket and withdrew a piece of paper, reading—"in Ms. Mae Bell Larkin's name."

Kelly glanced at Seth, who shook his head in confusion. "Did you do this?" he asked Clark.

Clark, smiling, shook his head, too. "Nope. Well, I helped load it and transport it this morning, but that's the extent of my contribution. No, this is a no-strings contribution to the Blue Moon Haven Drive-In, courtesy of my dad."

Kelly opened and closed her mouth several times, searching for a response. "I . . . well, I don't understand. This is one huge contribution. I mean, this thing had to run around forty thousand dollars or so—"

"Fifty-two thousand one hundred sixty-seven dollars and thirty-two cents, to be exact," Gerald announced, handing the paperwork he held over to Kelly. "The receipt, warranty and number for tech support's all in there, along with my number. If you have any trouble with the projector and can't find what you need there, just give me a call and I'll find out for you."

"But . . ." Kelly flipped through the paperwork. It was all there, as Gerald had said. Paid for, free and clear, and registered to joint owners, Kelly Jenkins and Mae Bell Larkin. "But I . . ." She looked at Clark. "There's no way I can repay your father. And I can't accept a gift this expen—"

"You don't have a choice." Clark smiled. "This is one thing I'm glad Dad was adamant about." His lips curved. "And before you start feeling all obligated or guilty, consider the fact that he did it more for his benefit than anyone else's. He had a great time out here last weekend and he's always been sweet on Mae Bell. Seemed that night sparked a renewed interest in this drive-in and in Mae Bell." His smile softened. "My dad's been feeling pretty low for a while now. Hasn't had that get-up-and-go like he used to, and his memory is fading. This place"—he swept an arm toward the large projection screen and open field—"breathed a new zest for life in him. Helped him remember good times he'd begun to forget. He's eager to come back out here tomorrow tonight—and as many nights going forward as possible—to enjoy the movies he used to love." He winked. "And to have a shot at spending more time with Mae Bell."

Seth laughed. "Watching a good film under the stars beside a woman you love." He met Kelly's eyes and smiled. "I can understand that being priceless to him."

Gerald reached into the back of the van and started sliding the large box toward him. "We'd best get this unloaded and up and running by noon—otherwise, I won't get the tip Clark's dad promised me."

Clark helped Gerald unload the projector from the

van, chuckling. "Don't get your hopes up. My dad is normally a cheapskate, which is exactly why he could afford to buy this monster."

Seth pitched in, opening the door of the projection booth and directing them to the appropriate location.

Kelly followed them inside and watched them work for a while, her smile slipping as they unboxed, installed and tested the projector. She was happy Mae Bell's dream now had a fighting chance. She just wished there was still hope for her own.

CHAPTER 15

Hours later, Kelly turned into the parking lot of the school and parked in the pickup line, waiting for Todd and Daisy to come out. As she watched, children of all ages trickled out of the front entrance of the school, smiling and laughing, some meeting one of their parents on the sidewalk, taking their hand and chatting a mile a minute as they walked to a parked car.

Kelly sighed and closed her eyes, praying for strength for the thousandth time since she'd left the drive-in, hoping she'd be able to maintain a solid, optimistic front for Todd and Daisy.

It hadn't been easy in any respect. After Gerald and Clark had finished setting up the new projector, they had hung around the drive-in for a little while, helping Kelly learn the ins and outs of operation and sharing a few troubleshooting tips. When she felt comfortable operating the new projector, she thanked Gerald and Clark again and asked them to pass along her thanks to Brighton, pressing a stack of free tickets to film screenings at Blue Moon Haven Drive-In for him to share with family and friends, along with an assurance of a lifetime pass to the drive-in for as many free showings as he'd like.

Clark had smiled, but it had been tinged with sadness. "The older I get, the more a lifetime doesn't sound quite as long as it used to, you know? Especially not for my dad." He'd smiled wider then and held out his hand, squeezing Kelly's as she shook it. "Thank you for helping Mae Bell reopen this place. It'll give my dad a lot to look forward to, and I plan on visiting frequently myself as well."

Kelly had hugged him. "I hope so. And please tell your father we look forward to seeing him tomorrow night."

After Gerald and Clark had left, Kelly had stood by the projector and stared at its sleek, modern lines, lost in thought.

"There's hours yet until it'll be time to pick up the kids," Seth had said, placing an arm around her shoulders and hugging her to his side.

She had hesitated, tearing up, then set her shoulders. "I'd better start packing some of their things so they'll be ready to leave when Zane is."

She and Seth had spent the next hour packing Daisy's toys and a few of Todd's clothes. Then, overwhelmed with an odd mix of anger and pain, she'd left the trailer, returned to the tree house and grabbed a two-by-four and hammer. Todd and Daisy had looked forward to enjoying the tree house, and though she couldn't change what was to come, she could at least give them one last thing to enjoy before leaving Blue Moon.

Seth hadn't said a word. He'd simply followed her out to the tree house, picked up a two-by-four as well and begun working on the other side of the frame.

They'd spent the next couple hours working in silence, and by the time two-thirty had rolled around, they'd finished.

The tree house was, at the very least, one last gift she could give Todd and Daisy.

The doors of the school's entrance swept open once more and Todd and Daisy emerged, holding hands again and glancing around with grave expressions. Spotting her car, Todd headed over, keeping Daisy close to his side.

Kelly hesitated as they climbed into the car and smiled as Daisy, growing more confident and independent each day, settled into her booster seat and buckled herself in on her own. "How'd school go today?"

Daisy shrugged and Todd just looked at her silently, his eyes peering into hers as though trying to read her mind.

A horn honked behind them, and Kelly started the car and pulled onto the highway, driving off toward the drive-in. Each mile they traveled made her chest ache even more, and she fought to keep a smile on her face.

"What's going to happen?" Todd asked quietly.

Kelly swallowed hard past the lump in her throat and focused on the road in front of her. "Your dad has decided to take you and Daisy back to Birmingham with him." At his silence, she glanced at him, the drawn expression on his face making her vision blur. She looked away quickly, wiping her eyes with her hand and forcing her smile back into place.

Daisy began to cry, her sniffles and soft sobs breaking Kelly's heart even more.

"He's missed you both very much," Kelly said, meeting Daisy's eyes in the rearview mirror and struggling to maintain her smile at Daisy's distraught expression. "He's looking forward to you all being together again."

"I d-don't want to go," Daisy said through her tears.

Kelly stared at the road ahead again. "I know, baby," she said softly.

Todd sat completely still and remained silent for the remainder of the drive home. Kelly couldn't bring herself to look at him, for fear of bursting into tears.

When they drove through the entrance of the drive-in, Seth and Zane were standing by the tree house, inspecting Seth and Kelly's handiwork. They turned at the sound of the engine and Zane waved.

"Seth and I finished the tree house today while you were at school," Kelly said quietly, cutting the engine. "We finished the walls and added a roof and wood siding. I really wanted you to have a chance to see it before you left."

Daisy sniffed and wiped her eyes with the back of one hand. She looked out of the window at the tree house in the distance, her mouth wobbling. "Can we c-climb inside?"

"Of course." Kelly glanced at Todd then, the hard clench of his jaw and tight set of his mouth sending a fresh wave of pain through her. "Would you like to take a look, Todd? Y'all worked hard to help build it, too. You deserve a chance to enjoy it before you leave. I'm sure your dad will wait long enough for y'all to spend some time in it."

Todd didn't answer, but after a couple minutes, he shrugged off his book bag, opened the passenger-side door and got out of the car. Daisy unbuckled her seat belt, hopped out and joined him, and they slowly walked, hand in hand, across the field toward the tree house.

Inhaling deeply, Kelly forced herself to leave the car and follow, hanging back a few steps to give them some space.

"There they are," Zane said, smiling. He dropped to

one knee on the grass and spread his arms, beckoning
Daisy closer. "How was your day, baby girl?"

Daisy looked up at Todd, and when he nodded, she
walked over to Zane and hugged him briefly, but didn't
answer.

"Todd?" Zane pulled him close and kissed the top of
his head, his tone softening. "Did Kelly talk to you? Tell
you what we decided?"

Nodding, Todd eased past Zane, walked over to the
tree house and paused as he put his foot on the bottom
rung. "You finished it," he said quietly, looking up at
Seth.

Seth, standing nearby, shoved his hands in his pockets. "Yeah. Kelly really wanted you to see it before you
left."

"It'll always be here, you know?" Kelly walked over
quickly and stood beside Todd in front of the ladder.
"When you come to visit." Her body trembled and she
glanced at Zane, suddenly afraid she might not even be
granted that bit of grace. "You will let them visit, won't
you? They're always welcome here at any time."

"Yeah." Zane dragged his foot over the ground and
looked away. "If they want to visit, I can make that happen." He faced Todd again and grinned. "But we'll have
lots to do back in Birmingham, won't we, bud? I'm
telling you, you're gonna love the new place I got. It's
right downtown, near all the best places. Restaurants
and shops on every corner. A park and bowling alley.
There'll always be something to do."

Todd stared back at Zane, then looked down and
slowly climbed the ladder. When he reached the small
platform that served as a balcony, he glanced around at
Seth's orchard, then returned to the ladder and held
out his hand.

"Come on, Daisy," he called. "It's nice up here."

Daisy, standing off to the side twisting her hands together at her waist, walked over to Seth and tugged on his elbow. "Will you help me, Seth?"

Seth smiled, bent down and lifted Daisy into his arms, propping her on his hip and carrying her over to the ladder. He placed her on a middle rung and helped her climb the rest of the way until she was standing safely on the platform beside Todd.

"You oughta go inside," Seth suggested. "Take a look around. There's a window on both sides so you can see both projection screens from inside or out on the balcony."

Daisy and Todd did as Seth suggested and went inside. Kelly stared up at the tree house as their footsteps sounded across the floor above her head and their faces peeked out from each window from time to time as they explored.

After a few minutes, Zane glanced at his wristwatch with a sigh. "It's about time we hit the road, kids. Why don't y'all come on down and gather up your stuff? If we leave early enough, we can stop and grab a bite to eat at this little bar-b-que place I like in Glenville." He frowned as he peered up at the opening of the tree house. "Y'all like bar-b-que, don't you?"

They didn't answer, but Todd emerged from the tree house's entrance and motioned for Daisy to follow him out onto the balcony. Todd and Daisy stood there for a moment, staring at Seth's orchard. Then Todd released a heavy sigh.

"All right." He walked over to the ladder and started climbing back down. "Come on, Daisy. It's time to go."

Kelly walked with Todd and Daisy to the trailer and helped them pack up the rest of their belongings.

Daisy started crying again when she picked up Cassie off the bed and hugged her to her chest. "Do you think he'll let me keep Cassie in the backseat with me?"

Kelly smiled. "Of course, he will." She tapped Daisy's chin gently with her finger. "Now, why don't you help me carry your bags out to your dad's truck, okay?"

Daisy hesitated, but agreed, grabbing a small pink bag that held her toys, which she started lugging toward the door.

"Todd?" Kelly asked, glancing in the bedroom. "Are you about ready?"

He continued folding his shirts, slowly and methodically. "In a minute," he murmured.

Outside, Zane, all smiles, stood waiting by his truck. "All right, gal, let's load you up." He rubbed his hands together briskly, took the bag from Daisy and loaded it in the back of his vehicle.

Kelly and Seth pitched in, and within ten minutes, Todd had finished packing, all of the bags were loaded and there was nothing left for Kelly to do but say good-bye.

Kneeling beside Daisy, she forced a smile and held out her arms. Daisy, clutching Cassie to her chest and gulping back a sob, ran into Kelly's arms and buried her face against her neck. Cassie's hair tickled Kelly's nose and Daisy's hot tears against her neck tugged tears from Kelly, too.

"I'm going to miss you," Kelly whispered. She buried her face in Daisy's silky hair, breathing deeply, filling her lungs with the child's strawberry-scented shampoo and trying to memorize every detail of how Daisy felt in her arms, close to her heart. "I'm always here if you need me. Always."

"Okay," Daisy whispered. She raised her head from Kelly's neck, grabbed her shoulders and pulled herself up to kiss Kelly's cheek. "Bye, Kelly."

Kelly hugged her once more and whispered good-bye, then watched as Daisy ran back over to Seth and hugged him. Finally the little girl walked to the truck and allowed Zane to help her inside the backseat of the cab.

"Kelly?"

She looked to her left where Todd stood, staring blankly at her. "Yeah?"

Todd bit his lip and looked down at his shoes. "I . . ." He met her eyes, his chin trembling. "I didn't mean to hurt you when I said the things I did to you. I just . . ."

His voice trailed away, his eyes filling with tears.

"Oh, Todd." She grabbed his wrist and tugged him into her arms, wrapping him in a tight hug, her tears flowing freely now. "You don't owe me any apologies or explanations. I just want you to be happy. That's all I've ever wanted."

A sob escaped him and he hugged her back, pressing his wet cheek tightly to hers.

"Todd, come on." Zane opened the driver's-side door of his truck. "It's time we hit the road."

"I meant it when I said you could come home anytime you want. Really *anytime*," she stressed.

"Okay," he mumbled against her skin.

Before she knew it, he'd slipped from her arms, hugged Seth and started walking toward Zane's truck, one of his bags slung over his shoulder.

"Todd?" Despite her efforts, her voice broke and she was unable to keep her words steady. She waited until he stopped and turned to face her, seeking out his eyes. "I love you, you know? And I've always wanted you. In my heart, you were always mine. Always will be."

A strong sob shook his shoulders, and he ran off, disappearing around Zane's truck and climbing into the passenger seat. Zane gave a halfhearted wave, then climbed in his truck, started the engine and pulled away.

Kelly watched them leave, staring at the dust kicking

up behind the tires as the truck moved along the drive-way and disappeared from view.

Seth's strong arm wrapped around her and pulled her close, holding her tightly to his chest. He kissed the top of her head as heavy sobs racked her chest and shoulders. Several minutes later, when her sobs had slowed, he whispered, "What can I do, Kelly?"

Throat sore and eyes puffy, she lifted her head from his chest and forced a smile. "You can help me make to-morrow night the best grand opening possible for Mae Bell. We can at least give her a happy ending."

Seth plugged in the popcorn machine, then flipped three switches to turn on the light, kettle motor and kettle heat. The low hum of the motor warming up filled the concessions building as he retrieved pouches of oil, salt and popcorn kernels from a box that sat on the counter nearby.

"How are things looking in here?"

At the sound of Kelly's voice, he glanced over his shoulder and smiled. She stood on the other side of the counter, lifting a large box toward him.

He set down the popcorn fixings, took the box from her and opened the top. "Going well so far. The pop-corn machine came right on, like it did during the trial run this morning, the hot dog steamer is fired up and ready to go and"—he tapped the countertop—"there's about ten thousand pounds of sugar-laden homemade candy stocked in the candy bins, courtesy of Tully."

Kelly smiled. "Is she here already?"

"She wouldn't miss it for the world." He pointed at the field behind him, visible through the open windows of the concessions building. "She went to her car to get the extra toilet paper, soap and paper towels I asked her to pick up for the restrooms. And she said she has one more surprise for you that she brought along as well. She's bringing it in as soon as she finishes stocking the restrooms."

Kelly blew out a breath. "Oh, she's a godsend. Both of you are. I never would've had time to pick up Mae Bell and Mr. Haggart from the nursing home and finish setting everything up in time for the gate to open."

"You ask and it'll be granted." He winked. "I'm always eager to please."

She laughed and leaned over the counter, kissing his cheek. "I know you are."

His hands stilled over the box as he savored her soft laugh. It was good to hear the sound again and see a genuine smile on her face tonight. For several hours this morning, he'd wondered if Blue Moon Haven Drive-In's grand opening would even occur, given the state Kelly had been in the night before.

Last night, after Zane had driven off with Todd and Daisy, he'd stood in the field and held Kelly in his arms while she'd cried for almost an hour. Eventually they'd sat down in the field and watched the sun set, her tears drying on her face and a desolate expression settling over her features. She'd stood slowly as night had fallen, squared her shoulders and announced that the grand opening would continue as planned, insisting they start working on preparations first thing in the morning.

Happy to see her focus on something other than her pain, he was eager to help with anything, so long as it eased her grief and took her mind off Todd and Daisy's absence.

"They would've loved to be here," she said now, her smile dimming. "Todd really wanted to see the look on Mae Bell's face when we started the first film." Her smile disappeared altogether. "I wonder what they're doing now. If they're safe and happy?"

Seth walked around the counter and squeezed her shoulders gently. "I'm sure they're safe and sound in Zane's new home, settling in now." Or at least he hoped that was the case. "I know you miss them, and that it's almost impossible to believe, but I promise you that things will get better over time."

A small smile returned to her face. "I'm glad to hear you say that. At one time, I wondered if you ever would."

He laughed. "Yeah. I was pretty tough to be around for a while, but I'm glad you showed me another way of approaching life." His laughter trailed away, his tone growing somber. "And that's what we're going to do now. We're going to move ahead as planned—just like you wanted—and make this the best night possible for Mae Bell, right?"

She nodded. "Right."

He turned back to the box and tapped one of the open flaps. "What's in here?"

Kelly smoothed her hand over her hair. "Popcorn bags. A ton of them. Should be enough to get us through the next month at least."

"Good." Seth walked back around the counter and started loading the popcorn ingredients into the machine. "Let me get this going and I'll go see if Tully needs help stocking the restrooms." Kettle full, he lowered the lid and closed the popcorn machine. "Are Mae Bell and Mr. Haggart settled at their table of honor?"

"Yep." Her eyebrows lifted as a mischievous smile appeared. "And so is Carl's dad. Brighton was the first one here, and I made sure his place setting at the table of honor was right next to Mae Bell's. He was already flirting up a storm when I headed in here to check on you."

Seth grinned. "That, I got to see."

Sure enough, Brighton Wellings was seated next to

Mae Bell. One of his arms rested on the back of Mae Bell's chair and the other held a glass of iced sweet tea that he tapped against the one Mae Bell held, toasting something he whispered against her ear.

Mae Bell laughed, her long silver hair spilling about her shoulders. "Brighton Wellings, you haven't changed a bit."

"I'm exactly the same as I was sixty years ago," he said, waggling his eyebrows up and down. "Except now, I have more experience."

Seth choked back a laugh as he approached the table. "Well, what do you think about the setup so far, Mae Bell?"

She closed her eyes and spread out her arms, the ice clinking in her glass. "It's wonderful, Seth. Simply wonderful. You and Kelly have done a fantastic job. I couldn't ask for a more beautiful grand opening, and from the looks of things, I think we're going to have a packed house."

Seth nodded as he glanced toward the entrance of the drive-in. Cars had been lined up for almost half an hour now, awaiting the opening of the gate, and the line of cars stretched out as far as his eye could see down the main road before disappearing around a curve.

"We distributed flyers in every town within a hundred-mile radius," Kelly said, joining him by the table. "We worked hard to get the word out. I think it all paid off." A horn blared at the drive-in's entrance and Kelly rubbed her hands together briskly. "And on that note, I think I should get on over to the ticket booth and start taking people's money before they turn around and drive away."

"Do you need me to take care of any last-minute details?" Seth asked.

"No." She squeezed his arm and smiled. "You've done more than enough. Please tell Tully thank you for me and that I'll catch up with her once I clear the cars out, okay?"

Seth nodded and watched her sprint across the field, her long brown hair fanning out behind her as she jogged.

"Oh, what I wouldn't give to have her energy," Mae Bell said. "Though being here tonight, seeing the drive-in back in business, takes me back to a time when I was full of energy, hopes and life." She patted Seth's hand and smiled at Brighton. "It's so romantic out here. There's nothing like a movie under the stars to get you dreaming again."

Something fell onto the table with a clink. "And nothing like a good root beer to make it more palatable." Seated on the other side of Brighton, Mr. Haggart tipped the bottle of root beer in his hand to his mouth and swigged back a mouthful, then motioned toward Seth. "You just keep 'em coming and I'll be a paying customer every night you open."

Seth smiled. "I'll make sure it happens, Mr. Haggart."

"Would you look at that?" Mae Bell said, her eyes widening. "I don't know if all of those people will fit in here."

For a moment, Seth wondered that, too, as he watched vehicle after vehicle enter the drive-in lot, drive to its respective projection screen and search for a parking space. Kelly's hard work attracting customers had definitely paid off. She leaned out of the booth at the entrance, selling tickets as fast as she could; but as soon as she admitted one vehicle, another drove up to take its place, and as fast as the line moved, it continued to stretch out of sight down the main road.

"I'll catch up with y'all a little later," Seth said, striding off toward the entrance. "I'm gonna give Kelly a hand at the ticket booth."

As he walked, his cell phone rang and Seth reached into his back pocket and pulled it out. He didn't recognize the number, but answered anyway. "Hello?"

"Is this Seth?"

"Yeah." Seth tensed, his steps slowing as he recognized the voice on the other end of the line. "What's wrong, Zane?"

"It's nothing like that," Zane said quietly. His voice sounded strained and subdued somehow. "But I need you to come out to the Glenville Motel, if it's not too much trouble."

"Why?" Seth's heart kicked against his ribs, his mind racing with possibilities he'd rather not face. "Has something happened to Todd or Daisy?"

"They're fine," he said quietly. "But it'd be good if you could make it out here tonight. Without Kelly, though. Just you."

Seth dragged his teeth over his bottom lip. "You want to tell me what's going on?"

Zane was silent for a moment, then, his voice tight, said, "Todd will tell you when you get here. Can you make it out tonight?"

Seth spun around and started walking, his legs striding briskly across the field. "I'm on my way now."

He ended the call and shoved the phone in his back pocket, breaking his stride long enough to stop by one of the restrooms connected to the concessions building where Tully was emerging, holding a roll of paper towels.

"Thanks for stocking the restrooms, Tully." He hugged her, then squeezed her free hand and pointed toward the ticket booth at the drive-in's entrance. "Do you mind giving Kelly a hand?"

Tully smiled and shook her head. "Not at all. I'm all finished up here."

"Great, thanks." He started walking again. "Do me a

favor, please? Tell Kelly I had to go do something, but I'll be back soon, okay?"

"No problem," she called at his back. "But where are you going?"

Seth didn't answer. Instead, he quickened his pace, almost jogging back to his house, where he unlocked his truck, hopped in and took off, counting the miles to Glenville and hoping Todd and Daisy were okay.

Seth had never been to the Glenville Motel before, but he found it easily enough after entering the city limits. It had only taken him fifteen minutes to get there—he'd made the drive in record time. He made a right and drove into the parking lot beneath the bright neon sign and parked by the front office.

He cut the engine, exited the truck and had strode halfway to the front office when someone called his name.

Zane leaned beside the door to room seven, holding a cigarette. "The kids are over here."

Seth hesitated, then walked down the sidewalk toward Zane, stopping when he reached his side. "What's going on? Are they okay?"

"Yeah." Zane drew deep from his cigarette, blew out the smoke, then thumped the butt onto the sidewalk and ground the embers out with his heel. "Like I said on the phone, they're fine."

Seth frowned. "Then what's this about? Why the urgency?"

Zane rolled his head to the side and jerked his thumb toward the red door beside him. "They're ready. They didn't even really unpack to begin with, so there wasn't anything for them to do but wait for you to get here."

Seth shook his head in confusion. "I have no idea what you're talking ab—"

"They don't want to live with me." Zane looked away and a muscle ticked in his jaw. "Took Todd all night to muster up the courage to tell me—then he just came out with it while we were eating burgers this afternoon. Just blurted it out like he could barely bring himself to say it." One corner of his mouth lifted. "Guess I should take that as a compliment of sorts." He looked at Seth, a pained look in his eyes. "You know, he didn't want to hurt my feelings and all? At least he has that much respect for me."

Seth bit his lip, unsure of what to say. Inside, excitement surged through him, urging him to enter the motel room, sweep Todd and Daisy up in his arms, bundle them in the truck and take them back to Kelly before Zane could change his mind. But another part of him winced at the downtrodden expression on the other man's face and the hurt in his eyes.

After losing Rachel, he knew the pain of losing a child all too well and wouldn't wish it on anyone.

"I'm sorry, Zane," he said softly. "Todd and Daisy have grown used to being with Kelly over the past months. They've settled in at Blue Moon and feel at home there. It's hard for them to leave all that behind now, especially when they're just now feeling secure."

Zane was silent for a few moments. He tipped his head back against the concrete wall at his back and looked up at the stars, his brow creasing. "I couldn't call her." He rolled his head to the side again and met Seth's eyes. "Kelly, I mean. It's one thing for Todd and Daisy to ask to leave me and go back to her, but it's another for me to have to call and admit she was right all along." A crooked smile appeared on his face. "You too, come to think of it."

Seth shook his head. "You've got nothing to be embarrassed about, and neither I nor Kelly want you to disappear again. Todd and Daisy still need you in their lives, and you're more than welcome to visit them whenever you'd like. There's plenty of room at Blue Moon Haven and you're always welcome."

Zane dipped his head and murmured his thanks. "Tell Kelly I've already called the lawyer and asked for the paperwork to be drawn up for her to become the primary guardian. I'll send her a copy as soon as I've signed it." He motioned toward the door. "Go ahead. Let 'em know you're here." His halfhearted smile was full of irony . . . and pain. "They'll be over the moon."

Seth gripped Zane's shoulder and looked him in the eyes. "Only a good dad would make this kind of sacrifice."

His chin lifted, some of the pain receding, and he pushed off the wall and patted Seth's back. "I've already said my goodbyes. Todd knows how to reach me if he needs me."

With that, he sauntered off across the parking lot to a neighboring restaurant and walked inside.

Seth, barely able to contain his eagerness to see Todd and Daisy, opened the door and poked his head inside. Todd and Daisy sat on the edge of the bed with their backs to him, watching TV.

"Hey, y'all," he called softly. "I hear you want to come back to Blue Moon just in time to see your first drive-in movie."

Daisy squealed, scrambled off the bed and ran head-first into Seth's legs, wrapping her arms around his knees. "You came!"

Smiling, Seth bent, picked her up and propped her on his hip. "Of course, I did. I've never been happier to take a drive in my life." He glanced at the bed where Todd, now standing, smiled a mile wide. "You ready?"

"Yeah." Todd grabbed one of his bags, slung it over his shoulder and headed for the door. "Let's go home."

Kelly dumped another scoop of popcorn into a bag, filling it to the very brim. "Here you go," she said, handing it to a young boy standing on the other side of the concessions counter. "Enjoy your popcorn and the show."

The boy smiled, evidently having lost a front baby tooth recently and lifted his chin as though to point it out. "Thanks." He dug his hand into the bag, gathered up a handful of popcorn and shoved it into his mouth as he left, leaving a trail of popcorn behind him.

Kelly smiled and rubbed her forehead, her body aching in muscles she hadn't realized she even possessed.

"Two snickerdoodles, one large popcorn and two sodas." Tully, standing beside Kelly behind the counter, served another couple and waved as they left the counter, chatting. When the line finally cleared out, she slumped onto her elbows and blew out a breath. "Whew! Who knew we'd go through so much food so fast! It's a good thing there's only about an hour left in the movies; otherwise, we'd sell out of everything before the night was over."

Kelly threw an arm around Tully's shoulders and gave her a squeeze. "Thank you so much for helping me out tonight. I wouldn't have been able to pull all this off without you."

And that was the honest-to-goodness truth.

After selling over two hundred tickets, Kelly had lost count and just focused on selling each ticket as fast as she could. Tully had shown up early on, pitching in and helping move the line faster but the relief they felt at having cleared the ticket line vanished as soon as Kelly caught sight of the people lining up at the concessions building.

It was to be expected. She'd planned on a big grand opening, but hadn't planned on being so short-handed. Without Todd here to run the ticket booth and without Seth to man concessions, Kelly had been forced to impose on Tully to see to those things while she started the films. Once the films were running, Kelly had hurried over to the concessions building to help serve refreshments. Thankfully, Tully had experience in the food service industry and knew several tricks to keep things going smoothly behind the counter.

Overall, the night had been a success, everyone seemed to be having a great time and Mae Bell hadn't stopped smiling since she sat down at her table. Only . . . there was still something missing. Or rather, several important people missing.

Kelly's stomach sank. Todd and Daisy she couldn't do anything about. But Seth . . .

"Did Seth say why he had to leave?" Kelly asked Tully. "Or when he'd be back?"

Tully shook her head. "No. He just said to let you know he had to go do something and would be back soon."

Kelly sighed and dragged a hand through her hair. "Well, I don't suppose worrying about it will make him come back faster." She touched Tully's arm. "You want to take a break, go sit down at the table with Mae Bell, put your feet up and watch the movie? You have free passes for life after all the help you gave me tonight."

Tully grinned. "I might take you up on that." She walked to the other end of the counter and tapped a small machine with a pink dome that she'd brought with her into the concessions building earlier. "I brought this surprise especially for you, but it seems everyone else got to it first. I'll make a fresh batch just for us."

She picked up two paper wands and a bag of sugar. "How much you want?"

Kelly laughed, eyeing the cotton candy machine. "A ton!"

Tully added the sugar and they both waited as the sugar heated up. When it began coming out in wisps of pink cotton candy, they dipped the paper wands in the bowl and rotated them until they each had a huge pink cloud of cotton candy ready to be enjoyed.

"This is a dream come true," Kelly mumbled around a mouthful of cotton candy. She closed her eyes and groaned as it melted on her tongue. "I can't believe you're giving this machine to us."

Tully laughed. "I'm glad you like it. Seth mentioned you were a fan of cotton candy, and after the business you had in here tonight, I think you can afford to buy a second one, if needed."

Kelly opened her eyes and took another bite. "That's definite. Guests are loving the cotton candy!"

They walked out of the concessions building and Tully sighed.

"I think I will take you up on your offer and go sit with Mae Bell for a while," she said. "You want to come with me?"

Kelly shook her head. "Oh, no, thank you. I'd just like to soak up the atmosphere for a minute or two."

Tully smiled. "You've earned it. You and Seth made tonight a success."

Kelly watched Tully walk over to the table where Mae Bell, Brighton and Mr. Haggart sat watching one of the films and listening to the sound on a radio. Mr. Haggart guffawed at the antics of one of the characters on the screen, and Brighton, his arm around Mae Bell, whispered something in her ear. Mae Bell tipped her head back and laughed, snuggling a few inches closer to him. The rest of the scene around Blue Moon Haven

Drive-In's lot was the same. Couples cuddled close in the front seats of their cars and in the beds of their trucks. Families sat on blankets they'd spread across the ground, eating popcorn and candy and laughing as they watched the film. And several people strolled by the Moon Garden, admiring the newly opened blooms and soft glow reflected from the full moon above. The sweet scent of honeysuckle drifted on the air and the distant chirp of crickets echoed in Seth's orchard.

Kelly strolled across the field back to the ticket booth, went inside and leaned on the counter, admiring the crowd of cars and trucks and the flicker of the films beneath the soft moonlight, happy that Mae Bell's dream had come true. Judging from the results of the grand opening, Blue Moon Haven Drive-In would thrive for years to come.

Only . . . it would have been that much sweeter if Todd and Daisy were here.

Kelly twirled her cotton candy wand between her fingers, fighting back tears and trying to focus on the good that had come out of moving to Blue Moon. She'd found a friend in Mae Bell, a comfortable home in the silver trailer, a thriving business in the Blue Moon Haven Drive-In and had fallen in love with the good, honest and handsome man who lived next door.

But . . . she no longer had Todd and Daisy. Her shoulders slumped, the tears finding their way down her cheeks.

An engine rumbled and headlights swept over the ticket booth.

Kelly held up a hand, shielding her eyes from the glare of the lights, then straightened as a truck pulled up to the booth. Holding the cotton candy wand with one hand, she reached for the roll of tickets, but stilled when the tinted window on the driver's side rolled down and Seth leaned his elbow onto the windowsill.

He smiled gently, his eyes roving over her tear-streaked face. "Is it a sad one?"

Kelly wiped her face and cleared her throat. "Is what sad?"

He pointed toward the drive-in lot. "The movie. Does it have a sad ending?"

Dredging up a smile and trying to infuse a teasing tone in her voice, she shook her head. "No. Blue Moon Haven Drive-In only shows movies with happy endings, sir."

Seth grinned. "Then this should be the best happy ending you've seen in a while."

Still blinking back tears, Kelly frowned in confusion as Seth slowly leaned back in his seat, revealing Todd in the passenger seat. "Todd?" She shot upright, her cotton candy falling onto the counter. "What—I thought you . . . What are you doing here?"

Todd, staring back at her with tears in his eyes, said softly, "We want to come home. We want to live with you." His voice broke. "You said we were yours." He hesitated. "So, can we stay?"

Hands trembling, Kelly clutched them together at her chest to still the shaking and smiled through a fresh onslaught of tears. "You're kidding me, right?" When his expression fell slightly, she hopped onto the ticket counter, swung her legs around and jumped out of the booth. "You never have to ask—you belong here!"

The truck door opened as she jogged around the hood and Todd met her halfway, throwing himself into her arms.

"I love you, Kelly," he said, burying his face against her neck and hugging her tightly.

Kelly squeezed him back and smoothed her hand over his hair. "I love you, too, Todd." She smiled so wide, her cheeks ached. "You'll always be mine, you know? Always."

Another small body hurled itself against her, and Kelly, laughing, lifted one arm to let Daisy wiggle into her arms as well, then hugged both her and Todd even tighter. As Seth walked over, she tried to speak, tried to ask all of the questions rolling around in her mind, but Todd and Daisy hugged her so tightly she could barely catch her breath.

"Todd told Zane he and Daisy wanted to come home," Seth said softly. "Zane thought it over and decided it was best to let them stay with you. Said he was transferring primary guardianship to you and would send the papers over as soon as they're available."

Kelly closed her eyes and kissed the top of the children's heads, savoring the moment.

Daisy was the first to move, lifting her head from Kelly's shoulder to smile from ear to ear and peer past Kelly toward the drive-in lot. "Is the movie still on?"

"Yep," Kelly said. "Two of them."

Todd straightened, too, smiling as he wiped his tears away. "Two? You got the new projector?"

"Yep," Kelly said again. "And there's fresh popcorn, cotton candy and tons of fun just waiting on y'all."

"Can we get some popcorn and watch it with you and Seth in the tree house?" Todd asked, grabbing Daisy's hand and leading her toward the field.

Kelly grinned. "I wouldn't miss it for the world. You two go ahead and grab some snacks, and we'll meet you over there."

Todd and Daisy scampered off, heading toward the concessions stand.

Seth moved close, wrapped his arms around Kelly's waist and kissed her softly. "Mmm. Cotton candy," he said, licking his lower lip.

She grinned. "We're getting another cotton candy machine exactly like the one your sister gave us and installing it ASAP. It'll be our new specialty—Blue Moon Haven Cotton Candy in a thousand fantastic flavors."

He drifted his thumb across her lower lip. "Cotton candy, model airplanes and a house with a red roof." He smiled. "I'd say this is the kind of happy ending you were looking for, wouldn't you?"

Kelly curled her arms around his neck and kissed him softly, whispering against his lips, "No. This is the perfect beginning."

Please read on for an excerpt from CALDER GRIT
by Janet Dailey!

**During the summer of 1909, a battle rages in Blue
Moon, Montana, between immigrant homesteaders and
cattlemen determined to keep the range free. In a
fierce struggle that echoes the challenges of today,
history is made.**

*As the countryside explodes in violence, the Calder patriarch
has the power to stop the destruction, though some believe
Benteen Calder is only stoking the flames for his own gain.
One man courageously straddles the divide . . .*

That man is Blake Dollarhide, the ambitious young
owner of Blue Moon's lumber mill. When Blake's spoiled
half-brother takes advantage of the innocent daughter of
a homesteading family, Blake steps in as Hanna Anderson's bridegroom to restore her honor and give her un-
born child his name. But Blake doesn't count on the storm
of feelings he develops for sweet Hanna. When the war
between the factions rages anew, everyone wonders if
Blake will stand by the close-knit community he serves,
or the wife he took in name only . . .

A marriage of love is more than Hanna ever dreamed
of. For her family, surviving the rugged trip west, claim-
ing a parcel of land and planting their first crops on the
vast prairie are the only things that matter. Which is why
the unexpected passion she feels for her husband is all
the more poignant. But even as she longs to trust the
strong bond growing between her and Blake, Hanna
knows it will take courage and grit to overcome the dif-
ferences between them. And even greater strength of
will to put down roots in this wild new country.

*The epic tale of the settling of the American West comes to
vivid life in this inspiring saga of love, hope and endurance.*

CHAPTER 1

Blue Moon, Montana
July 4, 1909

Hanna stood next to her stern-faced father, one foot tapping out the beat of the polka. Couples whirled around the rough plank floor to the music of the old-time accordion band. She would've given anything to join them. But Big Lars Anderson had already turned down three cowboys who'd asked to partner his daughter. Hanna would've said yes to any of them, just to get out there and dance. But Big Lars had made his position clear. Those rough-mannered men from the ranches, even the polite ones, weren't fit company for an innocent girl.

As if being guarded like a prisoner wasn't bad enough, her mother had forced her to dress like a twelve-year-old, in a white pinafore, with her long, wheaten hair in two thick braids. But even the girlish costume couldn't hide the breasts that strained the bodice of her gingham dress. She was almost seventeen years old, with a woman's body and a woman's mind. When would her parents stop treating her like a child?

As the music flowed through her limbs, Hanna gazed at the deepening sky, where the sun was just setting behind the rugged Montana mountains, turning the clouds to ribbons of flame. It was so beautiful. How could she complain after such a glorious day—a celebration of America's freedom in her family's new home?

As she breathed in the fresh, free air, her memory drifted back to the tiny apartment in the New York slum, where she'd helped her mother tend the babies that just kept coming. Her father had worked on the docks, barely making enough to keep food on the table. When her older brother, Alvar, had turned fourteen, he'd gone to work there, too. In the desperation of those years, the American dream that had brought her parents from Sweden had been all but lost.

But then the news had traveled like wildfire through the tenements. Thanks to the passage of the new Homestead Act, there was free land out west. All they had to do was get there on the train, build a cabin, farm the land for five years, and it would be theirs, free and clear.

Now the dream had come true. Hanna's family and their neighbors had claimed their parcels of rich Montana grassland. The fields had been plowed; the wheat was planted and growing. On the anniversary of America's independence, it was time for friends and neighbors to celebrate an Independence Day of their own.

The festivities had begun earlier that afternoon with picnicking, races, games, and now a dance, with fireworks to end the day. It was the homesteaders, like Hanna's family, who'd planned the event; but the whole town, as well as the folks from the big cattle ranches, had been invited. That included the woman-hungry bachelor cowboys who'd shown up hoping to dance with the daughters of the farm families.

So far, the cowboys hadn't had much success. The immigrant fathers had guarded their girls like treasures. They wouldn't trust rough-mannered ranch hands anywhere near their precious girls.

But the girls, even the shy ones, were very much aware of the men.

"That cowboy is looking at you." Hanna nudged her friend Lillian, who stood on her left. Lillian, an auburn-haired beauty, was only a little older than Hanna, but she was already married, which made all the difference in the way she was treated.

The cowboy in question stood on the far side of the dance floor. He was taller than the others, with black hair and a hard, rugged look about him. Hanna knew who he was—Webb Calder, son of the most powerful ranch family in the region. And yes, he was definitely looking at Lillian.

"Does he know you?" Hanna asked.

Lillian shrugged and glanced away, but not before Hanna had noticed the color that flooded her cheeks. She was married to Stefan Reisner, a humorless man even older than Hanna's father. Lillian wasn't the sort to play flirting games with men. But it was plain to see that Webb Calder had made an impression on her.

As if to distract Hanna, Lillian gave a subtle nod in a different direction. "Now *that* cowboy, the one in the blue shirt and leather vest. He was just looking at *you.*"

Hanna followed the direction of her friend's gaze. Something fluttered in the pit of her stomach as she spotted the rangy man standing at the break between the wagons that surrounded the dance floor. He was hatless, his hair dark brown and thick with a slight curl to it. His features were strong and solid, and there was pride in the way he carried himself—like a man who had nothing to prove.

But even though he might've been looking at Hanna earlier, he wasn't looking at her now. His gaze scanned the dance floor and the watchers who stood around the edge. He started forward. Then, as if he'd been called away, he suddenly turned and left.

Blake Dollarhide swore as he made his way among the buggies and wagons toward the open street. The Carmody brothers, who worked at his sawmill, had been warned about picking fights with the homesteaders. But with a few drinks under their belts, the two Irishmen tended to get belligerent. If they were making trouble now, Blake would have little choice except to fire them. But before that could be done, he'd probably have to stop a fight.

With the dance on, Blake had hoped to get a waltz or two with pretty, blond Ruth Stanton, whose father was foreman of the vast Calder spread, the Triple C Ranch. It was no secret that Ruth had her eye on Webb Calder, who would inherit the whole passel from his father, Chase Benteen Calder, one day. But there was no law against Blake's enjoying a dance with her. He might even be lucky enough to turn her head.

Taking anything away from Webb Calder would be a pleasure.

Ruth had been free for the moment. Blake had been about to cross the floor and ask her to dance when he'd heard shouts from the direction of the street. A quick glance around the dance floor had confirmed that the brothers weren't there. Dollars to donuts, the no-accounts had started a brawl.

Blake broke into a run as he spotted the trouble. The two Carmody brothers, small men, but tough and pugnacious, were baiting a lanky homesteader who'd probably left his friends to find a privy. The confrontation was drawing an ugly crowd.

"Pack your wagon and go back to where you came from, you filthy honyocker." Tom Carmody feinted a punch at the man's face. "We don't need you drylanders here, plowin' up the grass to plant your damned wheat, spoilin' land what's meant for cattle. Things was fine afore the likes of you showed up. Worse'n a plague of grasshoppers, that's what you are."

"Please." The man held up his hands. "I don't want trouble. Just let me go back to my family."

"You can go back—after we show you what we do to squatters like you." Tom's brother, Finn, brandished a hefty stick of kindling. Readying a strike, he aimed at the homesteader's head.

"That's enough!" Blake's iron grip stopped Finn's arm in midswing. A quick twist, and the stick fell to the ground. Finn staggered backward, clutching his wrist.

"I warned you two about this," Blake said. "I'm sorry to lose two workers, but I can't have you stirring up this kind of trouble. Any gear you left at the mill will be outside the gate."

"Aw, they was just funnin', Blake." Hobie Evans, who worked for the Snake M Ranch, was the chief instigator against the homesteaders. He'd probably goaded the Carmody brothers into targeting the lone farmer, hoping others would join in and give the poor man a beating to serve as an example.

"Don't push me, Hobie. This is a peaceful celebration. Let's keep it that way." Blake glanced around to make sure the farmer was gone and his tormentors had backed off. "Before I had to come out here, I was planning to dance with a pretty lady. For your sake, you'd better hope she's still available."

Blake strode back, past the wagons that ringed the

dance floor, intent on seeking out Ruth. But in his absence, something had changed. Webb Calder was on the dance floor with the pretty, auburn-haired wife of one of the farmers. Ruth was on the sidelines, looking stricken.

Blake nudged the cowboy standing next to him. "What's going on?" he muttered.

"Webb got Doyle Petit to talk the drylanders into lettin' us dance with their women. My guess is, soon as this dance is over we can start askin' 'em." The young cowboy grinned. "I got my little gal all picked out—the one in white, with the yellow braids. She's right next to that big farmer—he's her pa. See her?"

"I see her." Blake gave the girl a casual glance. She appeared to be a child, almost, in her white pinafore, with her hair in schoolgirl braids. But then he took a longer look and the bottom seemed to drop out of his heart. He swore under his breath. She wasn't a child at all, but a stunning young woman with an angel's face and a body that even the girlish pinafore couldn't hide.

"Ain't she somethin'?" The cowboy asked. "What do you think?"

"I think you'd better be damned fast on your feet," Blake said. "Otherwise, somebody else might get to her first."

Somebody like me.